The Fairy Rose in America

The Fairy Rose in America

Volume Two

A.E. Fortin

Copyright 2022

ReadersMagnet, LLC

The Fairy Rose in America
Copyright © 2022 by *Anita Fortin*

Published in the United States of America
ISBN   Paperback: 978-1-959761-02-0
ISBN   eBook: 978-1-959761-03-7

All rights reserved. No part of this publication may be reproduced, stored in a retrieval system or transmitted in any way by any means, electronic, mechanical, photocopy, recording or otherwise without the prior permission of the author except as provided by USA copyright law.

The opinions expressed by the author are not necessarily those of ReadersMagnet, LLC.

ReadersMagnet, LLC
10620 Treena Street, Suite 230 | San Diego, California, 92131 USA
1.619. 354. 2643 | www.readersmagnet.com

Book design copyright © 2022 by ReadersMagnet, LLC. All rights reserved.

Cover design by *Kent Gabutin*
Interior design by *Dorothy Lee*

Table of Contents

Book Summary 7

Prolong: Scotland In 1850 9

Chapter One: New York 19

Chapter Two: Joseph And James 37

Chapter Three: Uncle Emile Letter 49

Chapter Four: The Night Ellen Was Born 67

Chapter Five: The Fight Begins 81

Chapter Six: Girls With No Face 94

Chapter Seven: Going To Deilondolay 103

Chapter Eight: Francis And Marcos 115

Chapter Nine: Nightmare Was Safed 126

Chapter Ten: Misty Falls In The Pool 136

Chapter Eleven: A Shield Around Mic 153

Chapter Twelve: Mic's Last Year Of School 184

Chapter Thirteen: The Tornado Change Everything............ 200

Dictionary: Scottish Words And English Words 212

About The Author 215

2

Book Summary

IN THE FIRST BOOK. The Magic Fairy Rose. It started in Scotland with Thomas McGregor and Eleanor Heart. This book is a love story. However, it was much more. Thomas had to find out what happen to his brothers. His oldest brother had told Thomas. Someone was trying to stop him. His name was Marcos, and he was evil. Learn why this man went after Thomas family. You would have to read the first volume to know what he done. Thomas's father had asked him to bring his mother a rosebush home. It was a tradition that the McGregor men always brought a roses home for her. Discover what happen with the rosebush that he found.

In 1850 the Scottish were leaving the Highland's. Many of them were kicked off their lands with no place to go. They got on a ship heading to America. Learn how they broth three rosebushes to America without caring them. Tonight, there will be two ghost visiting Alexander MacGregor and Neil Heart. It took a hundred years before the magic rose was broth to America. Garret Heart made a promise. He said that one of his family members. Will always be there to protect a McGregor. Why you say. Meghalaya the storyteller. She told Thomas that an evil man will be coming after the next Thomas and Eleanor. Their mothers will call them Tom and Ellen. Discover why their fathers became a Navy Seal? Why was Tom and Ellen sent to a school in the Highland of Scotland. Discover the mystery why their memories were mass with. Who order one of their fathers? To take their names from them. Then to be put in a school that changes their names. To Tom became Mic and Ellen became Angel. Remember their will be a family member of Garrets to watch over them. Don't miss the twist at the end of the story. See what is next in volume three.

Prolong: Scotland in 1850

THROUGHOUT TIME MEN WENT TO WAR OVER RELIGION. In the 1700 Scotts started leaving Scotland. In the 1850 over 600,000 Scotsmen left their homes. They were told they could not worship their own religion. These days felt as if darkness had fallen over Scotland. Our land and way of life is being wiped out. The English liquefy the Catholics and Calvinists religion, by revoked religious liberties. The Treaty of Limerick forbade public worshipping. To be able to worship, Scots had to belong to the Episcopal church of England.

Many Scottish spoke out. *"The Episcopal Religion is not Ours."* There were property transactions set in place. To make it easier to take the clergyman land from them. Farming didn't bring in enough money to pay the rich landowners. They decided to remove the farmers. The farms were replaced with cattle or sheep. Soldiers were brought in. They were ordered to remove any recognition of Christian denominations. As well as handicapping, non-Anglicans. English liquefy the Catholics and Calvinists religion. Greed… forced many Scots off their land. Soldiers were ordered to make sure that the Scots follow the letter of the law. They forced the Highlands to immigrate to North America and Australasia. The Commonwealth and elsewhere in the UK, they took with them, over half of their people share of Scotland's skills and educated Scotsmen.

"We been bought and sold for English gold. No more…we Scotts will live the way we see fit. Aye! They took our land from us and forced us to leave our country. It's time to find another place to live." *****

High in the heavens Thomas and Eleanor watched over their family.

'Dear, do ye think it's time to pay our family a visit?'

'Aye, ye take Alexander. I don't think Neil will be good company after he gets a visit from his mother.'

'All right dear, ye know best.'

With the soldiers overrunning the Highland's, Alexander father. Thought to remind his younger son of the story that was passed down from father to son.

"Son, ye know the story that Meghalaya told Thomas?"

"Aye Dad. She said that a MacGregor will take the roses to America. Thomas believed in what Meghalaya had told him. I was talking to Neil about this. I know that I'm the one to leave Scotland. Ginger is now in America. The rose dropped into my hand for her."

"Does Neil want to go?"

"Aye! However, he will not leave his parents. The soldiers will be here next week. If there not gone. They will throw his parents off the land with nothing."

"Aye! I know all about this son. I have asked the Hearts to stay with us. Neil's father told me that they had made other plans. Son do ye know that his parents has magic."

"No! I thought that Neil grate-grandfather had given all his magic to the roses?"

"Aye! I thought the same thing. I was told that through the cross and rose they wear. This mark gives them their powers. The fairy magic knows when they should and shouldn't use their powers.

"The cross that Father Sinclair blessed Garret with. Garret had made more of those crosses. He then told his son to past them down from father to son. It not only gave him his powers. It also gave him powers from the fairies. With the cross, he kept with him. Through time Garret found that he could call on both of his powers. He also found that demons couldn't trick him. He knew if they were good or evil. Ye do know when Garret gave his magic to the roses. It protects our land and keeps us safe from evil. When ye were born. I knew ye were the one to leave Scotland.

The day ye told me that the rose dropped in your hand. I knew it was Ginger ye gave the rose to. Ye told me that ye were happy and scared all at the same time. When she breathed in the scent of the rose did ye know what it meant?"

"Aye! As I held her in my arms, I understood that she became my soul mate. Dad don't worry I will find Ginger once we get to America. However, I am worried about Neil. He keeps having these feelings there is something wrong with his parents."

"Aye! Neil should be worried."

"What's wrong with them?"

"Now that Neil sister is on her way to America. His father told me that his wife and he were dying."

"Dad, dying from what?"

"He didn't tell me. I believe they don't have much time left. They been using their magic to hide their sickness. What he did say he was going to put a spell on the land. It will make the land useless to grow grass for sheep. No one will be able to use their land."

"Neil said he was going to come here to sleep. I think I'll sleep outside near the pond. There is magic in the air tonight. Do ye mine if I get a bottle of scotch?"

"I don't mine. Aye! There is magic tonight. It could be coming from the roses. Neil will need more than one drink tonight. It's going to be a full moon with no clouds around. Aye, staying outside sounds like a good idea. What Neil's parents told me. Ye better get the roses tonight. If they put a spell on the land. Neil should leave the Highland soon. The soldiers will think. He was the one that put a spell on the land and killed his parents."

"I believe ye are right about that. Good night, Dad."

"May the Lord be with you tonight. Good night, son."

※※※

Neil Heart rode with his sister and newlywed husband. His sister was leaving Scotland for good. There wasn't anything there for her husband to make a living on. Her older brother rode with them. There been to many soldiers around. Neil needed to know his sister made it to their ship. Aboard the ship her husband can keep her safe. His skills of fighting were right up there with his own. At last the three of them found the location of the ship. Tonight, there would be a full moon. The temperature was a lot colder on the water. In town, there were soldiers everywhere. When the moon came out, it will be high tide. Neil watched the ship as it sailed out of sight. He noticed that the moon was extra bright tonight. It made it safe to ride home this late at night. As he rode Neil noticed that the trail of light, was getting smaller and brighter than before. All the moonlight was shining on him.

'This wasn't just moonlight. Neil thought this was magic.'

Quickly he stopped his horse. The vividly bright light made it extremely hard to see the trail. Suddenly, he heard his mother's voice.

'Neil, my only son. I hope ye know that your father and I love ye. Forgive us! Our health been failing us. We should have told ye what was happening to us. We used our magic to keep it from ye and your sister. Your father has put a spell on our land. No one! Will be able to use this land. It will not support any animals after we are gone. Do not be sad for us. Go on with your life son. I hope ye will have children of your own. If one of your children come back here. Tell them to come to the land that belongs to the Hearts. Use a drop of their blood at all four corners of the land. On the first Sunday go to the meddle of the property. Do it one more time with a drop of their blood. Come back at the end of the month. Ye should see the grass will be growing again. Take the deed that I gave ye. Pay the back taxes on the land. Tell them nothing! Of how ye brought the land back. If they ask what ye are going to do with the land. Tell them ye are going to raise horses. Son, ye have your full powers. The mark of the cross and rose, gives ye your power. Go to America with Alexander. Teach your sons how to help Thomas. Your father and I love ye. Always remember that.'

In his mind's eye! Neil found himself standing at the corner of his father's land. He watched his father placed one drop of blood at each corner of his land. He lit the blood with white magic. With all four corners done. He waved his hand, the white fire started making the box. Neil found himself inside the house. He watched his father draw out another drop of blood.

"Dad!" he cried.

His father turns and looked right at him. This can't be his father. Through the window. Moonlight shone on the mark of his father's chest. How could his sister and he be so blind? His father's face was all drawn in. The man looked as if he was already dead. Then his mother came into the picture. She looked at her son and, in his mine, he heard.

'Son place us in our bed.'

With the wave of his hands. Neil picked his father and mother up. In their room, he placed them in bed. White fire went red hot. Flames danced around their bed. Neil helped his mother to lay her head on her husband's arm. With the last of her strength her arm went over his chest.

Neil heard. 'I love ye son.' He knew then they were gone.

Neil opened his eyes. From out of no where's, came a red eagle. The eagle swooped down in front of him. It flew right past him landing on a stump. There was a bright flashed of light. Neil eyes cleared. The eagle was gone, sitting on the stump was Thomas MacGregor.

'Neil, do ye feel the mark that your grandfather gave to all his children's children?'

"No, should I? Ye are Thomas, the keeper of the magic roses. Ye are no demon."

'Aye, that is who I was. It's time to take the roses to America. This is yours and Alexander destiny. We didn't know what Marcos will do. If at any time, ye feel your mark burn ye, be where. For a demon is nearby. The new world ye will be able to find your mates. Your children's children will help the next Thomas.'

"Thomas, how shall we pay our way to America? I'm been told that America is a big place. Where shell we start?"

'That's being taken care of as we speak. Ye have till the end of this month. Ye must be on a ship. Before the soldiers come to your parent's land. If ye are still here. They will think ye are a demon with black magic. Your grandfather gave everything ye need to the roses. Neil, your parents kept this from ye and your sister. Do ye understand why they used their magic?'

"Aye! I know now. Don't worry about us. The time we had with our parents. Those were happy memories for us. I will make sure that Alexander will get to America. My children! They will know about the demons. They will also know what the cross and rose can do for them. Thank ye for tell me about my parents."

The ghost of Thomas said his good byes. 'Ye have a safe trip, Neil.'

Alexander was building a fire. When he noticed a cloud of smoke. The cloud looked just like a box. The location was Neil's parents land. His father needs to know about this fire. He went to run back to the house. When he stopped. In his mind's eye. Neil and he was walking through a covered bridge. Alexander thought he heard two lassies speaking. It was in his native tongue. Once they were out of the covered bridge. Alexander notice the lassies were close to their age.

Alexander spoke, 'Hello could one of ye lassies tell us where we are?'

'Aye! Ye are in Vermont. The town of Pittsford.'

Alexander wondered. 'What was that all about.' When his eyes cleared. There before him was his grate-grandmother Eleanor.

"Tell me! Are my eyes deceiving me? Are ye my grate grandmother, Eleanor?"

'Aye! Ye may call me Granny?'

"Granny are ye here to tell me about the roses?"

'Aye that is just what I'm going to do.'

"Could ye tell me where we are going to get the money?"

'Alexander, if ye let me tell ye about all of this. Then ye will know.'

"I'm sorry Granny. I saw a cloud of smoke shaped as a box. It was near Neil's parents land."

'Neil's parents are with their mother and father. There is a lot I must tell ye. Neil will be here in a while.'

The ghost of Eleanor floated over to Alexander. She then set on the grass near the fire.

'Come set with me.'

"Granny is Neil and I heading to Vermont?"

'Aye, so ye understand the vision ye had?'

"I believe we will be heading to Vermont. To a place that will remind us of home."

'That is right. Your vision was to show ye the way.'

"I understand Granny."

Granny nodded. 'Ones Neil is here. He has his magic now.'

"How did this happen? We were told Garret gave his magic to the roses. How would Neil have magic now?"

'He always had magic. The mark of the cross and rose he wears. Can give him the magic and can take it away. When Neil gets here. He could make everything ye are taking smaller. This way ye could keep it in your sporran and it won't break. When ye find a place. Ye must bury the tablet. If the tablet was broken. The roses will return to the Highlands. Ye know the story of how Thomas had retrieved the roses.'

"Aye! We've were told this story since I've been a young lad. My family try to figure out who would take the roses to America."

'Did ye figure it out?'

"Aye! Neil and I will take the roses to America."

'Ye will bring only the tablet and the deer skins. When ye remove the tablet. Everything will get larger. Ye will have two small pouches. One for the soil. Neil will fill the pouch using his magic. The soil keeps everything hidden. There are two vests. Ye must wear the vests while you're traveling. When there is a full moon. Place everything in the moonlight. The moonlight gives everything its power. For the last pouch. Ye said, ye need to pay your way. This pouch can help. Don't worry. If the pouch gets taken or lost. It will only work for a MacGregor. This pouch will always go back to the magic roses. Do ye remember when Thomas had Garret make two lockets for him?'

"Aye. My mother has one of the lockets. It was your locket."

'Aye. Ye will have another locket for your wife in America. Don't ye worry about the locket for now. The tablet is keeping it out of sight until it is needed.'

"Granny, what if I need the locket before I buy my land?"

'Neil will be able to take the locket from the tablet. All he must do is call for the locket. It will show itself to ye.'

"Thank ye Granny. It's good to know."

'Are ye going to try to fine Ginger?'

"I heard that her family was going to New York. The vision told me the name of the town in Vermont. It was the town of Pittsford.

"Granny my brother had a rose drop in his hand first. I tried it with Ginger. It also happened to Ginger, and I. My father had said, *she is my soulmate.*"

'Alexander did ye keep a few rose petals on ye?'

"Aye, and she has a locket with the petals inside it."

'Then ye will fine her. She is your mate. Be careful Marcos will have demons watching ye. Alexander when ye have your home remember this. Only your mate will find the right rose bush. She must work the soil with her bare hands. If she gets her finger picked on a thorn. Then the drop of blood will stay on the thorn. The rose bush will show itself to her. Ye must take the rose bush and plant it in your rose garden. Alexander, this is very important. Don't let your youth cloud your mind. She must stay a virgin. The lass must wear the locket when ye bed her. When you're in Vermont. Find a place. Read the journal. It will tell ye everything ye must know. It's time for me to leave ye. My husband is waiting for me. Be safe. Remember who ye are. We will keep an eye on ye.' There was a flash of light and she was gone.

Alexander heard a horse riding up. "Neil is that ye?"

"Aye! I hope ye have a strong drink, with ye?"

"Aye! I know about your parents. Dad told me. He had seen them when they were not using their magic. I was told that ye may need a drink."

Neil took the drink and toss it back. "One more."

Alexander then poured him another drink. Neil took the drink and tossed that drink back just as fast.

Alexander said, "I was told that my grandfather Thomas came to ye."

Neil taken his saddle off his horse, so he could graze. "Aye, and I know ye had a visit from your grandmother Eleanor."

"That I did. Eleanor is a bonnie lass. Just before my visit. I had a vision of where we are heading."

"So where in America are, we heading to?"

"Where sailing to New York. When we land, we will be heading to Vermont. I will get a map to show us the way. Then we can see which trail we will take. Before, we have another drink. Ye must use your magic on a few things."

"What magic are ye talking about?"

"Neil, the one ye was born with."

"Alexander what would ye do? If ye saw your mother and father dying. I need another drink."

"Neil, I know about your mother and father. I saw the cloud of smoke shaped as a box. Granny told me of your magic. No more drinking right now. We must get everything from the tablet and roses first. While the moon is still out."

"All right! Let us do just that."

The two men work and talk of what they had learned. Alexander was told there will be a ship leaving in four days. He told Neil that he has the money to cover the trip to America. When they land in New York. They must find a bridge that was in Alexander's vision. This bridge will lead them into a town of Pittsford, Vermont.

"Alexander, now that we have everything. I'm going to stay outside tonight. I think I'm going to get foxed. This has been a hell of a night."

With a wave of his hand. A bottle of scotch appeared. "Will ye, like to join me?"

"Aye, we will get foxed together. This will be our last time getting foxed in Scotland."

Chapter One: New York

ON THE FOURTH DAY, THEY BOARDED THE SHIP. Alexander and Neil were on their way to America. The days were long. There was nothing but water for miles. At last land. In front of them the Statue of Liberty. This will be their new home. The men watched as they pulled up to the docks. They were now in New York. After all papers were done. Neil spoke to an old man who knew all about the covered bridges. The man told them to take the train to Castleton. In Castleton buy yourselves some horses. You will be heading to West Rutland. In Rutland. There you can take a trail. This will lead you to the covered bridge called Gorhan. On the other side, will be the town of Proctor, Vermont. Alexander knew this place could be where Ginger lived.

"Alexander hurry up and get those tickets. Before we miss the train. It's getting ready to leave."

In Castleton they bought their horses. The trail to Proctor wasn't hard to fine. They had arrived at the covered bridge. The two of them dismounted their horses. It was good to walk after being in the saddle along time. Neil went over to read the sign that said Gorham Bridge, built in 1842. The bridge was Proctor's town line. They walked through the bridge with their horses. Alexander was hoping to hear the voices of women talking. Disappointed he got back on his horse and rode into town. Neil stopped in front of a barn. The sign had read. MacKay's blacksmith we also bed horses.

The Fairy Rose in America

Alexander looked at Neil. *"Stop looking at me. You're the one that needs to fine Ginger. See if it is Ginger's father. Your vision had gotten us here."*

Alexander nodded. *"Hello, Mr. MacKay are ye here?"*

John replied, *"Aye. I'm out back."*

Alexander went through the door that led outside. There was a man working on some metal. He had his back to Alexander.

"Sir, I was looking for a place to bed our horses."

"Ye found the right place. How many horses do ye have?"

"My name is Alexander. We have two horses. Where do I bed them?"

"My son Ben can show ye. He will be right back."

"I know a Ben and Ginger MacKay. Ye must be their father."

"Aye! They call me John. Do I know ye young lad?"

"Aye, that ye do. My father and ye were best of friends in the Highlands."

"Your voice sound familiar to me. How long has it been?"

"Six years, I was much younger then."

Ben came through the door with some more wood.

"Dad! Look who I found. Neil Heart. He said that Alexander MacGregor is also here."

Neil had yelled. For Ben almost hit Alexander.

"Look out Alexander."

Ben just missed his head with the wood he carried. The metal John was working on. He had place it in a barrow of water. When John turned around. He found not the boys but two young men.

John made the sign of the cross. *"Thank heavens. My prayers have been answered."*

He went and gave them a bear hug.

"Alexander, let me look at ye. Ye must be around twenty-two."

"Aye, old enough to marry your daughter Ginger."

John looked at Alexander, *"So ye couldn't get my daughter out of your mind."*

"Aye… she is in my heart and always in my mind. Remember I said. If it was for me to take the magic roses to America. I would be coming after Ginger"

John just smiled. *"Your father and I knew that ye were the one for my daughter. Six years to get ye stronger. To be able to bring the roses to America. Neil are ye married yet?"*

"No, all the young women were brought here to America."

"How did ye find us? Did ye ever find out who will father, Eleanor?"

"I don't know who will bring Eleanor into this world, not yet. Why do ye ask?"

"Father Paul is visiting my wife and me. When Father met the women, he said. So ye are the once that the men are looking for. Ye are their soulmates. Before he left the Highlands. Father Paul went to see your father. He showed him the painting of Thomas and Eleanor. Father Paul thought he heard a voice. It was coming from the painting of Thomas. The voice told him to go to America. Visit John MacKay and his wife Sue in Vermont. When the men come to Vermont. Ye must marry them to their soulmates Caroline and Ginger."

When Neil heard the name Caroline he asked. *"Who is Caroline?"*

"Caroline been staying with my mother and father. Her parents were killed."

"Ben, we have done enough work for today. It's not every day when we get to see someone from Scotland."

"Dad, I'll be a long later. I need to get this wagon done before tomorrow."

"I know son."

Neil looked at Alexander and spoke. *"If we help them. We could work to pay for the up keep of our horses. Then all of us can go to your place afterward.*

"That is a fine idea, Neil. Then we can talk as we work. Neil could ask some questions about Caroline."

John went back to his work and swore. *"Damn it, the fire went out again. It's going to take longer to get it started. The coals cool off to fast. I'll have to get some more hot coals to get the fire going again. Will be right back. Ben ye come with me. We're going to have to buy that piece."*

"Mr. MacKay here is some money to help fix it."

"Alexander ye will need your money to buy your land."

"Don't worry John. Maybe Neil and I could fix the fire pit."

After John and Ben was out of sight. Neil waved his hand and the fire came to life. He had fixed the problem on the fire pit. Alexander got the wood setup and ready to be cut.

"Neil, here is how long the wood should be. Can ye use your magic to cut these boards."

"Aye… ye can work on the medal to make more spikes."

When John and Ben came back the fire was ready. Alexander made ten spikes for the wagon. The wood was cut and ready for building.

"Ye two fixed it for me. They don't have the piece that I needed. This is great! The fire is going and ye have everything ready for us."

"That's what friends do. Let us get to work so we can put this wagon to bed."

John got to work and made ten more spikes for the next wagon. The wagon was done in less time with the four of them. It was time to head to John's home.

"Dad I'm going to get cleaned up. My wife and I will be there afterward. I think Father Paul was visiting with my wife and neighbor. I'll bring him with us. I live some ways down the road."

"We will see ye then."

After Ben was out of sight. Alexander started to ask questions.

"How is Ginger? Ye haven't told me anything about her."

"I'm just glad ye are here Alexander. We been having trouble with these two men. One of the men says he wants Ginger to marry him. He's been making life hard for the family."

"I don't care about that. What was Ginger's answer?"

"Ye know the answer to that question. It was No! She is still in love with ye. The men think were the ones keeping her from marrying him. She told him she was promise to ye."

"Neil, Caroline was only to stay with us until she was out of school. Her parents were killed not long after they sailed away. They gave us this letter. It's to be given to the one who will save her. I didn't understand what they were telling us. Until now. On the envelope, the day her parents died. May 10, 1850, appeared on the envelope. Today is May 10, 1850. It's to be given to the one who is a demon hunter. Neil, could this letter be talking about ye? Your grate grandfather always knew when demons was around."

"Aye... I was given that power also."

"Neil, we were told when Caroline is twenty-one. She will receive her powers. If anyone but the demon hunter, mates with her. Her powers will be lost forever."

The men rode into the yard. John's wife came running out of the house.

His wife called out. *"John, Caroline had another vision. She didn't want Ginger to go out today. She saw trouble in her vision, and it scared her. Ginger always listens to Caroline. This time she didn't. She wanted some blue berries to make a pie. Caroline tried to stop her from going out. When Caroline stepped outside, she then agreed with Ginger. It was as if the two of them were under a spell. It was over and hour a go."*

"Do ye know which way they went mum."

"Alexander is that really ye."

"Aye."

Quickly she made the sign of the cross. Then she saw Neil.

"It's true, what Ginger told us. The roses are here with ye. Neil, ye are the demon hunter. Ye are here to keep Alexander safe. Caroline has this letter that her parents gave us. The letter is for ye. Ye are the demon hunter."

"If there is trouble. Ginger and Caroline is in the thick of it. We better go and find them. Which way did they head?"

"Take the path on the side of the barn. It will lead ye to the rock wall. They should be some where's nearby."

"I'll go with ye two."

"No John! Ye stay here with your wife. We will take care of those men."

"Mrs. MacKay when we get back. I like to see that letter."

"Aye... Neil ye can call me mum. I will fix some food for all of us."

"If there are any demons. Will find them and take care of them. Don't worry."

The two men took off down the path on horseback. They had to find Ginger and Caroline.

Alexander wondered *'How would Marcos know about Caroline?'*

Neil had changed his last name to Angel-Heart. Could it be a new start for Eleanor and Thomas? We're not the ones that's going to have them. It will be our son's. Alexander cleared his mind. He cried out in his thoughts.

'Ginger my love where are ye? Ye have to hear me.'

He kept trying. There was no answer. Alexander stopped his horse. He reached into his sporran and took out a small cross. Ones again, he called to Ginger. This time he heard her.

'Alexander, I wish ye could help us.'

'I hear ye Ginger. Where are ye? I see where ye were picking blue berries.'

'Alexander are ye here in America?'

'Aye… Be quick and tell me where ye are.'

'They have us on the other side of the rock wall. There is a small cave in the wooded area. Two men is guarding us. There waiting for someone. I didn't know what they're going to do with us? I'm scared. What's going to happen ones that person gets here. Right now, the men are outside.'

'Don't worry. Neil and I will take care of those men. Do ye still love me Ginger?'

'Aye… I was yours the day the rose dropped into your hand. My heart will always be yours.'

Alexander yelled to Neil. He told him where they had to go. Neil waved his hand and the rocks disappeared. They rode hard towards the woods. Not far, they arrived at the cave. It was right where Ginger said it would be. They found in front of the cave two men standing guard.

"Neil, Ginger said there is another man that they were waiting for."

Neil had jabbed Alexander in the arm. He was setting on the ground not facing the cave.

"Alexander, another man just showed up. He's a demon."

"Neil, tell me again about that lass ye dreamed about."

"Now! What the hell are ye thinking of. When the women are in danger? This is not the time to talk about my dreams."

"Bear with me. I have a feeling that Caroline is part of all this. Ye said she has golden brown hair and bluish green eyes. In the dreams, do ye remember speaking each other's name?"

Neil went quiet. "No! I would remember that."

"I just asked Ginger what color hair and eyes Caroline has. She said golden brown hair with bluish green eyes. She is looking for the demon hunter. Neil it all fits."

"Damn it! Marcos is trying to stop both of us."

"Aye… Neil! Ginger and Caroline will give us a son. Our son's will be the ones to give life to Thomas and Eleanor. Marcos must have known I wanted to marry Ginger. Ye has told me many times that a demon was watching Ginger and me."

"Aye… There was one watching when we got on the ship. Even here in America they watch us. Marcos cannot come to earth himself, not yet. What if he doesn't know about the mark Garret wore?"

"Aye… that would be a good thing. Thomas don't want demons sneaking up on Garret. He went so far to asked Father Sinclair to bless Garret."

"That's right Alexander. Garret was a spirit back then. Ones he became a boy. He made sure his whole family wore that mark of the cross and rose. Marcos don't know that Garret didn't die. The demon thought he was by himself doing the magic. If the demon knew he was there. Then Garret had put a spell on the demon or a wall between them."

"Aye… Now what does Marcos know about Caroline? She could be your mate Neil."

"Alexander, if she is? What part does she play in all this?"

"Neil, we know she will come into her own powers, tomorrow. Her mother told her. At midnight before her birthday. A demon is going to rape her. Marcos sent this demon here to take care of both women. Ginger must be a virgin for the magic rose can help her. Ye must mate with Caroline before midnight. So, she can receive her powers."

"Who told ye about this? Did Ginger tell ye?"

"No, it was John. He talked more about Caroline then Ginger."

"No one is going to rape Caroline."

"Neil then ye are going to merry her?"

"Aye… The two of us will be marrying those two women. Alexander, ye are right. It will be my son that will give Eleanor life. Marcos don't want Eleanor to have powers. He doesn't want her to give him any trouble ones he's back on earth. All right, we cannot use my magic yet. These men don't look as if they could even fight. I'm feeling that they are going to become demons. Aye, right after we take care of them."

"Alexander I've been doing a lot of thinking. Who would know I would be here in America? In this very town. Right before Caroline's birthday. My father never talked about my grate-grandfather. I don't remember hearing anything about Garrets birth mother and father."

"Neil, I know a lot about Garret. Thomas told the family everything about him. Your grate-grandfather had strong magic. He had a sister who could see into the future. Before Marcos became a demon. He had met Garrets family. Marcos found out that the family could do magic. He also took a liken to Garrets sister. He had killed their parents. His sister was eighteen at the time. When Marcos had raped her. For her powers. She wasn't going to come into them until she was twenty-one. Garret sister died in child birth. He never found out what had happened to his sister's child. He was a young boy. He had his powers but didn't know how to use them."

"Alexander what are ye trying to say."

"Neil, that letter could be from Garret sister. Marcos may not want ye to mate with Caroline. Ye are my best friend. Remember Caroline's parents were killed. Her mother could be the one who has the powers. The demons will be after both girls. Marcos don't know about the locket that Thomas gave Eleanor. He may think if he has Ginger virginity. I may not want her for my wife."

"Alexander then we have to make are move now. The demon is heading for the cave. He may have a time limit. He must leave both girls not a virgin."

"Neil before we fight. Remember we don't know the laws around here. I can only hope these men are going to be demons. Then it will be a quick cleanup for us."

One by one Alexander and Neil took down the two men. The men disappeared right before they even hit the ground. Now they must deal with the demon.

Alexander yell for the demon. *"Come out here demon. We know who ye are. Your men are dead. They disappeared before they hit the ground. Tells us ye are also a demon. Show yourself."*

"I see that you've taken my men down. I won't be that easy to get rid of."

Neil had stepped out into the clearing. *"Ye underestimate us."* He through his dirk that carried his small cross and rose. The dirk landed deep into the demon's chest. Like the others, he disappeared. Only Neil's dirk and cross were left behind.

"Neil, ye stay here."
"No Alexander. If ye go in their Ginger will not stay a virgin for long. It's bad luck to see your wife to be."
"Damn its Neil! Why must ye be always right!"
"Alexander, think! We know that Father Paul is visiting Ben and his wife. I now know what Father Paul was talking about. All we need is the marriage licenses. Then the four of us can get married.
"Tell Ginger, I'm sending them back to the house. They must get change for their weddings tonight. The four of us are going to get married."

Neil relies that he never asked Caroline if she would marry him. Could she also hear his thoughts?

'Caroline can ye hear me?'
'Aye… I hear ye. Are ye the man of my dreams? The one that came from the first demon hunter.'
'Aye… my name is Neil Angel-Heart. Would ye marry me tonight?'
'Aye… I will marry ye tonight Neil.'

The men heard the women cry out… *"Aye… we will marry ye!"*

They heard two women that sounded like little girls. Neil needed more of his magic. He called append the magic of the Fairy Roses. He also needed the magic that he had with in him. With a wave of his hand, the women were sent home. Neil then made two licenses. They appeared in his hands.

Alexander had gone inside the cave. There was a fire burning. The two women were gone.

"This cave would be a nice place for one of us to stay for three nights. Neil, I can't marry Ginger without the locket. Do ye think we can get it without planting the roses?"

"*Aye! Take the pouch out. Hold it in your hand and think of the locket.*"

When Neil wave his hand over the pouch the locket came to the top.

"*Now take hold of the locket.*"

When Alexander grabbed the locket, the bubble popped. The locket was now in his hand. Neil never felt so much power before.

'*What else do we need?*'

Then he remembered their clothes. With a wave of his hand. They had new clothes on.

"*Alexander, that idea ye had about the caves is a good one. We will make two big rooms, with everything we may need.*"

In the cave was two fireplaces. Two big beds. Then two nice pools of water to lay in with their bride. Alexander just needed to say food, and it appeared. Neil placed a wall between them. With a wave of his hand. The men were sent to Ginger's parents' home.

"Here Alexander this is for your bride. I remembered, that she loved the roses. For my love of my dreams. I picked a flower from every place she has been in her life."

There was laughter upstairs. Ginger's mother and sister-in-law was helping the girls get dress. When the door opened. They handed the flowers to Ginger's brother. He took them upstairs to his wife. There was one red rose for his wife to carry. Neil was handed the letter from Caroline's mother. A scotch to drink was at the table. He opened the envelope. When his fingers touch the letter. Neil felt the power.

Hello Demon Hunter;

My name is Leslie, I am Garret sister. I know that ye come from my brother's children. Marcos was the one who killed my family. At first, I thought Garret had died. It was hard to see my brother standing there. Marcos had brought Garret into the room. He wanted to make sure Garret was dead. I screamed when he ripped my clothes off me. Then Marcos had me tied to the bed. I heard my brother's voice in my head. He was saying a spell as he tied my hands. A spell only our father would know. Garret had used both powers. His own and our father's. He took my spirit from my body. I didn't have any pain or knowledge when Marcos raped me. He had no idea that Garret took my spirit. I stayed with my brother until I was with child. When Garret put my spirit back. He had switched my baby spirit with me. I was given a second chance to live. He had helped me see into the future.

I'm sorry that no one was told what happen to me or my child. There was to many demons that could have over heard. My father and mother before they died. They gave all their magic to my brother. At the age of twenty-one, my magic came to me a long with my mother's powers. Thomas understood what was happening to Garret. When he killed the demon. Garret the boy was freed. Marcos doesn't want ye to mate with my granddaughter. He found out that she was my great, great, granddaughter. My brother knew, he had to keep his powers hidden from Marcos. Remember, Marcos thought Garret's body had the magic. He only had a piece of the boy's magic. With our father's powers. Garret kept hidden from Marcos. Along with his knowledge of how to use the magic. When his body died. Both magic's went with Garret spirit. When he was in with the demon. A wall of magic and prayers was put up. The demon didn't fine Garret any where's inside his mine. When I was born, the evil died with my body. I lived once again, through my daughter. Garret forgot everything, when his spirit came from the teenager's body.

This letter is for anyone that needs information. The one who holds the letter. Ye can ask about the past or things to come. Beware of this time frame. Salem kills witches. Stay away from there. Only use your magic when ye must.

There is a place in Dorset, Vermont. A hundred acres. Just right for two families to live on. I know there is a lot ye need to know. It was Garret who set this in motion. He made it possible for ye and Caroline to dream about each other. When ye see her for the first time. It will be as if ye grew up together. Your dreams started when ye were fifteen and she was thirteen. After your wedding ye will have just two hours to bed her. Your seed must spill into her. Marcos will still try to stop ye from mating with her. Go now and be quick about this. Keep this with the magic roses when ye don't need it. The power those roses have is strong. Give your wife the mark ye ware. Love her with all your heart. I know Caroline will love ye deeply.

Be safe demon hunter.

Love Leslie.

Neil went outside where their wedding was going to take place. Father Paul was waiting for the two grooms.

He asked them, *"Are ye going to do both weddings together?"*

"Aye..." Answered Alexander and Neil.

The men were in place. Ginger and Caroline came down stairs. John step between both women. When Neil first saw his bride. It felt he knew her for a long time. The wedding was over before they knew it. Neil kissed his bride. The papers were signed and there was a toast given to the two couples. He had told Alexander how to get to their room. Neil had left them a spell. All he had to do was say the words our room.

Then he pulled Caroline away from everyone. He took her to the bathroom. There behind closed doors he kissed her. While his hand found her heat. Caroline went very still as his finger moved inside her. Neil's tongue made love to her mouth. He found out that his wife wanted him now. Her hands ran over his back and under his kilt. He drew in air when she took hole of his heat.

"We're going to do just fine together."

Neil waved his hand and was inside their room. There were two glasses. One was a glass of wine. The other was a scotch.

"Neil, I feel a little tipsy."

"Forgive me. I must have ye now. Drink all of it. Your body will relax more with it."

Caroline giggled. *"Alright. I know we have a time limit. Do what ye must do. We will have time to enjoy each other later."*

She made it easy for him. Slowly she took off her dress a piece at a time. Caroline giggled, as she moved sexily in front of him. It was making Neil hot. She went and set on their bed naked. Her finger wiggle for him to come over to her.

On the bed she sat with her legs a part. With a wave of his hand. His clothes were gone. Caroline could see he wanted her. She smiled and giggled. Neil walked toward her.

"Did I do this?"

"Aye... that ye did."

Caroline ran a finger over his heat. It moved when she had touched it. She had giggled and place a hand over her mouth.

He went and sat on the bed. One hand cupping the back of her neck. The other hand moved slowly up her leg. She giggled and gave a little shiver. Quickly he laid her down. Neil bent his head bringing his lips to hers. He was making love to her mouth. His hand cup her firm breast. He was moving quickly. As his mouth drew in her nipple suckling it hard. Caroline grab his hand. She pushed his hand to the mound of curly hair.

"Neil do something here. I'm having strong feelings inside me."

"Is this what ye need."

Neil's finger moved quickly between her moist lips. He moved inside her heat until she climaxed. His mouth caught her cry of pleasure. While his tongue made love to her mouth. Neil knew he was moving too fast. He went down to her heat. His hands under her bottom lifting her. When his head was between her legs. She tried to move away.

"Neil what are you doing?"

"I need to taste you."

"What? I don't understand."

"Ye will my love. I need this for both of us."

Caroline's bottom was moving up the bed. Neil had to hold on to her. As she climaxed again. His tongue took her sweetness. He had his finger moving in and out of her heat. Her body was bucking under him.

Neil was mad at himself for moving so fast with Caroline. *'To damn fast.'* There wasn't enough time to do it right. Afterword, he will make it right. They will have time to get to know each other better. The hour was about up. His seed had to be inside her before midnight. With his heat in his hand. He guided his heat between her moist lips. Slowly he moved inside her until he felt her maiden head.

"Hold on to me."

Neil lifted her bottom up. He pushed passed her maiden head. Until he was deep inside of her. It hurt him when he saw a tear in her eyes.

"There now. Ye are mine. As I'm yours. The next time when we make love. Will have more time to enjoy each other."

"I understand. Neil, I feel some twitching inside me. Is that your heat doing that?"

"Aye!"

When he said that. Caroline took holed of his heat. She saw his eyes go wide. If he was holding back so she could get use to him. The thought was gone. She had grabbed his bottom. Each time he pulled out. Caroline pushed him back inside. The time was running out. She knew he had to climax before midnight. Together they moved, and when she climax. Neil climax with her. He pumped his seed into his love. There were only five minutes until 12:00. Breathless Neil dropped on top of her.

"Ye are mine! There is nothing anyone can do now. I sent the demons back where they came from. My seed is inside ye. No demon can take ye from me. Ye are my wife."

Neil pulled his wife on top of him. He covered them up.

"Before we sleep. Race up for me that's high enough. With my powers. I give ye the mark of the cross and rose. This will tell ye if a demon is around. Rest my love. Lay here with me. Let me stay inside ye. Afterward will wash and I'll do better next time."

The two of them slept for a while. Neil had to rest for a bit. Caroline needed to wash up. She slipped out of bed and into the warm water. With her head laid back she was remembering how he felt after he climax. His body went limp on top of her. His heart was beating so fast. She felt the moment he came out of her. He had stayed hard for quite a while. The next time they made love. She would like to try everything.

Neil knew she had left their bed. She looked so beautiful. He lifted himself up on one elbow. All he had to do was looked over her body. Her body had done it. He was hard again. Neil remembered how she felt when he was inside her. Caroline had fallen asleep in the water. With a wave of his hand. He had her on her back on top of him. His hands roamed over her breaths. Neil knew when she opened her eyes.

"I want to taste every part of your body. I think I'll start with your mouth. Then those nipples."

He had her up in the air. As he sat up. He turned her and parted her legs. Neil wanted to taste her sweetness again. Slowly his finger moved inside her. Her legs close around his head when she climaxed. Now she was face to face with him and under him. Her nipple was in his mouth. He teased the other nipple with his thumb. Then he was turning her over as he kissed her. His hands moved over her back. Caroline take me inside ye. Set up and feel how deep I am.

"What are ye doing to me?"

"Take it slow. There. Is this all right?" His hands were around her waist. He was moving her up and down on him.

"Aye… Neil more give me more." She had climax again.

Her body was reacting to everything he was doing to her. There were feelings she had that thrilled her. Other feelings that scared her at the same time.

When she climaxed. She cried out his name. *"Neil…"*

"Now, I'm going to enjoy your heat. I'm going to drink your sweetness and make ye come again."

Then he turned her on her back and spun her around. He moved her legs apart brought her heat to his mouth. His tongue went between her moist lips. Caroline cried out as she climaxed.

"Aye, ye are sweet tasting. I want more of ye."

He moved a finger inside her. His tongue played with her click. Caroline grabbed his legs and climax again. Neil enjoyed everything he was doing to her. With a wave of his hand. Neil spun her around and brought her mouth to his heat.

"I want more of ye. Take hole of my heat, put your mouth around it."

"Neil, please stop. This way is not for me right now. I want ye inside me."

Without thinking Caroline waved her hand and spun him around. Neil was floating over her. He could see in her eyes she didn't know what happen.

He gave a little laughed. *"I see ye have your powers. Happy Birthday my love. What would ye, like me to do?"*

"Neil, did I do that?"

He smiled, *"Aye that ye did."*

Then it was his turn. "Come up here. I have just what ye want."

Neil brought his love up to him. She was facing him. He took her hand and placed her fingers on his heat.

"Is this what ye want?"

"Aye... ye are wet and hard. Did I do this?"

"Aye... all I have to do is look at any part of ye."

Caroline guided his heat between her legs. She kept her fingers there. Neil was laying under her. Now she was setting on top of him. When they were back on the bed. She could feel how deep he went inside her.

"Is this what ye want?"

"Aye... I can feel ye are deep inside of me. Neil make love too me. I need ye. Oh Neil... those power scared me."

"Don't think right now. Will talk about this. *I will show ye the letter from your great grandmother. For right now. Let me make love to ye."*

"Aye, setting on ye like this. Is this the only way you're really deep inside me?"

"Ye want me deeper inside ye."

Neil had her get on all fours. He slid inside her moving in and out.

"Slide your hands down the bed. This way is going to be deep. I'll move slowly at first. Try to get yourself to climax with me."

He hoped he wouldn't get her with child yet. With his hand on her hips. Neil drove his heat inside her.

"Neil... Don't stop. Harder." When she climaxed.

Neil climax with her. She felt the power behind his climax. When it was time to give him a child.

This would be the way to go. Then she remembered she had powers.

"I love ye Neil. I don't want to hurt ye with these powers."

"*I love ye too. Ye make me feel whole.*"

They floated back down to their bed. They couldn't get enough of each other. An hour later they were in the water. He was enjoying touching his wife.

"*Neil, ye said that ye would show me my great grandmothers' letter.*"
"*Aye that I did.*" He handed the letter to Caroline.

Hello Granddaughter;

I'm feeling ye are fearing your own powers. My parents died because they didn't want to hurt anyone. They couldn't use their powers to even save them self. Evil uses power to control people. Because men like Marcus needs to be powerful. They use religion to control people that are weak.

I remember when I grew into these powers. Before my birthday, the woman who saved me. Gave me a book that was my mother's. Inside was this letter. When my father gave Garret his powers. The letter came to him. Aye, the letter that ye are holding. Everyone gets different information from this letter.

Ye see Garret made it so anyone who picks this letter up. Will have their question answered. This happens even before ye speak it. Your powers will not let ye hurt anyone of your family. The mark Neil gave ye, has the magic fairy rose on the cross. Ye can only see the mark on the full moon. If there is danger that someone will know ye have magic. The fairy magic will not let ye use your powers. Remember, your powers can be given to your children. Their powers could be strong in mine and body not magic. Ye and Neil have all these things. With your thoughts call to Neil. I know ye can hear him. He was able to hear ye. These powers Eleanor will need. Make them stronger for her. She will need that kind of magic. The stronger ye get in anything ye do. Will make your children, children's powers stronger.

Ye like to know if your child will give Eleanor life. Your child will not be the one to bring Eleanor into the world. It will be the third generation, around 1900. I cannot tell ye when it will happen.

What I can tell ye. When Eleanor is thirteen years old Marcos will try to rape her. Take care of each other. Time will tell. If Marcos will win or we will beat Marcos.

 Love,
 Leslie

Chapter Two: Joseph and James

SINCE 1850 THERE HAS BEEN FOUR GENERATIONS. The children of the MacGregor's and Angel-Heart's families that has passed. Leslie's letter told them around 1900. The birth of Thomas and Eleanor. A hundred years has passed. Here it's 1950, Joseph and James were just born. The two families were wondering if Leslie meant it would be after the fourth generation. Does this mean Joseph will sire Eleanor? James should be the one to sire Thomas. His father needed to know. If his son doesn't take care of the roses after he's passed away. It will drop into Thomas's lap. He will have to teach Thomas how to take care of the roses. His son must marry soon. Leslie's letter has gone missing. The MacGregor family couldn't fine the letter any wares. It should have been with the three rose bushes. They don't know if Thomas would arrive in this time frame.

James found being around his father was getting harder to do. All his father talks about is the roses. If not that question. His father is asking, who is he going to marry? His brother Brandon had to go to Scotland. There was no son to take care of the roses. In America, the same thing will happen if James don't have a son. James and Joseph had a meeting with their father's. They were trying to find out what plans their sons had forgetting married.

James was talking to his father. *"Dad, I don't want to take care of any roses. I'm sorry, but I don't believe in the magic rose. I want to* become a Navy Seal. To do impossible things. Work with men who is protecting our country."

Joseph try to tell his father about the Navy Seals. *"Dad, James and I wrote to uncle Emile. He sent us what the test will be for a Navy Seal. James will be eighteen soon. I just turn eighteen. We're going into the Navy. After boot camp, we are volunteering to become a Navy Seal."*

"Sir and my father. We mean you no disrespect. I think I know why you're so upset with us. I hope I'm wrong about this. You're thinking, that we may have a death wish. I ask you this. Do you think, Emile joined because he has a death wish?"

Both fathers said, *"No. Emile is a strong man. We found that he could do anything."*

It was Joseph father that relies what his son was doing.

"So that is why you been over here. You been working on your swimming and running, haven't you?"

"Dad you know I have. I've been working on the things Emile has told us to do."

James had spoken up. *"Sir and Dad. Do you think it's easy to become a Navy Seal? We must pass the endurance test. Do you think they would throw us into a team? No! As a team, if were unable to hold up our end. We could get someone killed. Before that happens, they will kick us out."* Both fathers looked at each other.

Joseph father had spoken first. *"Alright. We can't stop you. Be careful. Keep in mind that you still could be the once to bring Thomas and Eleanor into these families. There is one thing the two of you should do. Go to the waterfall. You don't have to dig the roses up. Just lay down over them. Let the fairy magic call to you."*

James father spoke. *"Son, you and Joseph have been best friends as your father, and I have been. Have you ever thought about Desiree and Malaya? The four of you have known each other for a long time. Have you ever kissed Desiree since your older?"*

James spoke, *"No! She's like a sister to me."*

Both fathers started to laugh. Where have we heard that before. Could history be repeating itself?

The two boys looked at each other.

Joseph spoke. *"Alright we will go take a nap under the tree. We will see if anything happens. Beside the four of us are going to go swimming today. Will see, what the fairy roses will do with the four of us together."*

<hr>

James and Joseph followed the path that led to the waterfall.

"Joseph, what do you think about the talk we had with our father's?"

"James, are you talking about the roses, or our sisters? If you're talking about our sisters. Say were at boot-camp. You find out that Desiree was going out with Max. You do know that Max been trying to date her. Would you be alright with that? What if he had sex with her? What would you want to do?"

"Damn it! Joseph why are you asking me these questions?"

"James, you know why? It's what our fathers had said. What if their right? Do you want me to say it first? I will! Yes, I do have feelings for Malaya. Ray been asking her to go out with him. I don't like him at all. If he hurts her…I'd…"

"Alright, you made your point. I do have feelings for, Desiree. Your right about everything. Let's take that nap over these magic roses. I hope they will show me what I need to do."

When they started to lay down, the sunlight got brighter. The light was coming closer to them. There before them stood Eleanor MacGregor.

'Joseph and James why are ye trying so hard? Ye already know who ye want to be with the rest of your life. Ye are acting like my husband and brother did back in my time. Tell me this. When ye are away from Malaya. Do ye go over her house once ye get back. Just to see her?'

Joseph looked at Eleanor and wonder if his daughter would look like her.

"I'm sorry Eleanor. I was thinking. I'm sorry was that question directed to me? I know that you're not my grate grandmother. What may I call you?"

'You may call me granny. Aye, that question was for ye. Ye were thinking. What your daughter may look like. Malaya has hair like mine.

Her skin is also similar, to my own. What would ye say? When your mine has been only of Malaya.'

Joseph spoke, "Granny, I feel like Thomas did. My father is being like Thomas father. Should I see if Malaya has feelings for me."

'Aye! Ye should find out. At the same time ye will know about your own feelings. Ye must tell them, about the secret. Be honest with them.'

Joseph spoke, "Granny, it's hard to think of Malaya feeling that way. I don't know if she could stand being a wife of a Navy Seal. What Emile had written us may be hard for them to be a part of."

'Are ye sure about that. Do ye think they would run from anything?'

Joseph spoke, "No, I'm not sure. How do you know about all of this? Do you know how they feel?"

'Aye… I may know. Ye will have to find out yourself.'

James spoke, "If you're telling us the truth. Do you know what she would say? Could she handle being a navy wife? On top of dealing with a demon?"

'My poor boys. Tell me this. When ye go see them, has either of them ever dressed up for ye?'

Joseph spoke, "Yes, she did. I remember I couldn't take my eyes off her. Damn it, how blind can a person be! That day I watched her walk away from me. I thought she sure has a nice bottom. I love those long legs of hers."

Joseph shook his head to clear his mine. "Tell me this. These thoughts I'm having. Are they my own? You're not putting your thoughts into my mind, are you?"

'No, they are your own thoughts. I was just asking ye questions. Just so ye would think and remember. The way she looked at ye. Things that they had done for ye.'

Joseph replied, "I do have feelings for her. I don't understand these feelings. Malaya is more than a sister to me. She is a beautiful woman, that I enjoy being with. If anyone hurts her I... Damn it. Granny are you saying everything is going to happen, the way it was in your time?"

"Will it be the same for us? When Thomas and William new that they loved each other's sisters."

'No, this is your time. It's not mine. Somethings are mint to be the same. It's up to ye. The four of ye will have to find your way.

James, I'm sorry ye don't like to take care of the roses. Without a MacGregor male taking care of them. The roses will all die here in America. We need your son to take care of them. Can ye see yourself without Desiree?'

"Granny, you don't play fair. She is Joseph sister."

Joseph spoke, "Yes! Desiree is my sister. Malaya is yours. What is the difference. I have strong feelings for Malaya. I thought it was the way I feel for Desiree. I know that it's been hard to take my eyes off her. When she looks so sexy at times. I'm going to say it. It makes me want her in that way."

"Joseph are you saying you're in love with my sister?"

"James you know that answer. I believe I am. Come on James. I saw how you looked at Desiree.

You can tell me that you don't have strong feelings for her. Something gives you away. If you know what I mean."

Joseph, I'm pleased that ye were able to know your own feelings. Ye had found out that ye were in love. James ye are trying too hard. Stop being blind about this. Ye won't say one way or another. Ye two love each other's sisters. James ye may not say what ye are thinking. Your heart speaks for ye. Ye both had saved each other sister. James when Desiree got hurt. Ye were scared that ye would lose her.'

James spoke, "Yes, I kissed her on the lips. I said a prayer that she be alright. I knew you saw me kissing Desiree. Yes, it scared me to see her like that. I would love to kiss her again. Where she could kiss me back or slap me in the face. Granny, how do we go about this?"

'My poor boys let your heart lead ye. Try to go slow. Remember, a man has two brains. Don't let the little brain take over. Good luck my boys.' Eleanor then disappeared.

"James do you think we should take that nap."

"Joseph that's a big yes. Let's see what the fairy roses have for us. Maybe it will make a believer out of me."

"James, that's a very good idea. Maybe it will tell us how to go about all this."

James and Joseph laid near the roses. They listen to the waterfall to fall asleep. It worked! The two of them dreamt of each other sister. They didn't know that they were being watched. Joseph hadn't felt the mark on his chest. The demon would make sure the boys wouldn't remember the talk with Eleanor. The only thing they would remember is seeing her.

It was the first day of summer. It's been hot weather for a week. The water was warm enough to go swimming with the girls. The boys have been swimming for two weeks. They been trying to get use to cold water.

"Joseph, how should we bring up the idea to go out with them? I don't know what to do. I know that talk with are fathers got me thinking. I've notice, Desiree been dressing up and acting different around me."

In the back ground someone was watching. He waved his hand to make trouble.

"James, your right about that. The girls have been dressing up. I started to think about being away from Malaya. You can say it did the trick. I didn't like the thought of her being with another guy. I thought of her kissing someone else. It upset me. No! It made me angry. James, I wonder how Thomas felt with his best friend was dating his sister?"

"Joseph you're my best friend. It's your sister? Would you mind if I start dating her?"

"James you're not alone. Yes, you can date my sister. I always see the two of you together. I thought the same thing with another guy taking Desiree out. It also upset me. To be true full it made me angry also. would you mind if I date your sister?"

"James, I can't see Desiree with anyone else but you. There is only one thing we could do. Test the water."

"Joseph, I know what you're talking about. Right back at you. It's time we found out how the girls feel. See if they feel the same way. They know everything about school and the magic roses. They even know about us going into the Navy."

"James, we have to tell them about us trying out for the Navy Seals. First tell them about the Navy Seals. Then show them Emile's letter. If their okay with it. We can ask them out."

"Joseph, I don't have the letter with me. Should I go get mine?"

"James don't worry about the letter. I have mine with me."

"Joseph it would be nice to know how your sister kisses back. You can't tell when there unconscious."

"James, we must be careful. We can't have them with child until were in the Navy. To be able to touch them. To know if it's just sex. What am I saying! Where did that come from?"

Joseph was trying to wake-up. Something wasn't right. Why was James yelling at me?

James raised his voice. "Joseph just don't have fun with my sister then dump her. Because you found out that you don't love her."

Joseph spoke softly. "James, you know me better than that. Stop it!... We're being watch. I'm not talking about the girls. There is a demon around."

Joseph saw a man behind the tree then he was gone. Now he knew he had the mark that Garret had given his family.

Joseph spoke, "So, it has started. I have some of my powers. We must be on the right path, and just in time. There's the girls."

James spoke, "Oh boy!... they have new swim suits. I think there trying to get us to notice them. Wow!... I think we're in trouble!"

James and Joseph got out of the water and went over to help them with the food. James took Desiree away from Malaya and Joseph.

Malaya spoke, "What do you think Joseph? Do you like my new swim suit? Joseph, will you turn around and look at me."

"Malaya, I have to tell you something first. It's about my plans for the Navy. Forgive me for not looking at you. What do you think of me signing up to become a Navy Seal?"

"I can't believe that Thomas was right."

"Malaya did Thomas MacGregor come and visit you today?"

"Yes, he came while Desiree and I was outside. He told us that things are changing be-tween all of us. Has it? I have a right to know."

"Malaya, after are talk with our father's. I was thinking. I would like to date you. To see if it could change between us. Then Eleanor came, I don't remember what she said to us."

"Thank you, Malaya, for telling me. I have a letter from Emile. Let's see what happens after you read the letter. It's about the test we will have to take to become a Navy Seal."

"Let me see it."

Malaya took the letter from Joseph. After she read it. She brought it to Desiree and came back.

Joseph took hole of her hand. *"Will you come with me. We can swim across the pond. I think we have a lot to talk about."*

"Joseph how do you like my swim suit?"

"Malaya do you want me to tell you or show you."

Malaya didn't know what to say. *"Joseph, just show me. Then I'll tell you what I think. Of you being a part of the Navy Seal team."*

Joseph took Malaya by the hand leading her into the water. *"Come on. Let's swim away from James and Desiree. You're sure about me showing you."*

She was wondering if she made a mistake. They swam across the pond, side by side. At the end of the pond they climb the rocks together. On top, he took her by the hand and led her behind the large boulder.

"Malaya, tell me what you think of me becoming a Navy Seal? I need to know."

"Joseph, why do you need my okay. Just to become a Navy Seal? Is there more to this? You always call me your sister. Has your feelings change about me?"

"Damn it, Malaya! Don't you know why. Yes, my feelings have change."

Joseph pulled Malaya into him. His arms went around her back to hold her close. He felt her soft bare skin on his arms and hands. When their eyes met. He knew he had to kiss her. She closed her eyes and felt his lips on hers. After the kiss ended.

"Joseph, what does this mean?"

He was kissing her face and down her neck. His hands went to her breast.

Malaya had pushed him away from her. *"No! Stop it! I don't want you to touch me."* She was angry with him.

Joseph didn't know what to say to her. *"Malaya I…"*

He had let his little brain take over. Joseph had turn away from Malaya. Would she understand? It's time to tell her how he feels.

"Malaya, I'm sorry. Your skin felt so soft. You look so damn sexy in your swimsuit. It brought out feelings that I thought I would never have. Not with you. I always thought of you as my sister. I know now.

I'm in love with you. It's not the kind of love I have for my sister. The moment I saw you today. It was as if I just met you for the first time. I wanted you. It was my little brain that took over. Every part of you was different. The talk with our fathers got me thinking."

"Joseph, I don't understand what you are saying. What do you mean a man has two brains? You're saying it was your little brain that woke you up? Where do you keep this little brain?"

"Damn it… Malaya stop this game you're playing. You know what I'm talking about. I'm not playing games with you. I love you. I always knew that I was in love with you. I'm glad you stop me. I can't have you with child, not yet. Not intel I'm in the Navy. When I get my first pay, I like to buy you a ring. Malaya, do you love me?"

Then she burst out laughing. Something was not right. Malaya was acting strange. This isn't the way it should be. She wouldn't wear a swimsuit like she has on.

"Malaya would you follow me, when I go in the Navy?"
"Why should I?"
"Because I love you and want to marry you. We can use my class ring from ROTC. After boot camp, I can get you a better ring."
'Why is she laughing at me?'
"Why would I marry you? Couldn't you come up with better way to tell a woman that you want her. It's not me. It's my little brain making me hot for you. Now you want to marry me. Then you tell me that you can't have me with a child. Who said I want to have children with you? I didn't tell you that I love you. Now did I!"

⁂

Desiree and Malaya were on the path to the waterfall. They had a picnic lunch with them. Up a head they saw a man. He looked like James, Desiree's brother.

'Why would her brother have on a kilt?'
Malaya spoke, *"James is that you? Why do you have a kilt on?"*
As they got closer. This handsome man looked older them her brother. He was the ghost, of Thomas.

'Hello Lassie. Aye, your brother looks just like me. I'm Thomas MacGregor. I'm here to tell ye about your future. Ye two women will have Eleanor and Thomas. Both of ye will have two children. A girl and a boy.'

'Malaya, ye will be with child the day your husband goes on their first mission. Your men will be gone for seven months. Malaya, your child will not be Eleanor. Eleanor's brother will be eleven years old, when she is born. Thomas sister will be nine years old. Ye will not remember what I told ye. Only on the day it happens. Ye will remember seeing me. My wife and I will always be watching over ye and the children. Until Marcos is out of your life for good.'

Then Thomas was gone. The two of them felt light headed.

"What just happen to us Malaya?"

"I don't know Desiree. Come on let see what the boys are doing."

The day was beautiful. They headed to the waterfall, after seeing Thomas. When they reached the water. The boys weren't any where's to be found. They headed up to the top of the falls. Malaya's father told the girls where to find them. Right next to the magic roses. The boys were fast to sleep. Both girls looked at each other.

Then Malaya heard Joseph. '*Malaya, I love you. Don't leave me I need you. Did she hear what Joseph said? This is new. Will I always hear him from now on?*'

Malaya spoke, "*Desiree did you hear anything?*"

"No, I didn't. What are you going to do?"

"It's time to make our move. I'm going to show Joseph I'm not his sister. I'm a woman, who's in love with him. I'm having trouble thinking he is my brother. I want to touch those mussels of his. Desiree, I don't know what you're going to do. I saw you looking at my brother. Your eyes went wide when he took his shirt off."

Desiree spoke, "All right you caught me. What are you going to do, Malaya?"

"I was thinking of kissing him. Desiree, I've waited so long for Joseph to make his move. I've dressed up sexy for him."

"I know Malaya. You've been in love with Joseph since we were thirteen. As I have been in love with James. All right! It's time we make are move. Once there in the Navy they could meet another girl. Let's do it."

They went over to their man and got down on their knees. Quickly, they laid next to them. They couldn't wake them up. To give them a kiss. So, they placed their hand over to the side of them. The girls lifted themselves up on one elbow. Malaya placed a kiss on Joseph lips. It surprised her when he reacted. His arms went around her. There he pulled her against him. The kiss lasted longer them she thought it would. Slowly he turned her over. His tongue was moving over her lips. Could this be really happening to her? Malaya then let Joseph push pass her lips.

In her mind, she cried out. *'I love you Joseph. Please see me as a woman. I'm not your sister. I need you.'*

He could taste cherry on her lips. This kiss is not a dream. He started to make love to her mouth. No... this is not a dream. He could feel her finger nails on his back. He opened his eyes quickly and sat up.

"Malaya, what are you doing?"

"Joseph don't you know when your being kissed? I know that you kissed me back. I've been with you for a longtime. Haven't you wonder what it be like to kiss me."

"Malaya, I guess I have. We're not kids anymore and you're not my sister. James, wake-up. Your kissing my sister. It's time we do what we have talked about."

Joseph watch James open his eyes and sat up. Both girls had done the same thing. *'So, his sister was in love with James. Could Malaya be in love with me? Did I hear her voice, when I was kissing her?'*

"James, you are staying here for now. Malaya, do you have your swimsuit with you?"

"Yes Joseph, it's under my clothes."

"Then go get change into your swimsuit."

Malaya felt shy right then. She could still feel his lips on hers. Did he just say that she wasn't his sister? She went quickly behind the tree. Her face felt hot. When she came back. Malaya had a two-piece bathing suit on. The bottom had a skirt to it. Joseph couldn't take his eyes off her. The dream made him unsure of himself. He took out the letter and gave it to Malaya.

"*Malaya, I like for you to read this letter. Then give the page to Desiree to read. Don't say anything to her about it. Just hand it to her and come with me when you're done.*"

As she read the letter. Her thoughts wondered. Would she be strong enough to handle what-ever came at her? She would have to watch Joseph leave. Their training is also dangerous. What about the time he's gone on a mission? Joseph saw fear in her face. It came and went just as fast. Each sheet was past to Desiree to read. As she read on. Joseph took off his shirt and pants. Malaya saw him from the corner of her eye.

'It felt so good to be in his arms. How can I get him to kiss me again? Joseph could you love me like you did?'

Right then, Joseph looked over at Malaya. *'He was wondering was he hearing Malaya's thoughts?'*

As Malaya she could feel Joseph eyes on her. She felt that he feared what she thought of this letter.

Chapter Three: Uncle Emile Letter

I'VE BEEN THINKING ABOUT YOU TWO. It's a big step volunteering to become a Navy Seal. You boys wanted to be just like me. I've heard this also from your fathers. I think I made those stories to glamorous. I'll tell you a little bit about how I became a Navy Seal. As you know I joined the Navy in 1943.

After the attack on Pearl Harbor. They started an Amphibious Training Base. This base was adapted for both land and water. The units UDT-1 and UDT-2. The Birthplace for UDT-Seal teams: was Waimanalo, Hawaii. The service took men from the Air Force the Navy, Army, and Marine Corps. I became a diver for the UDT that they called a frogman. They were the first Airborne Frogmen. Not only went under water. These men took on difficult assignments. They would jump from a plane landing in water with full diving gear. In 1948, a team of three men in a small submersible. Made the first docking with a submerged submarine on the USS Quillback's. These men work on the Sea. In the Air, and on Land. They go to were ever they are needed. Their history from the elite frogmen of World War 11. They were given Special Operations missions in all operational environments. To be trained for "Amphibious Roger." At the Scout and Ranger school at Ft. Pierce, Fla.

In 1962, President Kennedy. He had set up SEALS Teams ONE and TWO from the existing UDT Team. To develop a Navy Unconventional Warfare Capability. The Navy Seal Teams were designed as the maritime counterpart to the Army Special Forces *"Green Berets."* They deployed act at once to Vietnam. They work in the deltas and thousands of rivers and canals in Vietnam. These teams effectively disrupted the enemy's maritime lines of communication. The SEAL was so effective that the enemy named them, *"the men with the green faces."*

"Two months ago. I send your father a letter. In this letter, I told him what they had to train for. Joseph it's not all fun and games. For twenty-five years, I have been a Navy Seal. BUD/S is a 6-month SEAL training course. It's held at the Naval Special Warfare Training Center in Coronado, CA. You'll start with five weeks Indoctrination and Pre-Training as part of a Navy SEAL Class. Then you will go through the Three Phases of BUD/S. Called Basic Underwater Demolition/SEAL.

I'm writing this letter. The way we would describe to anyone who would want to volunteer for the Navy Seal. This is all true what I'm telling you. It may change your mind on volunteering. This part I'm not going to sugar coat it. I'll tell it like it is.

First, Phase is the toughest. It consists of 8 weeks of Basic Conditioning. It peaks with a grueling segment called *"Hell Week."* This is midway point, where you'll be tested to your limits. Hell Week: Is a test of physical endurance and mental, tenacity.

Tenacity: to see if you can stick to a goal. If you have staying power to keep going.

Teamwork: Efficiency of the whole team, and courage. There can be 2/3 or more of your classmates that call it quits or *"ring the bell."*

Physical discomfort and pain will cause many to decide it isn't worth it. The miserable wet-cold approaching hypothermia will make others quit. Sheer fatigue and sleep deprivation. Will cause every candidate. To question his core values, motivations, limits, and everything he's made of and stand for. Those who grit it out to the finish will hear their Instructors yell the longed-for words,

"Hell, Week is secured!"

There will be an exceptional few. With the burning desire will persevere them. Were their bodies are screaming to quit yet continue. These men experience a tremendous sense of pride, achievement, brotherhood and a new self-awareness.

"I can do anything I put my mine to!" The most outstanding among them. The man whose sheer force of will becomes their example. He inspires his classmates to keep going. When they're ready to quit, he Will become the *"Honor Man"* of the Class. These determined men will continue.

Second Phase: 8 weeks of Diving.

Third Phase: 9 weeks of Land Warfare. Most men who have succeeded in Hell Week make it through these phases. If not, it's usually due to academic issues.

For example, dive physics. In the Dive Phase, or weapons and demolitions safety/ competency issues. In the Land Warfare, weapons and tactics Phase. After BUDS is completed, trainees go through 3 weeks of Basic Parachute Training.

At this point, training shifts from testing. In how the men react in a high-stress, called *"gut check."*

Environment: The circumstances, objects, or conditions by which one is surrounded. To making sure the trainees are competent in their core tasks.

The men go through a final 8 weeks of focused SEAL Qualification Training. In mission planning operations, and tactic, techniques. Upon completion, they may wear the coveted Navy SEAL Trident insignia on their uniform. SEAL training ends with the formal BUD/s Class Graduation. Here the proud few in their dress Navy uniforms are recognized for their achievement in the presence of family and senior SEAL leaders. The Commanding Officers and senior enlisted advisors of the Naval Special Warfare Groups and SEAL Teams attend. The BUD/S graduates, as their newest Teammates, will be reminded of the special group they have entered, to be worthy of the sacrifices of the courageous Frogmen who came before them, and the great honor it is to serve as a U.S. Navy SEAL.

Joseph, this part is for the woman that you would like to marry or go out with. My wife said I need to tell you everything about Navy Seal. Some woman will have to be able to deal with this if they get out.

Many women can't deal having their man gone all the time. This is also any part of the Air Force. The Navy, Army, and Marine Corps. It takes a special kind of woman, to be able to dill with this.

"As my wife said, she will handle it when it happens. To think about what he is going through is too much. He has a job to do. She also has her job. To take care of their children and their home. If the children are all in school. She may have a job."

A SEAL must devote 100% of himself to his job and having a family needs 100% of a man's attention! One element in his life is going to suffer and most of the times it will be his family. His family can take a lot more than a job as a SEAL.

If you don't show up to your child's game nothing happens. Your child gets used to it, or he will start to resent you! A relationship with a Navy Seal is a tough one! A SEAL is on call about every moment that he stays a Navy SEAL! If you and your SEAL boyfriend are having a wedding ceremony. He could be deployed right in the middle of it if it was necessary! They are constantly in war zones that are extremely dangerous, and unforgiving.

In these zones. His mind must be on what he is doing. It could cost him is life. If he is thinking about the fight with is child, or his wife. Which means you are constantly worrying about them coming back home safely! Their training is very dangerous. Some have said that he has almost died more times in training than in actual combat! Seals are always training. This means, even if there isn't a war, they could die in training! Many Navy SEAL's can't even tell you when they will be deploying! It's also hard to get a Navy SEAL to quit his job! Imagine being the best of the best at everything. Surrounded by amazing people from all over the world. Doing everything, shooting, blowing stuff up. Going on adventures. Taking risk. Jumping out of planes. Occasional you get a shot of adrenaline throughout your body. It's hard for them to retire. When you come back after all that you have done. When it will hit you. How could he top all of this? He wonders what to do next! For the past many years, all you have known is grind, grind, GRIND, and now there is nothing! Let the girls know about this.

Good Luck, Joseph.
Your Uncle Emile

When Malaya was done with the last page of the letter, she passed it to Desiree. She went over to Joseph and gave him her hand. The two of them went down the hill holding hands. They stop at the edge of the water. Joseph turn to face her.

"Malaya, I'm so mixed up about all these feelings about you and me. Do you know why I never dated another girl for very long?"

"Joseph, I believe it had to do with the magic roses. You know where that letter from Leslie is hidden. Leslie told you and my brother something. Could it be you're the once to bring Ellen and Tom into the world. Am I right?"

"Yes Malaya. Do you also know who she said will be my mate?"

"No! Joseph why are you looking at me that way?"

Them Joseph smile at Malaya.' *"So, you're not wondering how long we knew?"*

Malaya shook her head no. *"Well I'll tell you. Since my uncle told us about the Navy Seals. Why do you think I kept away from other girls? I knew then I wouldn't fall in love with anyone else. You know I tried. It just didn't feel right to me. Malaya, how long have you known that your brother and I had the letter?"*

"I knew from the age of thirteen. After that you changed. The days you took all those girls out. It went on for months. Then something happened to the two of you. Now you two were working out, doing some running and swimming. You started to let me run with you. Sometimes I got to swim with you. On days James couldn't go. You ask me. It was the same way with my brother. I saw the look you had on your face. On the day I went out with someone else. I thought that you would have hurt my date. All through school you kept me around. You wouldn't let me get close to you or another boy. When I touch you. You let me but not for long. Joseph, in my mind I would yell at you."

"I know Malaya. You would say, can't you see I'm a woman. I'm not like anyone else."

"Joseph you could hear me?"

"Yes! I couldn't handle the feelings I had for you. When I received my powers. I made a spell. I took our feelings and put them in a bottle. It was James eye dear. The two of us couldn't handle what we wanted to do with you two. I made the spell for both of us. You and Desiree were the only ones that could break the spell. I change our love. To the love for a sister. My dreams of you. Told me I lost you. The need to touch you in my dreams. Every time you ran from me. I saw a demon laughing at me. He said that Ellen will never be born to me. It scares me to know my daughter will have to fight off Marcos. I need to become a Navy Seal. I have to teach you and our daughter how to fight."

"Joseph, what I read in that letter scares me. I pray I will never have to deal with the death of you. In my heart, I have always loved you. Teach me what you will have to go through. Show me your strong enough to endure it. I love you with all my heart. I know it's not the kind of love for a brother. It never has been."

"Malaya I'm sorry. You and I became best friends. Damn it… Malaya, I keep telling myself your James sister. I couldn't think of you any different. Until now. You're not my sister. Not any-more. You broke the spell. Those feelings are out, and I need you. When you kissed me. I wanted to touch you. To have you under me, more then you should know. I could tell you everything. You and James are my best friends. Come on, we have a lot to talk about. We will put the letter back after you and Desiree look at it. Do you know you're my mate?"

"I wasn't sure about that. I wanted to hold you. When you looked at me. I prayed you come over and kiss me. You never did. I was afraid you would meet someone else."

Joseph pulled her into him and kissed her. It had left Desiree hopeful. *"Come on let's talk about this behind the bolder."*

The two of them dove into the water. They swam together to the other side of the pond. In the water. What he had dreamt of some parts was coming true. As they climbed the rocks. His thoughts and feelings of everything was coming back to him. They went behind the bolder. He could feel the need to hold Malaya. Joseph didn't know if she would be angry with him.

"Malaya, I'm sorry about that spell. I am going into the Navy. I must try to become a Navy Seal. I keep getting these feelings about Marcos. I will be dealing with him as a Navy Seal. You said that you hope you won't have to deal with the death of me. You also said you love me. Those words weren't the love from a brother."

'Does she really love me. Would she marry me. I'm scared of her answer. I don't know what I do without her.'

Joseph was up against the bolder. He was running his hand through his hair. He watched Malaya as she looked toured the mountains. This was the hard part. She had their lives in her hands. Her back was to him. Then his eyes went toured her bottom. The bottle up feelings was coming out fast. Too fast. He had to get a hold of himself before he does something he shouldn't do.

'How he wished he could touch her. He knows now they would have been lovers. When she kissed him. It felt as if he had kissed her many times before. All the girls he went out with. There kisses didn't feel like hers does now. How am I going to start getting her ready for me? I don't know if I could stop myself. Right now, I want to go all the way with her. My Lord, this scares me. I must be in the Navy first. We have all summer to get to know each other. Just after I get out of boot-camp we can marry. Will she marry me? Damn it... What have I done to us?'

Malaya was still looking at the mountains. Tears ran down her cheeks. She could hear Joseph's thoughts. Malaya knew he would become a Navy Seal. She didn't have to see the letter. In her heart she knew that they were the once to have Eleanor. She would call her Ellen, her little Angel. Slowly, Malaya turned toured Joseph.

He was now pounding the bolder with his fist. He couldn't hear her thoughts. He was to upset with himself. She went to Joseph and put her arms around him. Malaya heard his thoughts that she was going to leave him and not marry him. The dream was coming true. Joseph froze the moment he felt her arms around him. In his mind, he heard her say.

'I love you Joseph. I always loved you. Please kiss me. Let me feel your hands on me. You haven't lost me. I have been waiting for you to make up your mind. If I was going to be just your friend or your lover. I can't be your sister any more. When I want so much to feel you inside me.'

Joseph felt her hands move over his chest, and down to his heat. She boldly took hold of his heat and said.

"This is mine. I'll have your heat inside me, today. I do know Joseph it's not the time yet. I want to get to know you. To know each other's body.

It's time, please, kiss me and touch me. I need you, I've been waiting for you for a long time."

Joseph had taken her hand when she went inside his swim suit. He had felt her cheek was wet. She's been crying, her tears were on his back. Just the touch of her fingers made him hard.

"Malaya, stop. If you keep going, I will have you today. Let me touch you. I want to kiss you and make love to your mouth. Let me touch you for now."

Joseph took a deep breath. He held her hand and turned in her arms. He pulled Malaya into him and took her lips.

'Oh yes, I need more of her.'

Joseph turned Malaya. He had placed her up against the bolder. There was a part of the bolder he could lay her back more. Her arms went around his back. He wasn't close enough to her. She wanted to feel his heat against her. With her hands on his bottom. She pushed him into her. It made his heat push against her swim suit.

"Joseph, what's happening to me. It aches here between my legs. I can feel how hard you are. Touch me I need you. I need to feel the way when lovers are together."

"Is this what you're talking about."

His hand was inside her swim suit. She knew it was his heat that made her ache for him. She tried to push his hand closer to her own heat.

"Malaya slow down. Let me give you what we both need. I can't have you with our child. Not yet."

Joseph put her leg between his legs. He lifted her top and took her nipple into his mouth. He sucked on her nipple until it was hard. How he loved her and enjoyed touching her.

"Joseph," Malaya cried.

He took her mouth. While his hand played with her curly hair. His tongue made love to her mouth. Malaya needed more from him. Boldly she took hold of his hand. She tried to push his finger inside her.

"I got this. Let me make you cum."

Joseph felt two moist lips. Her hand plunged his finger into her heat. The moment his finger dipped inside. She felt an explosion with in her. Malaya climax for the first time. His mouth was taking her cry of pleasure. She opened her eyes and looked at him. Malaya held his hand there. Until she couldn't feel that wonderful feeling anymore.

"Malaya let me move inside you. I can give us what we both need."

"Joseph, wait, wait until it stops, please. These feelings are wonderful and new to me."

"Malaya, I need you. Take hole of my heat. Help me to climax. Let my heat slide between your fingers. I'll make you cum again. Just let my finger move in you."

Malaya did as he asked. She didn't think she would have cum again, but she did. In her hand, she held his heat. She felt when he came. Then she relies Joseph was too big around. He had just a finger in her. She was too small for him.

Tears ran down her cheeks. "Malaya why are you crying. Did I hurt you?"

"No… Joseph I'm too small for you. Your much too big to be able to come inside me."

"Malaya, my love. This is where our children will come out of you. You know that. The more we kiss and touch each other. This will open more. You climax twice. I can almost put the tip of another finger in you. When you can take three fingers of mine. You will be able to take me inside you. Before I leave for boot-camp. We will go away for the weekend. On that day I will come inside you. I won't be able to give you my seed. Once were married. I won't need to wear anything. I will make love to you as often as you let me. We will know each other quite will by then."

"Joseph, I just remember I can't marry you. If I do, then Thomas won't be able to marry Eleanor. Our blood line will be to close together. Your sister and my brother. Now you and me. The blood line is too close."

"Just wait." First, he had cleaned them up. "I have something to show you."

Joseph waved his hand and a piece of the rock moved a side. There on top was just a piece of folded paper. Leslie's letter, the magic paper. To help all the families that came after them.

"Malaya take the letter. Asked if you and I will have Eleanor?"

From a blank piece of paper, it changed to having words on it.

Hello Malaya;

Let's get to the heart of all this. Yes, you will have Eleanor. Joseph will be the father of her. How can that be? The answer to this question. James is not your real brother. The MacGregor's had adopted you. You became their daughter the day you were born. Your real mother is a distant cousin of Eleanor's. When Eleanor was sixteen her cousin mother was giving a coming out party. Eleanor's cousin had been missing for nine months. They found her dead. You could see she was killed after given birth to her a little girl. Their mother is the grate-grate-grate granddaughter. The family tried to make what happen to her mother go away. They thought that the child was evil. The child left and came to America. She tried to get away from the past. It was the child blood line. Marcos blood is what kept coming up.

The ghost of Thomas came to two women, Eleanor's cousin and Albert Huascaran daughter. These women blood line took a part in what happen to Thomas and Eleanor. After the MacGregor and Angel-Heart women had their first child. When it was time to have another child. Two years started going past. Many times, the women tried to conceive a child. They found that they couldn't get pregnant again.

They sought-out Leslie's letter. She had told both women. The two families will adopt a little girl. They found out that a demon placed a spell on them. They couldn't get pregnant. Think of this. You now can marry Joseph.

Desiree real mother is the grate-grate-grate granddaughter of Albert Huascaran. Marcos thought that Albert was his son. He had a magic locket made by Garret. The locket would go into Albert's chest. Then Marcos spirit could take over his body. Albert spirit would have been sent to Marcos master.

James didn't like being told he was going to mate with Desiree. He was thirteen and Desiree was ten. She didn't know about Leslie's letter. James wanted to burn the magic letter. Joseph understood, that the letter needed to be hidden. Then he put a spell on him and James. Only the girls could break the spell. A kiss of love. Once the spell was broken. The feelings for the girls would come back. You are at that point. Remember the girls cannot be with child until you two men are in the Navy. Remember it won't take long to get Malaya ready for you. Use a balloon over your heat. Leave room for your seed. Malaya when you receive Joseph seed. On that day he will give you, the cross and rose. It will be place on your chest. This will tell you if demons are around.

For Ellen, she will have a little of Marcos in her. She will know when he is around. Remember, when you and Malaya cannot please each other. Stay strong, use the balloon, when it gets too much for the two of you. Tell James there is a locket that Desiree will wear when he gives his seed to her.

For Tom and Ellen. She will have to wear the locket the first time he beds her. Ellen must stay a virgin. There will be hard times for the two of them. Malaya, Joseph and James will be fine with the Navy Seal. You will make a fine Navy wife for him. He will not die in the Navy.

Good Luck.

Love, Lesli.

"Joseph, should we tell James?"

"No… James must fine out like I did. When you kiss me. It broke the spell. The magic I used on us is no more. I couldn't fight those feelings. At first, I thought it was a dream. The more I kissed you the more I needed you. When Desiree kissed James. All his feelings came back to him in full force. He did what I had done to you. When he was on top of Desiree. Her arms went around him, and she was kissing him back. When he can't keep his hands off her. I will show the letter to him again. It won't take him long to know he's in love with Desiree."

"Joseph you will have to show Desiree the letter. She will have to know that you're not her brother."

"*You worry too much. My sister knows she was adopted. I don't know why they didn't tell you.*"

"*It may be the same reason that James was up-set. It's because of the blood line of Marcos. I'm older now. James will be able to understand that Marcos has no control over me.*"

"*Malaya don't you know?*"

"*What am I supposed to know?*"

"*That Lesli is the sister of Garret. He had placed his sister spirit into the baby. Lesli's body had taken the evil spirit. Marcos killed the baby that was placed in Lesli's body.*"

"*So, there will only be a piece of Marcos. I know why I'm having this bad feeling. He will try to stop Ellen from being born. He knows she will have strong magic. Do you think that I may know some of his plans? Maybe our daughter will also know what he may be up to.*"

Joseph took Malaya into his arms. "*We will remember this and when the time comes. I will put a protection spell on the room. Our daughter will be born.*"

"*I've been thinking of the people who brought the roses here to America. I've noticed each person has ties to the ones before us. There's magic this time. Our daughter is going to have Magic.*"

"*Yes, Ellen will have magic when she is twenty-one. I had asked Lesli about this.*"

Joseph put the magic letter away. He smiled when he took Malaya into his arms.

"*Joseph you have that look when you were going to touch me. You know kissing me would lead you to touching me again.*"

"*Yes, your right. This time, I want to taste how sweet you are. Malaya, would you let me taste you?*"

"*No… my love! You shouldn't have shown me Lesli's letter. Where moving too fast. We should go in the water to cool off. Joseph you're going into the Navy. Do you think you could keep your mine on your job as a Navy Seal? When you can't keep your hands off me. If I let you. I will be pregnant with are son. My love! You have magic. Make a place for us in the dream world. There you and I could go all the way. When your away we could be together in the dream world. Make-it that no one will know what we are doing. Tonight, I will let you taste me.*"

"There I will make you climax again. Each time you do. I will take my tongue and drink your sweet nectar. I will make this place where we can sleep together. Where I can have my way with you.

Now I know why I love you so much. You always kept me balance. When I come inside you in the dream world. I will give you the mark I wear. The day we go away together. You will be given the mark I wear."

"Joseph, I hear them. There in the water."

"I will make a place where our families can go and be together. Malaya were going under the water by the rocks. Hold on to me. Take a breath."

Before Malaya knew it. They were under the water coming to the surface.

"Malaya are you okay?"

"Yes, I'm fine." Joseph kissed her again. Quickly she called out to her brother. Before they started touching each other again.

"James were over here."

The two girls looked at each other. They moved away from the boys to talk.

"Malaya, what were you doing under the water?"

"Just coming to the surface. How did it go with James?"

"It was wonderful being kissed by him. He touched me. I never felt something like that before." Malaya smiled. She knew just what had happen to Desiree.

"Let's go swimming with the boys. Maybe we can get more kisses from them."

"Desiree, do you think later we can touch them?" All Desiree heard after was giggling.

***

A storm was raging outside the hospital. Joseph was in the delivery room with his wife, Malaya. Their son was waiting with the MacGregor's family. Emily was setting next to Raymond in the waiting room reading. A young boy sat at the window watching the trees move violently back and forth.

"Daddy." cried Tom.

"What's wrong son? Is the storm scaring you?"

James walked over to his son and sat down next to him.

"Tom, what do you see out there?"

James could see his son didn't like what he saw. *"I see evil out there in the trees. He's calling for Ellen and me. He said his name is Marcos. Tonight, Ellen and I are going to die."*

"Tom, how do you know all this?"

"The beautiful lady with the golden-brown hair. Told me that Ellen will be born tomorrow night. I told Uncle Joseph, yesterday about all of this. I also told him that evil will try to get in to the hospital."

"What did Joseph say about that."

"He asked me who told me this. I said, it was the beautiful lady Eleanor. She comes to see me often these past two months. Marcos has been upsetting Ellen. When we talk. I told her he won't hurt her. Her daddy knows about Marcos. She knows that her daddy is going to put a protection spell when her mommy will give birth."

James heard a man's voice yelling. *'Get the boy away from the window. Now!'*

He grabbed his son. Quickly he brought Tom over to the other side of the room. Ones there, a tree limb broke through the window. Right where Tom had sat, a sharp piece of glass was left. The limb would have hit Tom. The glass would have gone right into his son killing him.

"Daddy why does Marcos want to hurt the baby and I?" Desiree took Tom into her arms.

In James, mine he cried out. *'You can't have them. One way or another we will stop you.'*

"Baby Ellen is here. She safe, she doesn't like to be cold. Marcos had scared her. Ellen gave her momma a hard time. I told her everything will be all right. Mommy can you hear her crying?"

"Tom, how long have you been able to hear her?"

"About two months."

Raymond spoke, *"Momma told me. Tom has the gift to talk with his mate. My little sister is Tom's mate."*

Then Raymond felt his mark. *"There's evil out there. He's trying to get inside."*

Tom jumped off his mother's lap. He went for the broken glass turning the point out-wards.

"Be Gone Satan! You can't have her. Ellen is my little Angel."
"Tom what are you doing son."

Quickly Tom thrust the point into the open space. Everyone heard a cry of pain in the wind. On the tip of the glass dripped blood.

One of the ghosts spoke. *'Be gone Marcos! Ye cannot have her or the boy. Go back to your master. Tell him. How Tom took the glass and thrust it into ye. He beat ye Marcos. A baby boy beat ye.'*

Raymond waved his hand and the window was fix. He then put a protection spell around the room. James took the broken glass. He then checked his sons' hand. There was no cut any where's. In a blink of an eye the glass was gone. The door open standing in the doorway was Joseph. In his arms wrapped in a pink blanket was a baby girl. Joseph looked at everyone. He knew that something had happened.

"Is it safe to bring her into the room?"

Joseph saw his son wave his hand in a circle when he opened the door.

"Raymond, what are you doing?"

"I just made the room safe. Can we all see my little sister?"

Joseph sat down in a chair. He then opened the blanket revealing his daughter. Raymond and Tom looked at her with loving eyes. They looked up at Joseph. In Joseph and James mine, they heard.

The ghost of Neil spoke. *'Ye done well my boys. Your children are strong and brave. Raymond powers are strong for his age. He will do will when he needs them.'*

The ghost of Alexander spoked. *'Thank ye for listening to Tom. I couldn't stop Marcos. He thought if he scared Ellen. She would die. I heard Tom talking to her. He told her no one will hurt her or her momma. Tom will need that power when their older. There will always be one of the family close to them. I wished that this could have been stop in my own time frame. Be careful, Marcos will do anything to take the two of them to his master. Teach them everything ye know. One of the family will keep an eye out for Marcos. Be safe.'*

James knew who was here. In his mine, he heard his great-great grandfather who brought the roses to America.

The ghost of Alexander spoke, *James, Tom is a brave boy. He's older than he looks. In action and in thought. It was your son who knew just what to do. He could see what Marcos was up to.*

Then everyone saw the two ghosts of Alexander and Neil.

Neil spoke, *Are family will watch over all of you. Marcos will be back on earth soon. We will also be here. On the day Ellen turns thirteen. Will be around until Marcos is unable to come back to earth.*

James went over to his wife and children. Ellen still had Tom's and Raymond finger. The adults smiled at the two boys.

Tom said. "Raymond, Ellen is glad you are her brother."

Today Ellen turn four years old. The gift for her birthday was ballet lessons. She was so happy to see a ballet outfit. Tom smile as she tried to dance in her tutu.

He called to Ellen. *Angel, you look so pretty in your tutu. Do a spin for me.*

Ellen gave Tom a big smile. *Mic, will you dance with me?*

Yes, Angel I'll dance with you.

On Monday, Ellen had her first lesson. Tom took karate lessons also that day. An hour after Ellen's ballet class. He had asked if he could watch Ellen. From then on. The mothers would take turns, bringing the children to their classes. A month later Tom notice how strong Ellen's legs were getting. She was moved up to another group. It also moved her to a different day. Tom had also change groups. He stepped into a new level of karate. At her new ballet class. He noticed that this class had older boys' dancing. Tom remember seeing two of the boys that played football. After the class was done. He asked one of the boys why they took ballet.

"Hello, my name is Tom. I like the way you dance and play football. Is that why you like dancing? Does the dancing help you be a better football player?"

"Yes, it helped improve my balance and movement for football. I can jump hire over the guys with the football."

These boys were older then Tom. *"Beside football. I enjoy dancing with the girls. Are you hoping to dance with that pretty young girl?"*

"Yes. She shows me everything she had learned. When we dance it's like dancing on a cloud?"

The older boy spoked. *"So, you know what I mean?"*

"I believe I do."

Tom enjoyed dancing with Ellen. 'He thinks he may ask his parents if he could take lessons with her. It's been helping his balance. His legs are stronger, and it's improved his karate.'

On Ellen next lesson Tom join the class. He had to show how much he knew about ballet. Ellen was advance two years in her class. She went over to talk to her teacher.

"Mrs. Macule, Tom has been dancing with me. He helped me with the couple's parts. Could we show you what we can do? I've shown him all the steps. May I dance with him?"

"Will see Ellen. Hello Tom. Ellen has told me you can lift her over your head."

"Yes mam, her brother made me lift weights. Until I was strong enough to lift her with no trouble. First show me how high you can lift Ellen."

"That was very good. All right you can show me what you two could do. Be careful doing your dance."

"Tom, we will do all the dances that we worked on together."

In Ellen's mine she called to him. 'It's just you and me here. We can do this. It's up to you that if want to be in my class?'

In Tom's mine he answered her. 'Angel, I always love dancing with you. Your brother made be stronger. I could pick you up and put you over my head. You may have two years of dancing. I also have two years in dancing and in karate. I'm move quicker and jump higher. I love dancing with you.'

"Tom it's been fun. I fine teaching you the moves got me thinking. This will help me to teach others later. Maybe you could teach also."

They moved together as one. Ellen's teacher couldn't believe what she was seeing. When they were done everyone clapped their hands.

"Wow... that was beautiful. Tom, have you dance before?"

"No, I only dance with Ellen. I've watched her dance from the start. Sense I been dancing with her. I fine that my balance and movement has been much better. I'm stronger and it's helps me in a lot of things. I like dancing with Ellen. Do you think that we could dance together?"

"Yes. How long have you been dancing with Ellen?"

"We been dancing together from her first lesson. Ellen and I would work on what she had learn. She had told me it would help me in karate. I been watching her. I saw that she was too tall for the younger boys. All the other girls had their partners. I like having better control over my arms and legs."

The teacher asked Tom. "Could you always been able to lift Ellen?"

"No. The first time. Raymond stayed near us. He caught Ellen before she got hurt. Now, I have no trouble lifting her. Thanks to Raymond. I'm much stronger then I was."

After that they enjoyed dancing with each other. It was eight wonderful years. Until everything changed.

Chapter Four: The night Ellen was born

IT WAS A COLD RAINY DAY. Joseph and James had just finished training. Tired and wet, they made their way to the showers. The CO, AD, came over to them. He had a message from the commanding officer of the base. The message read, come to my office after your shower. The CO.

A soldier came out of the CO's office. He carried a listening device. An officer was sitting in the CO's chair. He was looking over two sets of records. When Joseph and James step into the room. The officer looked up, he dismissed the CO. The CO had stopped to speak with the men.

"I don't know what's going to happen too you men. Whatever it is good luck. From this point on you are in his hands. Don't worry about your teammates. All of them will be going with you."

When the door closed the officer stood up. He looked as if he had been one of the Navy Seals. The Officer held himself with pride. He had brown hair with blond streaks. Could he have served with their uncle Emile?

"Good afternoon men. I guess you are wondering why you're here. I've been looking over your records. Very impressive skills. You men have been a Navy Seal for fifteen years. During this time. There hasn't been a man killed or come up missing under your command. Your last mission something happened to one of your men. You always knew were the

other team was. If that is so. What happen to your teammate? Why is he missing?"

"Joseph, you were inside the building. The plan was to place the explosives. Get pictures of any plans and machines that was used. James you took the upstairs doing the same thing. The man that was missing. He went to the basement by himself. Why was that?

"The missing man was Jackson Chamber. Their men called him Lightning Jack. One moment he was there and then he was gone. Did you know Jackson was studying you and your family? That his twin worked at your son's school? I see that you had spoken to the CO about him. After Jackson had asked you if you know anything about psychic abilities.

"What would you say. If I told you that I know you two have psychic abilities. The skills I'm talking about. It's your ability to talk to each other and not out loud."

"Joseph, why isn't this in your records? Your great-grandfather Garret Heart was a wizard. Do you have the ability to do magic?"

Joseph asked. *"Sir, I don't know who you are. Our CO spoke, that we are now under your command. May we see the orders?... Sir!"*

"No! Not yet."

"James didn't Garret save Eleanor Heart? She's your great-grandmother. She was able to talk to Thomas. Did you know she had psychic abilities?"

Joseph asked. *"Sir, were did you fine this information? How do you know this is true or not true?"*

The Officer kept talking. *"Back in the 1700. A man called Marcos was able to steal Eleanor's spirit. It's been told she had floated near Thomas. Marcos Huascaran had a vendetta against your family. Is that right James. He tried to wipe out all the MacGregor men. He made a deal with a devil. If he died, he could come back to kill all the MacGregor men. The deal was to take Thomas and Eleanor's spirit. He failed to do so."*

The officer saw James fingers twitch.

James said. *"Sir I have a right to know why you're looking into my family's history."* Again, there was no answer.

Then Joseph tried again. *"Sir, what does this have to do with you putting us under your command?"*

Joseph didn't get and answer from the officer. He just kept talking. While the man spoke. James asked Joseph.

'Joseph is this man a demon? My mark says no. How about you?'

'No, he's no demon.'

'Joseph, how would he know so much about my family. Only Marcos would know all this information. Your family would know only what Garret told you.'

The officer went on speaking. "*With the help of Eleanor and Father Sinclair. Marcos couldn't take Thomas spirit from him. It was Thomas who killed the demon. This demon-controlled Garret's body. He didn't know the child. Thomas freed the young boy who hid from the demon. Garret had used his older body to trap Marcos. He was able to send him back to hell. It took Marcos a hundred years to come back to earth. Joseph he's coming after your daughter.*"

Joseph asked the officer. "*Sir, what part of the Heart's or MacGregor family are you from? We have a right to know when it pertains to our families.*"

"So, you have the ability to find out that I'm not a demon."

"My name is Murdock McKinnon. My family calls me Jim. I'm the cousin of Thomas MacGregors mother, Franceam."

Joseph said. *"All right you're a distant cousin. I saw you had this room swipe for listening devices. Where does Marcos fit in to all of this?... Sir."*

"*Always a soldier. Not when it comes to your children. Joseph, with your powers. I can imagine I wouldn't have my head for long.*"

"Sir! I don't know what you mean about powers. Are you a Navy Seal? If you are. You better be stronger and quicker than me."

"Well said. Yes, I am! Take a seat. I have another story to tell. Do you believe that our family can come back from the dead? As a ghost or spirit?"

Before Joseph spoke. He waved his hand to see if there were any recorders.

"*You do have magic. Now that we got that out of the way. This is what I know to be true. The ghost of our cousin Peter McKinnon came to me. I was fourteen years old. You would say I was a hot head. I thought I knew everything. My father told me a story about the Hearts and MacGregor family. I didn't believe a word of it. Until, Peter came to me.*

He told me to be careful. The demons are looking for people to help take down Tom and Ellen. He said acting tuff will get me a demon to pay me a visit. Peter told me that my father was going to send me to America. I will be eighteen, when my father will enroll me in the Navy academy. Before Peter left me, he placed a cross on my chest. I was told the cross came from Father Sinclair. The magic rose was on this cross. Time past, on my eighteenth birthday. I was place on a ship to America. My father made me work on that ship. He didn't pay my way to America. What my father couldn't teach me. The skipper did.

"*Before we left Scotland. I had a visit from a man called Marcuse. He told me. A young man like myself could go far. I found out why Peter place that cross on my chess. The story about that cross my father spoke of. I knew Marcuse was a demon. I felt the cross go hot quickly, then it was gone. Marcuse said. Once the country develops the parts. I will build a machine that can control someone's mine. Other countries are working on it as we speak.*"

"*I've been looking for Marcuse. He is also in a movement to bring the world to an end. Even by taking down one country at a time. There are people working on ways to control the minds of the weak. Marcuse said it's a way to get souls for his master.*

"*That assignment you two was on. Your men were to take pictures of blueprints, files and machines. When you went to blow up the building. Jack was nowhere to be found. You had a job to do. There were soldiers coming down the road. You did what you had to do. You blow the building up and got your men out. Did you use your magic to find out if Jack was inside the building?*"

"*Yes sir. He wasn't in the building. Sir.*"

"*Did you find him before the building went up?*"

"*No sir.*"

"*One of my men saw someone running in the woods. He looked to be Jack.*"

"*Who was the man that saw him?*"

"*Bill Colman, he took the place of our teammate who retired.*"

"*James, your son wants to become an engineer. His dream is to build a machine to help people with their nightmares. Tom is like you. Strong in many ways. He is an engineer, he can build anything. A young man like your son. They would love to get their hands on him.*"

Jim watched James face change slightly. "Sir where did you get this information from?"

"The information came from Bill. I had place Bill on your team to get to know Tom. My men have been watching over your two families. At the school that your son goes to. A strange man was seen. He was asking questions to some of the children. My man said a teacher came over to that man. She made the children wait inside for the bus to come. James, one of the children was your son. With that said. Do you trust Bill Colman?"

"Yes sir. There is something very familiar about Bill. We thought he was going to take a while to get up to speed. He knew just what we were about. Bill became one of the family."

"He should, Bill is one of Garret's grate-grandsons. Bill's mother comes from Garret oldest daughter. I'm putting Bill to watch over Tom when he gets out of school. He will be on your team until then.

"Marcuse has planned this for a long time. He has money and power. His base is deep in one of the mountains. There are tunnels all over the nearby towns. There is a big movement to fine people with psychic abilities. The machine you destroyed. They were using it to enhance the psychic abilities. These psychics could do it without help from the machine. They could control weaker mines in their sleep, or even kill them. There are new drugs being develop. There using these drugs to soften many of the young adults. Did you know that Jack Chamber, was a Scientist and a master of disguises?"

Joseph heard James swear. 'Damn it! Jack used us.'

The officer went on talking. "You said his neck name is Lightning Jack. Marcuse gave me a code word. It was Lightning Jack. When you get to Russia. Fine that mountain were these people disappeared from. They may be the once with psychic abilities. The name of the mountain has been covered up. Before, we discuss which men will go with you.

"I need to talk to you about Tom and Ellen. We need to get your children in a safe school. I know of two schools that the two of them can go to. You know I'm not a demon. The men were going after. If they could get their hands on your children, they will. They don't care what happens to them. I understand Tom and Ellen has some of your psychic abilities. Joseph do you think Ellen will have some magic soon?"

Joseph answered. *"It's hard to tell. Sir. It may happen when she turn's twenty-one. I don't know what kind of magic she will have. What I do know. Tom is not going to like being away from Ellen. You don't want to see him angry. Tom has been protective over Ellen since she was born. He took on a demon when he was a year old."*

"I know of all this. We need Tom in that school. We must keep him safe. Ellen can't go to her new school. Not yet, she's too young. The good news with her IQ, she can go next year. I don't need Tom out of school not yet. I know the school he is in now. They want to skip a grade or two. I need him safe. Tom can take college courses at this school. I found out from Peter that Marcos can use different bodies. It's said Marcos will be going after Ellen when she is thirteen years old. School will be out soon. Send them to your grandparents for the summer. I have place men at the ranch. They will help keep an eye on them, until school starts."

James said. *"Why do we have to send them to these schools?"*

"It's because of, what had happened in Tom's classroom. They had people come to talk to the children. Tom's class was giving talks on psychic abilities. This man had given a test to the children. He wanted to see who had the psychic abilities. Tom's teacher got scared. The man was focusing just on Tom.

"I've been placing some of your men in the Government. Arthur was one of your teammates. When he got out of the service. He took over the line of ships that his family runs. Arthur has many Government jobs. He has a ship picked out, with the best team around. Bill will be getting out around that time. He has four years left. Until he reaches twenty years.

"Joseph, your son Raymond. Taken ROTC in school. I wish all the children did that. He then went to the Navy academy and became a Navy Seal. This report said. He's able to get out of any where's. I have a place already picked out for him. Does he have any magic?"

"Sir, you would have to ask my son yourself. It's up to him to answer that question."

"All right… I will do that if there comes a need to know."

"James, I see that Raymond had married your daughter. This school that will send Tom to. They will hide the identity of the child. A school that will keep them safe. It has two sides, boys and girls. For the boy's side is Deilondotay. The girls Deilondolay. Raymond will watch over

his sister on the weekends and holidays. During the summer also. James, your brother Brandon is in Scotland. I like for him to watch over your son on the weekends and holidays. During the summer also. I know this is too much to take in. In this school Tom and Ellen will not know each other. They will not know any family member. Raymond and Emily will not be allowed to remember Ellen is family. The same with Brandon. His family can play the part of uncle and aunt. The same with Raymond. He will be her family for four years. You all have a strong mind. No pictures with the family. This is one of the school rules. With your children, their mines will not take to hypnosis. To keep them safe, it will have to be magic. Joseph, you're the only person that can-do magic."

James said. *"You sure you're not working for Marcos. If Joseph did what you said. Marcos will be able to get in closer to Ellen. This Marcuse is he Marcos?"*

"What I understand. Marcos can use any evil body. He can make them do whatever he wants. Do I believe Marcos is Marcuse? Yes! Remember, he had a hundred years to pick who he wanted to be. We are an undercover group. I need more members to help us. Marcuse must die. I need you on my team.

"Joseph, your parents have a ranch like James. Do you think they can keep Ellen safe for a while?"

"Yes. In this school, why would our daughter not know her family?"

"This schools take their name from them. The child can pick the nickname he like to be called. What name would Tom pick for himself?"

"It would have to be Mic. Ellen calls him that when they were little."

"Why the name Mic?"

"It's for Mickey mouse. The show that the two of them watch together when they were little."

"All right, what name for Ellen?"

Joseph said. *"It would have to be Angel. Sir!"*

"Joseph, I'm aware you're not happy with me. I know these children are special. The magic roses need them. This school I don't think they will let Ellen used Angel. It's part of her last name. Marcuse gassed his own people. There were women and children that he did this too. If he did that. Do you think he care if Tom was killed?"

Joseph said. *"I had enough of all this. Why should we truss you? You haven't showed us our orders yet. When it comes to our children. With our wives we will make the plans for them. We haven't said if we were going to be part of your team. I feel there is more to this story. What else haven't you told us?"*

"I told you about the mountain in Russia. What do you think will happen? If Tom don't go to this school. Marcuse could get his hands-on Tom. He will take him to that mountain. The strongest man hasn't been able to with stand the torture. They had taken one of my men. They sent him back to us. This strong man was nothing but a vegetable. They will brake Tom. He will do everything they want him to do. With Tom out of the way. Marcos will get what he wants from Ellen."

The summer went by fast. Tom was swimming at the waterfall with Ellen. The two of them hadn't seen much of each other. Soon it will be time to go back to school. It was already the beginning of September.

"Tom, something is going to happen."

"Angel what are you talking about?"

"Tom that's just it. I don't think where going back to Virginia. I heard my grandfather talking to my dad. Granddad said he's in roll me into school down here. I will be in my last year of junior high. There using my test scores to see how many grades I can skip. It's going to be used next year. The test said I can go up three grades. I'm going to another school some where's far away".

"Where?"

"I don't know Tom."

"Ellen you and I know that the two of us could have been in Highschool together."

"No Tom, you're not going to school in Virginia."

"Damn it!" Tom let of the breath he was holding. *"You're right. I heard Granny talking to mom. Mom said, that it's hard to pack up all are things by herself. She said, that your mom must pack their things also. One-day mom helps your mother and the next day your mother helps my mother. Ellen your right. There is something happening."*

Then they heard their grandparents calling for supper. Tonight, she was staying the night.

"Tom, we don't have much time together anymore."

"I know Ellen. Tonight, come to me in your dream. Meet me at the waterfall. I believe you can use your magic in our dreams. You will have more psychic Energy. Swim across the pond. I'll be waiting for you on the flat rock. I love you Ellen. This is the only way to be together. Were too young now. Our bodies can be older in our dreams. When were together we must be careful? The way I feel now is wrong. In our dreams we can be lover's. Tonight, in the dream world. Be with me. It's important that we have this link to our dreams. There is someone going to split us up. I have something I want to give you."

Tom took out a small locket. It was in a pocket in his swim suit. He held it out to her.

"I asked your brother to make it. Can you see the angel holding the rose?"

"Oh Tom. Yes, it's beautiful."

"I'm glad you like it. On the back there is a cross, your brother had it blest. He put a piece of my hair in it when he made it. There is a magic rose with it. Now you can tell if demons are around you. He made me a cross from a piece of your hair and mixed it with metal. It's had been blest and has a magic rose with it. If we keep it with us always, will be safe. I'll see you to night in our dreams. Remember, always at the waterfall."

"Tom, why do I feel this has to work. It scares me, to know where not going to be together much longer. What if my psychic energy is not strong enough?"

"Ellen, it's going to be all right. When your twenty-one you will be able to boost it with your magic. Don't doubt yourself. Walk with me."

They walked outside in the moon light. He had taken her to the barn away from the house. Tom leaned on the door jamb. These last few days he found himself studying Ellen's face. He took his fingertips and ran them over her cheek.

"Tom, what's wrong?"

"I've been thinking about you and me. Wondering what you will look like when your twenty-one."

"That's part of it. What else are you thinking about." Tom then ran his fingertips over her lips. What would it be like to kiss her? To hold her in his arms. Tom was feeling he needed to know this.

"Like always you know me to well. I been wondering what it be like to kiss you? To hold you in my arms."

"I been thinking the same thing. Yes, it would be nice to be kissed. Are you going to kiss me now?"

"Yes… I'm going to kiss you."

Tom took a step closer to her. He ran his hand through her long hair. It felt like silk as he cupped the back of her neck.

"Ellen have I told you I love your eyes. There the color of the ocean a beautiful bluest green. Angel when you're older a man could drown in your eyes." He pulled Ellen to him. *"Do you know I fell in love with you. The day you were born. I just didn't know it. On the day of your fourth birthday. You dance for me. I knew then I was in love with you."*

He bent his head and kissed her lips softly. When he looked up at her. Tom knew he wanted more. He took her hand and brought her to the back of the barn. A way from the barns light.

"Ellen, I don't know what's going to happen to us. All I know is I need to hold you and kiss you. You can go if this scares you. I will understand."

"No… I'm not scared of this. I was hoping this was going to happen."

Tom smiled and pulled her to him. His tongue ventured passed her lips. He made love to her mouth.

"Angel I think that will be enough for now. It's getting late."

They walked to the house holding hands. The two of them said their goodnights to Tom's grandparents. Together they went upstairs. There were two rooms on each side of the bathroom. Ellen's room was the one on the left side facing the bathroom. Tom had his hand on the door. He bent down and kissed Ellen one last time.

"Call to me, when you get to the waterfall."

"I will. Tom I'm in love with you too. I'll see you in my dream."

Mic was at the waterfall first. He wondered why he always came here. For a long time, it's been his safe-haven. Here at the waterfall the sun always shined. Mic stood on the edge of his dream world. He was trying to see the other side of the water's edge. Something was wrong? He couldn't see anything.

'Where is the waterfall? Why is everything black here? Mic touched the stuff. It felt thick like tar.' His cross went hot.'

He cried out. *'Angel be careful. Evil is in the spirit world.'*

How would evil get into the spirit world? Unless he can dream. A large black cloud moved over the sun. Mic then was plunged into darkness. He heard a laugh. The voice was deep. Why would that voice sound familiar to him?

'Marcos, so you found a way to the dream world.'

'Very good... for a young boy. You can call me Marcuse. You know she's not coming. When you're gone, Eleanor, will be mine.'

'Never... my grandfather Thomas beat you. Eleanor is Thomas's mate. If you think Ellen will be yours. You are wrong. She is my mate. I'm called Tom. We will stop you. Marcos, Marcuse, whoever you are. You think too much of yourself. Ellen is stronger than you can imagine.'

Marcuse laugh again. *'No, she's just a woman. Girls are not strong. You won't be around to see it. For you will be dead.'*

Mic knew he was in trouble for the darkness changed. There before him, was two big magical hands forming. Mic tried to wake up. In the dream world he looked around. There was no where's to run. The hands went around his neck. His air was being cut off. Try as he may, he couldn't pry the hands from his neck. Mic was strong for a boy of fourteen. This was magic. He needed the strength of a man. Angel was walking down the path to the waterfall. She couldn't see the rock from the water's edge. Then her locket went hot. There was evil in the spirit world. She heard the name Marcuse.

Marcuse was going to kill Tom in his sleep. She knew Mic was in trouble. Here in the spirit world she can save him. A boy can't fight off a man with magic. Angel had to change herself and Mic. She lifted her arms and cried out.

'I call upon the magic of Garret. He is my grandfather. Here in the dream world I asked to be twenty-one. Evil has come to do harm to us. Marcuse brings the darkness of death. He has the power to enter the dream world. Help me Grandfather! I need to help my mate! Marcuse is trying to kill Tom in his sleep. Give me the power of magic to save my mate. Marcuse must be stop here in the dream world.'

Angel pictured herself... As a woman, Mic as a man. She felt a wind starting to blow around her. Her hair felt longer. As the wind pushed her hair across her face. Angel was even taller than before. Her breast felt bigger. Her arms and legs were stronger. She had the build of a dancer.

While this was going on. Mic was also changing to a man. His arms and legs got bigger. He was now stronger and able to fight off Marcuse. Angel could feel the power running through her body. This was too much power for just her. Her grandfather was giving Mic some powers of his own. She stretched out her arms toward him. There she focused all her energy on the wall of darkness. As a woman of twenty-one. She had her powers and her grandfather's powers for Mic.

Mic felt his strength growing. He was able to pull the hands away from his neck. He drew the needed air into him. Marcuse went after Mic again. Their hands locked together. He was able to push Marcuse backwards. Mic heard Angel's voice. He needed to get away from the edge. To be able to break away from those hands.

'Mic...hear me... My powers are your powers... we are as one. I call to the light of goodness. Come to me. Fill my body with the brightest light of all. From me... Into Mic and through his fingers. Together, we will take evil from our dream world's, forever.'

Angel focused on the powers flowing through her body. There was a bright light building with in her, until she started to glow. With a flick of her wrist. The light exited from her fingertips. It bursts into a magical beam that cut through the darkness. The magic beam went into Mic. The two of them was as one. He was now twenty-two. Mic focused was on his mate. He felt Angel's powers. The more he held back the brighter his body became. Marcuse big hands were gone. The light was pushing him back. Mic knew the moment he had all Angel's magic.

Then he heard a voice. *'These next powers are yours Tom. Thomas saved me… these powers use them to take down Marcuse.'*

Mic raced his arms and cried out in a loud voice. *'Be gone Satan! You have no powers here anymore. Feel Angel's powers. The powers given to her by her grandfather Garret. Know my strength. Now know my powers given to me by Garret. Together we will take you down again.'*

Mic flicked his wrist. The magical bean lit up both of their dream worlds. It cut through the tar leaving the color of black ink… cutting Marcuse hands off. They heard the scream. There was black ink bubbling until there was no more. The sun came out it shined through the darkness. With the power spent Mic fell to his knees. He drew in air as if he came from the bottom of the pond. It took all his willpower and strength to stand. He had to get to Angel. If he was that weak. Mic knew Angel had to be weaker than him. He had to fine Angel. Then he saw her. She was near the edge of the water. He couldn't see if she was face down. Not thinking he dove into the water just missing the rocks. With his powerful arms Mic moved quickly through the water. He was by Angel side in minutes.

'Angel… my love.'

He quickly checked to see if Angel was breathing. *'Thank heavens. She must have passed out from exhaustion.'*

His hand brushed the sand and hair away from her face. Mic found that he had to rest for a bit himself. Afterward, he took Angel to the top of the waterfall. There he laid with her on the patch of grass. He had her head laying on his arm. Angel's body was close to him. A bit of time went by. Slowly she woke-up. At first, she didn't remember what had happen. Her hand was laying on top of a man's chest. She knew this because only men had hair. Quickly she sat up.

'Who's… lying next to me.'

One look and she knew it was Mic. Everything came back to her.

'This is Mic… Wow!'

Angel then ran her hand over his arm. He was a young man of twenty-two. She could see he kept up with weight lifting. His legs were like his arms strong. He was everything she had pictured in her mine. She wondered what he would do if she woke him with a kiss? Softly she placed a kiss on his lips. Then his arms came around her. Mic had taken over. She was now under his firm body. His lips moved over hers. Gently he used his tongue to push between her lips. There he made love to her mouth. When he lifted his head to look at her.

All she could say was… *'Wow!'*
'Angel are you, all right?'
'I'm fine Mic. Is this what we are going to look like?'
'Too bad we couldn't ask Leslies letter. We would have your answer.'
'I know where the letter is.'

Angel sat up and waved her hand. *'I seek the letter of Leslie. Come to me. We need some answers. Come out of your hiding place.'*

The letter came to her. When Angel opened the letter, she found there was a message already there.

Chapter Five: The Fight Begins

I KNEW MY BROTHER'S CHILDREN IS STRONG WITH THEIR MAGIC. Mic you been given some of my brother's magic. Your grate grandfather was a good man. Garret knew Marcuse was going to use everything he could. You two did well fighting off Marcuse. It's not over yet he has plans for your father's. You must check on them now. Your fathers think their hunting down Marcuse. Not sleeping. Tonight, he is sending demons after them. He thinks he can kill them in their sleep. Angel your father will think he is awake. You know he will not use his magic. The two of you must stop them from going into their dreams. I know your questions.

Yes, this is what you two will look like at the age you are now.

Yes, Mic you will have magic when your twenty-one.

Yes, you may make love to each other now. However, you must go to the magic rose in Scotland. Kneel before the magic rose Mic. Remember she is Ellen. Do what your grandfather told you to do. When it's time to take Ellen as your mate. You must do what you did in your dream.

Tonight, safe your father's. Then go to the magic rose in Scotland. Mic be careful after next week you will be heading to Scotland. The two of you will not remember each other. Angel, a boy at your new school. He will be under Marcuse powers. Be careful around him. This boy will write for the school paper.

Yes, the two of you will find each other again outside the dream world. Until then. You will run to the waterfall in your dream. There you can be together. Your hunger for each other will be satisfy in the dream world. You will have to work hard to find each other.

Good luck. Angel and Mic.

We have to stop those demons before they kill our father's.
Angel, I understand what you're saying but how will we do this?
You have Garret's magic. Any time we come to the dream world you will have Garret's magic.
If that is so. You help my father and I will help yours. Together we can slip into their dreams. Tell me how we should do this?
First, I need to give you this.

Angel turn toward him and put her arms around Mic. She needed to feel his arms around her. One more kiss before we leave.

Mic, I wish we could do this in the real world. I guess this will have to do for now. Take my hand and think of each other's father. We must go to their dream world before the demons can kill them.

They close their eyes and thought of each other's father. Joseph was fighting with his knife. He had taken down a few of the demons. Mic yelled at him.

Joseph, use your magic. You're in your dream. There trying to kill you in your sleep. If you die in the dream world. You will die in your sleep.

Mic raced his arms. He flicked his wrist and bright light came out of his fingertips. Joseph couldn't believe what he was seeing. Now he knew that he was dreaming. Mic saved him from dyeing in his sleep. The two of them wiped out the demons. Then Mic heard Angel calling for him.

Joseph, Angel needs me. Can you take care of the others?
Yes! I'll be there as soon as I'm done here. Take care of my daughter.

Joseph use bright light to kill all the demons. To get to James he thought of him. He found himself in James dream. Joseph then saw is daughter. Angel was beautiful at the age of twenty-one. Mic had a strong built of a man of twenty-two. They were fighting with magic. They must have had to fight off demons. Angel must have called to Garret for some of his magic. She knew her magic wasn't strong enough to split in half.

Joseph watched the two of them hold hands. They were stronger when they held hands together. With a flick of their hands. A bright light burned the last of the demons. Joseph was helping James when the last one was killed. When it was over. Mic told them that Marcos has taken a new name. It's now Marcuse. He is showing the demons how to takeout people in their sleep.

'Mic told their father's what Marcos tried to do to him. He didn't think Angel could help me. He knows you and my father are trying to take him down. Be careful Marcuse is taking it to the next level. Angel and I have to go one more place before morning.'

Now they were in Scotland and standing in front of the magic rose. Angel looked around. She wanted to remember this place. Inside her, she knew this place was going to be very imported to them. With the rose in his hand. Thing started happening quickly. Then she had the rose petal in her locket. The two of them were back at the waterfall. Mic made love to her by the magic roses. When he pushed into her, she felt a burn on her chest. When Mic came, he also felt a burn on his chest. Then he found himself on the flat rock looking at Angel. Mic wondered, when will he see Angel again as twenty-one. In the moonlight he saw the cross and rose.

'Angel you have the mark of the cross and rose.'
'I do. You also have the same mark.'

⁂

Tom was on the porch when he saw car's pulling up. The first car was Ellen and her mother and father. Ellen ran to him to give him her present. It was a stuff animal of Mickey Mouse. Then she gave Tom a kiss and whisper something in his ear.

"It's to remined you of me. The first time I called you Mic. We had fun watching Mickey Mouse as kids."

It was his turn. Tom gave her a present. His present was an angel with ballet slippers.

"Oh Tom! I will miss dancing with you."

That's when she kissed him on the lips. Ellen felt like crying. Today will be the last day she would see Tom.

'Don't cry my Angel. I will always be with you. The rose will tell me if you need me. I will come to you were ever you are.'

Joseph and Malaya knew this was going to be hard on them. He had to take the young man away from his daughter. Then he had to erase Tom's memory. All his family and love ones. Only Joseph had the magic. His son couldn't do it to his sister. Then how in Sam hell is he going to be able to do it himself.

He told his wife he would be right back. He had to run to the waterfall to talk with Leslie. At the waterfall he called to Leslie. Come to me quickly I need your help. The letter appeared in his hands. You know my heart. How can I keep them safe?

Hello Joseph;

The spell you are looking for. First do not take the memories away. Only block the memories of his name. When people see him, they will not remember him. Let Ellen and Tom dream of each other. Be careful Marcuse is not able to get to their dreams. You must put a protection spell around them. Do not do the spell without it. Marcuse will do anything to keep them apart. To the point of killing him. Tom's name will be block from him and anyone who knows Tom. When he steps into the plane the spell will start. The spell must be place on Tom and Ellen at the same time. Her spell will start when she is on her way to Scotland. Don't worry about them. Their love is strong enough to find each other in that school. Remember, the spell is to block the name Tom's MacGregor. Make the spell strong. Ellen's and Tom's magic will be strong enough to brake your spell with a kiss.

Good luck

Joseph knew what to do now. When the letter was gone. A demon took a part of what Leslie said away from him. *"Why did that hurt?"*

He joined his wife and said hello to them. *"Hello Tom."*

"Hello Sir." Tom could see the pain in Joseph's eyes. He went and gave Malaya a hug.

"Tom call me uncle like you use to. You even can call me Joseph."

"All right Joseph. I don't feel uncle is just right for me to say."

Another car pulled up. It was his father and mother. He stayed where he was and let his mother and father come to him. Then he saw another man get out of the car. Tom did the same thing to his father.

"Hello Dad."

To his mother he went right to her and gave a hug and kiss. To the men he gave a cold greeting.

"Tom this is Arthur Stanley he will be taking you to the school. He will also introduce you to the family that will watch over you in Scotland."

"Hello Sir."

"Hello Tom. It's nice to finally meet you. I heard good things about you. Are you ready to leave?"

"No Sir! …I am not ready. I haven't seen my mother and father for a while. It will be four years when I will get to see them again."

Joseph asked. *"Arthur ease up. You have four hours to wait before the plane takes off. Everything is already on the plane."*

"Joseph, he has to see that doctor before we leave. It may take some time."

James gave a dirty look at Arthur. *"Tom will not see that doctor. Your man will not work on my son. We will take care of it from here."*

"All right James."

James asked his wife to take Arthur into the house.

"Son will you and Ellen take a walk with us. We like to ask you two something."

"What would that be dad? Could it be about the dream you two had?"

"Son you had magic like Ellen. How did that happen?"

"It's okay Tom. I better tell what I had said. Tom had said that we could become older in the dream world. Then I remembered that my

powers will come to me when I'm twenty-one. Marcuse thinks women can't do anything. I had to try for my magic. I called upon the magic of Garret. I asked to be twenty-one. I knew that my powers may not be enough to take down Marcuse. I asked grandfather for Garret's powers. Here in the dream world. I asked to be twenty-one. Evil has come to do harm to us. He has the power to enter the dream world. Marcuse brings the darkness of death. Help me! So, I may help my mate! Marcuse is trying to kill Tom in his sleep. Give me the power of magic. For my mate and I can stop him. I told grandfather what was happening in the dream world. He gave me the powers. I shot the power into the darkness. I knew Mic was dying. He had to become a man of twenty-two. To be strong enough to fight off Marcuse. This time around Tom must have magic. Garret knew this."

"Daughter in your dream are you his mate?"

"Yes! Mic is my mate. Only in the dream world."

Tom said. "Uncle Joseph please, don't get upset. I know what I had to do to become her mate. We went to Scotland and I was given the magic rose. In the dream world she wears the mark of the cross and rose."

"Daddy Mic has the mark also. When we become lovers. We will have the locket with the magic rose inside it. Only when it's time for it."

"What is happening here. It's making the two of you grow up quickly. All right this is what's going to happen. I will not take your memory from you. Everyone you meet will not remember you. Once they say your new name. You will be that person from that moment on. In the dream world. I will not change anything."

"Ellen, you knew just what to do. Calling for the magic of Garret. He gave you powers to give Tom. I didn't ask Leslie about the powers Tom has. However, our great grandfather must know that Tom will need that magic. Now Leslie told me. Not to worry that Angel will fine Mic in school. She said that your love for each other is very strong."

Mic didn't remember much about the trip to Scotland. He thought they left in the afternoon. *'What did they give me? Whatever it was. It made his mine feel like he was in a dace.'*

He remembered being place in a seat. There was a man buckling him in. Once again Mic fell asleep. He didn't remember how long he was sleeping. When he was able to stay awake. He found himself on a private jet. Mic didn't understand what was happening to him. He felt he needed to be on guard.

'How would he do that when he can't keep his eyes open.'

When Mic slept. He couldn't understand his dream. He heard this girl's voice. She kept saying.

'Mic meet me at the waterfall.'

He answered her. *'What waterfall? How can I hear you? Who are you?'*

Mic heard crying after he said all that. In the dream he thought he sat on a rock. Everywhere he looked he saw darkness. Even in his thoughts he felt like he was losing his mind. It didn't help when he woke-up. Mic would look out the window of the jet. All he could see was pitch black.

He heard a man ask the pilot. *"How far are we from Scotland?"*

"Were about two hours out Mr. Stanley."

After a long flite to Scotland. Mic then was place in a car. He was handed a glass of something to drink.

"You should be waking up with this Mic. Drink it all down."

"Where am I?"

"Were in the Highlands and driving through a town. Slowly he was able to stay awake.

"Where are you taking me."

"To the family that will look after you. I will go and set up everything at the school. Your new family will bring you to school."

Mic looked around. He saw a school. Part of the castle was called Rose Hill elementary. Then the car turned into a driveway that led to a ranch.

"Were here. Be nice to these people."

"I don't understand. Why am I here? Why can't I remember things? What did you do to me?"

Mic didn't like this man. He would ask him something and wouldn't get any answers from him. What he did say to Mic.

"I had a job to do. I did what I was told. Whatever you do behave yourself. These people are very nice to take you in for the weekends and holidays for four years."

Mic got out of the car and walked with Mr. Stanley. He felt like he was going to be sick. As he got closer. Mic thought he knew this man. He couldn't put his finger on who he looked like.

"Mr. & Mrs. MacGregor. I would like you to meet Mic T.M."

All he could do was stair at Mr. MacGregor. There was a picture that was trying to forum in his mine. It was Mr. MacGregor, who spoke to Mic first.

"Hello Mic. If you like you can call me Uncle Brandon. This is my wife Kimberley. You may call her Aunt Kimberley. We take care of our granddaughter. It will be easier for her to understand that your family. Did you have a nice flight here to Scotland? You came to us on a beautiful day. The sun is out and it's very warm."

"I'm sorry sir. I don't feel good. Why do I feel sick to my stomach? If it's warmer out. Why am I so cold?"

Mic felt scared and dizzy. It must have shown in his face. Kimberley walked over to him. She then put her arms around him. Mic buried his face into her shoulder.

"I'm taking the boy in. Make sure we get all of Mic's things. Good day Mr. Stanley."

"Aunt Kimberley. I think I'm going to be sick."

He made it to the bathroom where he got sick in the toilet. Afterward he started feeling better.

He laid his head on the tub and closed his eyes to rest. When he heard the voice of that girl.

'Mic are you alright? You're not mad at me. I'm sorry I started crying.'

'No! What is your name? I was sick and didn't want to think.'

'I don't like this Mic. They took your name from you. They made it, so I can't tell you my real name. We can only say are nick names. You call me Angel. Mic I know we are six hours different from each other. I don't know if we can talk to each other much.'

'Can you tell me about this waterfall, Angel?'

'There is a path we go on to get to the waterfall. We must swim across to lay on a big rock. A lot of times you wait for me there. Angel I'll try tonight. I don't know if we can see each other. We can talk at least.'

'Okay Mic. Until tonight.'

Mic thought he was lucky to have an Angel. He will need one to look after him.

'Until tonight Angel.'

Mic came out of the bathroom. As he looked around. Mic felt like he's been here before. Part of him thought he knew this place. Right off he found his things in one of the bedrooms. He had to get out of these clothes. Then he saw a kilt in the closet. There will be time to learn about this kilt. He put all his things away that was staying here at the ranch.

The next day he was told they were going to the Highland games. Kimberley started to show Mic how to dance. Mic notice that they want surprise that he could do it. The three of them had fun doing the dance. Kimberley told Mic to get his kilt on. Everything you need is in the closet.

At the Highland games. Mic got to his feet and danced with his aunt. He also fought with the sword with his uncle. He was good with that sword. Mic through the dirk and hit the target every time. A man came up to him and asked if he was a MacGregor?

"No sir. I'm not from here. It's like throwing darts. The dirk maybe bigger. I guess I just like games."

"How about the sword. You can fight like you been doing it all your life."

Then Brandon came over to them. *"Mic go over to Kimberley. It's time to eat."*

"Alright I'll help her with Emily."

Uncle Brandon had brought Mic to school. This place was just for boys. In the low land of Scotland. He helped him fine his room. Mic was told that there was over a hundred-fifty acres. What he didn't like was that large gate. The fence he saw went around all the acres. What could be on the other end of this fencing? This place felt as if it was a jail… not a school. He thought a lot of guys could get really scared.

After saying his good-byes to Uncle Brandon. Mic went back to his room. He left his stuff animal of Mickey Mouse at is new home. It was hard at first… not being able to remember his full name. Why, was he thinking of the stuff animal of Mickey Mouse? Try as he may. Mic couldn't remember anything about it. All he got out of it was a headache. He told himself to think of something else. Why would there be a hundred-fifty acres for just one school? Another boy came down the hall. Don. D.M. He was Mic's roommate.

"Hello, my name is Don. D.M. Are you my roommate?"

"Yes, call me Mic. It's nice to meet you Don. D.C."

"You can drop the D.C."

"That sound good to me. I don't like to have to say Mic. T.M."

"Mic! I just found out there's another school on campus. It's for girls. Between the two schools is where we get to meet them. They say you must try out for some of the sports. Are you any good in any sports?"

"I can hold my own. Did you happen to see what kind of sports?"

"I haven't seen the list. However, I heard to meet any of the girls. You must go for the competitions. They pick only the best. There's an upper-class man a cross from us. His name is Cal. C.L. He said that there is a girl name Misty. Cal told us. Misty shouldn't have been her name. Bossy's fits her better them Misty."

"Hay Don. Don't scare him off. He looks to be a strong athlete. Until we get some girls with some back bones. Misty will have her friends in the competitions. Hi, my name is Cal."

"Mic."

"Have you had time to eat?"

"No, I just haven't felt like eating."

"Come along with me. Deilondotay does have some really good food. I'll tell you all about Deilondolay. What kind of sports do you like?"

"I do a lot of running. I try to run five miles a day. I work out on weightlifting. I also did some dancing, horseback riding and swimming."

"Wow… Everything the school needs. One other thing, are you in High school or College?"

"I'm in College. Why?"

"Grate… for the school not for you. Because Misty is going to be after you. How about you and I be roommates? I'm in College also. You and I should do some running together. Eat-up I'll show you around."

A teacher came over to Mic. *"Oh good you two already met. Mic have you unpack yet?"*

"No Sir, not yet."

"That's good. Because you're going to be roommates with Cal."

"Grate… We have a lot to talk about. Let's go get your things after your done eating. While you eat, I'll tell you about Misty."

Cal gave a run down on Misty and Hawkeye. Those two are brother and sister. Hawkeye has another sister. I wish she was here and not Misty. She is going to another school for the arts because of Misty. My sister Sunshine. She likes Hawkeye. There is one rule to follow. Don't fall in love with a girl that is an under-classmate. Like my sister I fallen for Hawkeye's other sister. He told Mic be careful around Misty. She does this thing with her eyes. If your weak minded, she can get you to do anything for her. Misty will be an under-classmate to you. This will be a good thing.

Today was Ellen's first day at school. She had two friends that live near the ranch. MaryAnn Colman and Stephen O'Connell were in the hallway with her. When she felt her locket get hot. She looked around and saw a boy staring at her. He had blond hair. Ellen could see he was small for his age. When he smiled. It made him look like a devil, with his hair sticking up.

'*So, you're the one who been sent to take me down. No way!*'

"*Stephen, who is that boy? The one with the devilish smile.*"

"*That's Francis. He's living with his uncle in town. His mother sent him here. He was always getting in trouble. I guess if I had that name. I would try to make myself look tough too.*"

MaryAnn said. "*I can see why. The first time I heard his name I thought. He's one of those people. It doesn't help when your small like he is.*

"MaryAnn that would be to easy."

"Ellen too easy for what?"

"How did you know he was there?"

"Oh! Did I say that out loud? Sorry Mary Ann and Stephen. Ask me again when there is no one around."

Ellen knew who's going to try to rape her. She's not going to be alone with him, if she can help it. School was going by fast. Everyone found out that she had a high IQ. Many asked her for help in their school work. MaryAnn and Stephen were always asking her for help. The two of them wanted to go into law. They had a hard time studying. Beside her own school work.

She was also an assistant to the ballet teacher. She showed Ellen how to handle people. One day when there was a new student giving Ellen trouble.

Her teacher said. "*Show them the hardest move you know. Then say your turn. There is always someone knows the form and the steps of ballet. They think their better than the teacher.*"

At school Francis tried to get Ellen alone. She was always one step ahead of him. One-day Stephen asked her again how she knew Francis was nearby.

"*Stephen do you believe in fairy magic?*"

"Yes… Ellen when you're an Irishmen. You learn to believe in things that happens and no way to explain it. Both of my parents are Irish. Now you can see why I have red hair. Now tell me how you know."

Ellen just pointed to her locket. Then said, "It has fairy magic. It gets hot when evil is around."

"Ellen that's good enough for me." The two of them never talked about that subject again.

The school year was all most over. At home Ellen went into the kitchen. On the table was paper work from Scotland. It was from the school she was going too. It had said that she will be place under a protection order. It talked about everyone's ID are place in a vault underground. These schools name Deilondotay for boys and Deilondolay for girls. There is ten miles that is fence off. This is where the boys and girls can work together on dancing and competitions. This will be the only place where a boy could meet some girls. This place you could be involved in the competition. The girls and boys each have twenty acres away from each other. They sleep, eat, work, and play on their own acres. The last ten acres was left for competitions. You would start off with riding horses then get into jumping, bicycling over hills. After biking it was the test of running. You had to pass the baton and finish the race as fast as you could. After that the last test was swimming.

This place sound scary to her. Could Mic be at Deilondotay for boys? It's been getting hard to talk to him. Every night Ellen would call to him. Did Marcos found a way to stop them? She remembered she hasn't been able to get to ren sleep. She has too much on her mine. This must be blocking her from the dream world. He has a demon that keeps me on my toes. Could a demon be working on Mic all so? Something is going to happen soon. Each night when Ellen woke-up. She found her pillow was wet again.

"Why do I have to cry every night?" Closing her eyes, she cried out in her thoughts.

'Mic, how much longer until we meet again?'

Chapter Six: Girls with No Face

FOR THE MONTH MIC COULDN'T GET TO REN SLEEP. He would think of Angel. Even try to call to her. What was happening? He been cut off from his Angel. Without a good night sleep. Mic's been very jumpy. Everything was getting to him. Cal was right about Misty. She didn't act as if she was on a protection order. It seems that she was place here for behaver problems. She was bossy and didn't care about anyone, but herself. Next year would be her last year here. She didn't go into any college courses. When Misty found out about him, she wouldn't leave Mic alone. Everywhere he went Misty was there. The only place she couldn't go was the boy's side.

She would always say. *'Mic could you help me with my homework?'*

Mic had tried out for some of the sports, even dancing. Misty even got him as his partner. She was a heavy girl. Some of the ballet movements, made it hard to lift her. Mic wasn't weak. The reason he had Misty as his partner. He was the strongest in the group.

'It's funny she said she liked him a lot.'

If she was falling for him it's too bad for her. She knows the rules. Never fall in love with under-classmen. He did his best not to be mean to her. However, the day came when she wouldn't put up her hair. Misty's hair was black. It was very thick and long. Too long for a dancer, hers went down to her bottom. When the girls dance. Their hair was to be in a tight bun. It must be on top of their head. The girls must be slim to do some of the moves. Misty wasn't slim but heavy. She was heading for a fall. What Mic was afraid would happen, did. She had half her hair down. He had told her to put it all the way up.

"No Mic! It's too thick. I can't keep it all up."

"Misty you're working on my nerves. I don't care how you do it. You can thin out your hair, so you could put it up."

"No Mic! I won't do it. I like it this way"

"Misty, don't you understand. Your hair is getting in my way. If you won't cut some of your hair. Then quit. I don't care if I don't dance this year. If you get hurt, then the two of us are out of the competition."

"No Mic! I'm not going to quit. You're not quitting either."

"Misty if we keep going this way. You're going to get hurt."

"Then fuck off Mic. This is the best I can do. We have to practice."

Mic notice Misty was doing something with her eyes.

"All right! Don't come to me crying if you get hurt. If I had my way your hair would get cut or you leave. I know about your eyes. It won't work with me. I have a high IQ, and I don't love you. So, back off."

They started again. When they came to the part where Mic had to lift her to his shoulders. Misty's hair found its way between his fingers. He couldn't free himself from the hair. She couldn't stand on his shoulders. She was bent in half. One foot on his shoulder the other wrapped in her own hair. She was high enough to land on her elbow braking it.

"Mic I hate you. You did this on purpose. You'll pay for what you did to me."

"Misty, I told you this would happen. You're so thick headed. Just like your hair. It's always having to be your way. Let me help you up."

"Don't touch me!"

"Misty stop moving. I can see your arm is not right. I have something to in mobile lies your arm. Then we can get you to the doctor. Before you start swearing at me. Don't! I've taken all I can from you. I never worked with a girl like you before. This will be the last time working with you. I won't work with any girl that acks like you."

Mic went over to his bag and got something to in mobile lies her arm. He knew there was a teacher in the other room. Mic had asked if someone could watch them. He had a bad feeling something was going to happen.

"Misty… Are you going to let me help you?"

"No… You can go to hell Mic. This is not over with. You're going to pay for what you did to me."

"Misty it's over for me. I will never work with you again. From here out. Fine someone else to help you with homework. I'm done with you."

It was a good thing that Mic had gone to one of the teachers in the building. She had been watching them. Mic had changed his shoes and picked-up his things. He looked at the window and place the rap on the chair.

"Misty good luck with your life. One thing I like you to do."

"Go to hell… I'm not going to do anything for you."

"All right Misty. Then I will do it myself. I'm not your boyfriend. I never was and never will be your boyfriend. You're not what I would call, a girlfriend. Come to think about it' You never were."

It was over. Misty and Mic was out of any competition. Thank heavens he didn't have to work with her anymore. There was always next year for him. He wouldn't dance with Misty again.

Before bed Mic wondered where he learned how to dance. *'Who did he dance with? I hope I can get to ren sleep. With Misty off his mine. He could ask Angel if she knew.'*

Mic was hoping she would be there. In his dream, he was dancing with Angel. They were on stage dancing together. My Angel is back. Mic took her in his arms. He lifted Angel high over his head. When he brought her down Mic pulled her into his arms. The two of them was now older. They were on the patch of green grass by the waterfall. Their clothes were gone. He was kissing his Angel and making love to her.

'I thought I would never see you again. Angel I need you.'

'I need you also Mic. Please let me feel you inside me again.'

'I thought you never ask.'

The two of them were together again. Mic was moving inside her. The more he gave. The more she took. Until they came together. Mic had turn over bringing her on top of him.

'Angel I needed you so much. I couldn't get to ren sleep. There is this girl I was working with. Her name is Misty. I know she is evil. I believe she is working with Marcos. Next year when school starts. I think you're coming to the school in Scotland. If Misty is there, she will fight to get me to work with her.'

'Mic it will be alright. I will be there on the girl's side. I saw the paperwork on it. I too haven't been able to get to ren sleep. Marcos has Francis after me. He works for the school paper. Francis has been trying everything to get me alone with him. Mic we got to be careful. I believe that Misty will get back at you. It may happen when you're not on guard. If I can get out of school without and accident with him. I'll be very happy. I'll tell you this. They were doing a good job keeping us away from each other. Tonight, we are together. We still have some time left. Before you and I must get up. Make love to me again.'

She took hold of Mic inside her. He felt her bringing him higher. His hands took hold of her waste. She drove him into her until he cried out.

'Angel I love you so much.'

To feel Mic cum inside her it was wonderful. Angel said a prayer. In her mine she prayed that they could enjoy each other when they become this age. Until then she will make love to Mic in her dreams. This was hope that one day she will have his children.

'Time to get wet. Come on get up.'

'Oh, Mic do I have too? I like to stay like this.'

'All right Angel. Will do it the easy way'

With a wave of his hand. They were under the water. They had parted and went to the surface. The two of them went to laying on the sand. Mic pulled her on top of him.

"Angel one last time before we part."

She took him inside her. When they both came. Angel laid down on top of Mic. As she was coming down from her climax. Angel's face changed. She had remembered what happen when Mic went to the school in Scotland. Does this mean they couldn't come here again?

'*Mic I'm scared.*' She sat up.

'*Scared of what Angel.*'

'*When you left to go to Scotland. We couldn't see each other for a very long time. Is this what's going to happen to me? That I'm not going to know you.*'

'*Angel we got through it. Will get through it with you. This time we will be able to see each other. I will find you there. Don't worry my love.*'

In the morning. He felt rested after being with Angel. She might be right. Thinking about what she said. This could be their last night together for a while.

At art class Mic was having day dreams. He was seeing a young girl taken care of roses with a young boy. He couldn't see their faces. He draws them how he saw them. The girl had long hair. It looked to be a golden brown. She always had her back to him. Her body looked to have a nice shape with long legs to top it off. This girl could be a dancer. He had a feeling he knew who they were. Then another picture of a baby. She had blond hair her eyes were a deep blue. There was a boy. Who looked to be a toddler? The baby was holding the boy's finger. The next girl had golden-brown hair. As he drew them. Mic had no faces on them. She was dancing with this boy that had no face. As the teacher walked through the rows. She had noticed Mic's drawing.

"*Mic this is very different. Why isn't there a face on the older girls? You're making them to have a ghostly image. I like the way the baby's hand is holding on to the little boy's finger.*

"*Mic, you should put this in the art show? The toddler dancing is so sweet. Even the little boy you can't see his face. Now the young lady with her back to you. You made her as if she had wings. I hope you will put it in the art show. If you win. It will be put in the art gallery for four years.*"

Mic went to his study room. He was finish with his homework. Now he had an idea for a story. He wondered if he should put it in with the painting?

Little girls
"Who are these little girls? There's a little boy with her.
Are they a part of me? Am I that little boy? Did we grow up together?
Here is a baby. Whose finger is she holding?
Do I know this baby girl? She is holding that little boy's finger.
Why can't I see their faces? I feel she is an Angel.
This Angel is bigger now. They are toddlers.
He's always with her trying to keep her safe.
An Angel who dances. A ballerina in her tutu.
Who is this little Angel? Why can't I see her face?
The passing of time they are older.
He's dancing with his Angel.
Will he ever see her face? Where is his Angel?
She's nowhere to be found.
There're mountains in the background.
Am I dreaming here on this rock? The sun is shining.
Where is his Angel?
He can hear water and turns around.
He sees the waterfall.
Here he watches the sun dance over the water.
The water is twinkling like diamonds. Is he dreaming?
This place is made of magic. Will he see his Angel here?
A tree with a patch of green grass. A place to lay with an Angel.
He's a man in this place. Does he come here to be with an Angel?
There she is. With her long golden-brown hair.
The wind blows as the sun dances over her hair.
This place has strong magic.
Between us is water. Can you hear me Angel?
Here we are older and in love. We can dance together
We are free here to dream. To play and to make love.
My beautiful Angel. I finely see my Angel's face.
November 20, 2017

Mic had taken an engineer class. His teacher asked for them to come up with an idea. He thought of a dream machine. It's been on his mine for some time. He had been working on his blue print. Nightmares and just dreams would be a good subject. The building where he sleeps. Across the hall from them. One of the boys had bad nightmares. After the blue print was mapped out. He would look for someone to program his machine. Mic never thought a dream machine could be dangers. He would find out when it was in the wrong hands.

It was Christmas time. School would be close for one week. The class was told when they came back to school. They were going to build a model of their blue print.

It was good to be back on the ranch. Uncle Brandon had asked Mic to clean the last stall for him. He had done quick work with the stall. Now to place fresh hay. With that done he went inside the house to clean up. There was a note saying. Gone to the store be back in an hour. When the phone rang.

He picked up the phone. *"Hello, MacGregor resident. Mic speaking."*

There was a long pause. So, he repeated. *"Hello, MacGregor resident."*

"Hello Mic. This is James. I'm Brandon's brother. Is my brother around?"

"No sir. I just came in. I was in the barn cleaning out one of the stalls. Your brother and his wife went to the store. I could let him know you had called."

"No, I will call him back. So, how are you doing in school Mic? My brother speaks of you every time we get to talk."

"I'm doing much better. Now that I don't have to dance with Misty. She made my life a living hell. This year is almost done. My grades are A and sometimes A+. I'm helping others with their homework. It helps to make the time go faster. Hold on I believe the truck just pulled in. Please hold."

Mic went to the door and call Uncle Brandon. *"Telephone, it's your brother James."*

He went back to the phone. *"Sir your brother will be right in. It was nice talking with you. I'm sorry. I seem to have dump my frustrations out on you."*

"Mic that was quite alright. I enjoyed the talk with you. You have a good day."

"I will. Where are you calling from?"

"I'm in England. My daughter is here with her husband."

"Before you past the phone. My brothers said you are having trouble sleeping?"

"He talked to you about me?"

"Yes. We talk about things that mean a lot to us. I am the oldest. We try to take care of each other when we can. Your now part of this family. So, we like to take care of you."

"A while back I was having trouble sleeping because of Misty. She's not the problem any more. I'm sleeping fine. It's just when I dream. I can't see any faces. It's the same girl repeatedly. Thank you for listening to me. Your brother just came in. I'm going to help bring in the bags of groceries. It was nice talking to you. Merry Christmas. Before I say good bye. If you call again. What may I call you?"

"What would you like to call me?"

"If I'm going to be part of this family. How about dad. It feels right to me. You don't have another brother, do you?"

"No, I don't have another brother."

"All right I'll call you dad. I'll see you later dad. Take care of mom."

"Good bye, Mic. I'll let mom know that you said hi. It was good talking with you."

"Hello James. It's good to hear from you. I'm sorry about that. I forgot that Mic was going to be here."

"It's all right. I thought I would find out how Mic was doing. It's been hard on Desiree. She's missing her children. So, you can see why we're here visiting Emily."

"Are you going to be there for Christmas James?"

"Yes, that was the plan."

"James, then come up here. It sounds like Mic needs a family. He called me uncle and it sound like your dad and mom. Bring Emily and Raymond *with you*. Then Mic can meet you all."

"I'll give Arthur a call and see what he thinks. Raymond has duty before Christmas Eve. I will talk with them and see what their plans are. I will let you know later."

"Brandon, I told Joseph about Mic's dream. He doesn't understand why this was happening. Ellen will be in school there in September. Joseph is wondering if it's the spell. He told them to forget what they look like. He believes once she meets Mic it may change their dreams. Ellen said that they talked a little. She must plan it just right when she goes to sleep. There is five hours different for each other."

When Mic came here Arthur told me that he brought Mic to a doctor. He said that he didn't think we knew what we were doing. So, Mic is under a spell and hypnoses. You should let Joseph know. Last weekend he was fine. He got to be with Angel. This week he doesn't know which way to go. He can see her but not her face. Let Joseph know about this.

"Before you hang up James. I been having a bad feeling about this Misty. She threatened Mic. If Mic's right about her being evil. Marcos might be behind this. You may tell Arthur about this. Just don't say anything about the doctor."

"I believe I will call Arthur. Brandon don't worry. I won't say anything about what we talked about. I will tell him about Mic. She upset my son. He never talks to anyone that he doesn't know. In less he knew it would be safe to talk to me about anything. I think deep down he knows I'm his father. He would like to call me dad."

"I believe you have it right. Mic took to us quickly. Call me when you find out anything. We have enough food for all of you. My wife had a feeling she would need more food. She called it a woman's intuition."

James quickly called Arthur and it was okay with him.

Arthur said *"If he doesn't remember you. It means it's holding. Just be careful that no one will follow you to Mic."*

Chapter Seven: Going to Deilondolay

RAYMOND HAD SENT THE FAMILY TO THE HIGHLANDS. Brandon picked them up on Raymond's land. After his watch he went over to Bill's place. They had sent Bill to England to work with Raymond. He was also told to get to know Mic. After Mic was out of school the two of them will be working together. It will be on Arthur science ship. Mike Corban will oversee the two men. He had worked with James and Joseph. The night before his shift. Raymond called on his grate-grandfather Garret. He found out that Bill was one of Garrets sister's children. One-day Raymond thought he saw the mark like his. This mark was given to all of Garrets and his sister's children. Garret sister had just a daughter by Marcos. Through the years, there were many boys born. Only a hand full had powers like Raymond. He found out that Bill didn't know about any powers. Things he had done he never understood how he did it.

"Hey Bill. How would you like to go to Scotland for Christmas?"
"That sounds grate. How are we getting there?"
"Were flying."
"Do you have a license to fly."
"Yes, don't worry how we will get there. Do you know we are distant cousins?"
"What are you talking about?"

"It's all right Bill. Leslie is the sister to my grandfather Garret. We are the team to make sure that Mic and my sister gets together. We will talk more when we get back. Remember Mic will be there. You have to get to know him."

With a wave of his hand they were sent to the castle.

"Raymond you didn't say we would be the planes. How did you do that. Do I have powers like yours?"

Raymond just laughed. He told him the story about the magic roses. They walked to the ranch where they saw Mic. It was hard for Raymond. He had to act like he didn't know Mic. Mic was like a little brother to him. The magic spell didn't affect Raymond. He wondered if the spell would have any effect on Bill.

Joseph and Desiree where at his family's ranch. The phone call from James upset him. He knew it had to stay this way. The name Tom MacGregor was taken away from his little girl. It was time to get her ready for Deilondolay. Everything had to be done slowly with her. She does have powers, being his daughter. He had to take his time with her.

Today, was Ellen's Christmas ballet. It was hard to see her dancing without Tom. Ellen has been a teacher's helper. James told him that some of the guys came to Mic on all the ballet dances. When Joseph saw his daughter leap high in the sky. He was so proud of her. All her girls dance flawless. Her spins she could spin for a long time.

Desiree, Ellen's mother use to dance. She had gotten hurt and couldn't do the ballet dances anymore. At the hall where the dances were taking place. Joseph felt that evil was here. At the end of the dance recital. Joseph stood up and started looking around. He found a young but not so tall of a boy.

Then another boy stood up in front of Joseph.

"His name is Francis. He's been a thorn in Ellen's side. You must have the same mark."

He whispered. "My I ask your name?"

Stephen felt strong powers in him. "My name is Stephen O'Connell. This is my girlfriend Maryann Colman. I see that Ellen never told you about Francis."

"No! My daughter is still mad at me. She must believe she can stay away from him. This is my wife Desiree. It's nice to meet both of Ellen's friends. Maryann why don't you show my wife were Ellen is. I would like to talk with Stephen."

The two of them walked a bit. Joseph asked Stephen.

"Has she talked about the man called Marcos?"

"No sir. She's closed lips about everything."

Joseph saw Francis watching them. He then waved his hand. In his mind, he spoke.

'Francis, you will never have my little girl. I could kill you with my bear hands. They will think you were choking to death. Just like now.'

Joseph slowly close his fingers. As Stephen watched Francis. Quickly Stephen turn his head and saw Joseph fingers closing.

"Sir this isn't the way to do this. Please stop." Stephen place a hand over Joseph's hand.

Joseph looked at the young man and smiled. This young man is seeing more than he is letting on.

"Shell, we go see Ellen?"

"Yes! I would love to tell her that I fallen in love with ballet."

Joseph liked the young man. He knew how to take charge of the moment. Ellen picked her friends wisely.

※※※

The last six months went by fast. Yesterday, was the last day of school. Ellen asked if she could take her friends swimming at the pond. Her grandmother told her it would be find. She will give her a basket of food to take with them.

"Ellen the three of you have to saddle your own horses. Someone took a big part of the fence down behind the ranch. All the men had to help your grandfather. Some of the horses got out. If that's not enough there is a young man coming for lessons. His name is Jim and never rode a horse before. He will be here at 9:00. Max will be back just before 9:00. Could you get another horse saddle for him?"

"Granny I be happy too. Thank you for making us a picnic basket."

"*You been working very hard helping your grandfather with the horses.*"

"*I've been enjoying helping. Granddad showed me a lot. My friends should be waiting for me at the barn.*"

When she looked out the window, Ellen saw Mrs. Foemen.

"*Granny, it's Mrs. Foemen coming up the walkway. She didn't fine granddad. The look on her face. Doesn't look to be happy about it. Would you like me to tell her your busy?*"

"*No dear. You think Mrs. Foemen is unhappy now. If we did that, I think we must put a new roof on the house. Go take care of the horses. I will handle Mrs. Foemen.*"

"*Now, I got it. She would blow her top. Gran that was a good one.*"

Ellen went out the back door. She had felt a different kind of evil. She had just brushed it off.

'*No demon is going to stop me today.*'

At the barn she saw her friends.

"*Hi there. We have food for a picnic. Stephen could you get another horse out for me. Make it Lulu. Someone is going to take lessons with Max today. Here Maryann could you take the basket. I'll get the saddles.*"

Stephen said. "*I smell chicken and potato salad. Wonderful! It will go good with the little cakes I brought. I'll be right there after I get Lulu.*"

For a minute. Mic felt strange. He was going to the tac-room to get a saddle. Then he felt his cross get hot. Quickly he looked around. There was nothing there. As he got closer to the barn. He could smell chicken and potato salad. He had just eaten two hours ago. Where is this smell coming from? At the barn his eyes started playing tricks on him. The barn looked different to him. Mic rub his eyes trying to clear them.

"*All right demon. Stop messing with me.*"

Inside the barn. As Mic got closer to the tac-room his cross went hotter. What would be in that tac room. He knew whatever it was its evil.

'*What the hell do they want with me? I'm not a MacGregor... Am I?*'

Mic looked between the door and the wall. Inside the tac-room was a small boy. He was holding a log. Mic couldn't see his face.

There was a mass over his head. This person had plans to take him down or kill him.

'Mic was thinking. He wants to fight me. So be it.'

He found a long handle that was metal. Now he will be able to block that log. Mic stepped inside the tac room. Right off he blocked the first blow. For the size of the boy. He had the strength of two men. The hit could have killed him. It just missed his head. It had brought Mic down on one knee. Before the boy could take another swing. Mic swung first. He slammed the metal handle against the log. The impact knocked the log out of the boy's hand. Mic kicked him in the stomach. The blow took the boys breath away. The last blow was to the back of the neck. Mic needed to know who this boy was. When he went to take the mass-off. The boy was gone.

"What the hell is going on. Am I going crazy?"

Mic went out of the tac-room. Outside he heard a man's voice.

"So, you thought you could get away from me. You belong to me. Did you think Thomas could help you? Think again Eleanor. Damn it! Why can't she hear me? That's right her name is Ellen. She can't see me ether."

Mic looked again between the door and wall. This time he saw three people. A boy that was laying on the ground. A man standing over the boy looking enrage with him. The girl with a long braid of golden-brown hair. This time he saw a sideview of her face. Still not the whole face. The face was still clouded.

"Can't anyone tell me what is going on? Who is messing with me?"

Mic's cross went to burning him. Then he understood. There after the girl with the long braid. She is the one in trouble.

Ellen went over to the boy. She had to make sure he was breathing.

'That's good' she thought. He's okay.'

She made quick work of tying his hands up.

'Now, who is this boy? She knew he was evil. He's not that big for her cross to be burning her.'

When she took off his mass, she saw Francis. Then Ellen heard laughter. Her cross was staying hot. When Ellen looked up. She saw Marcos the demon. He was standing over Francis.

"I know you from my dreams. Your Marcos." Ellen looked around, all she had was a cross to protect her with."

"You can hear me Ellen. I was going to let Francis have you first. For some reason he couldn't take you down. Even when I was helping him. You should be dead."

Mic knew what he had to do. The metal handle wasn't going to help them now. When his cross stayed hot. Mic took hold of it and stepped inside the tac-room. Somehow the cross brought him to where Angel was. He then dropped the pipe near Angel.

"Hello my Angel, my love."

Mic pulled her into him an gave her a kiss. He then placed his hands around her waist and lifted her up. Angel needed to be to his right. The demon just stood there looking at the two of them. When Mic took Angels left hand. The two of them became older. They had their powers now.

"Hello Marcos, or should I say Marcuse. I told you, Angel is mine. She is my mate."

Marcuse kept looking at the two of them. *"This can't be. You're in Scotland."*

"You don't remember? So, your master doesn't let you remember. Then let me tell you. Angel called for her great-grandfather Garret's powers. Garret gave his magic to me. This time around we will have powers to fight you on earth. In the spirit world and in the dream world. We will send you back to hell. You're no longer welcome here. This boy that you used. He's going away for a while. Tell you what Marcuse. I have had enough of you. You can think about this in hell. When you see your master. Have fun trying to tell him why Angel and I is not with you."

Mic bellowed, *"Begone Satan. You have no powers over us. I will always go where Angel needs me. You took Garret's family from him. Thomas save Garret. Garret saved his sister. Through them we have powers to fight with. You will not win this time either."*

He looked at Angel and smiled. This time when they lifted their hands together. Their magic shot as a bright light from their fingertips. It bored into Marcuse's chest. The light exploded inside his body. He screamed as the light spread through Marcuse. In doing so they sent him back to hell in pieces.

Bill was driving to rose hill. It was a beautiful day. He was to meet Mic and learn how to ride a horse. He bought some snacks for them to eat on the trail. Bill was all most to the barn when his birthmark went red hot. He knew Mic was in trouble. Bill's training took over. He pulled into the yard. He ran full out the rest of the way. Bill was ready for anything. As he moved in closer to the tac-room. He heard fighting as he looked between the door and the wall. There was a flash back. Inside he saw Angel was there and two others. How did the others get here? Bill saw Mic with a metal handle. He had step in front of Angel. A small boy with a mass on. There was a demon inside the boy? They took a swing at Angel. If Mic didn't have a metal handle. The swing would have killed Angel and Mic.

'He knew Mic wasn't in Scotland. A time-warp. He is fighting in the spirit world with Angel. There they have their powers. The cross that Mic wears. What did Raymond tell him? This cross was made from Angel's hair. It was put together with magic and the magic rose petals. Raymond had it blessed. Bill heard Mic call the demon Marcuse. As the two of them sent him back to hell. He felt there was someone else nearby. Another boy was watching Mic and Angel.'

"Angel I knew someone was in danger. I couldn't see the girls face. My heart knew it was you. I will always come to you when you're in danger. I don't care where you are at. I will find you. I love you with all my heart."

"Mic I will always find you also. I love you Mic."

"My love. You have good friends here with you today. I don't think you will remember this. The boy on the other side of the boards will know what to do."

"I don't want to leave you Angel. Being away from you has been hard on me. My mine has been messed with. I didn't know the girl with no face. I'm glad my heart knew. The love I have for you brought me right to you."

Mic pulled Angel into him. He took his last kiss knowing he had to go back. This boy had seen everything that Mic and Angel had done. Bill and Mic knew that the boy wasn't evil. When Marcuse was gone the cross went cool. The boy knew, that Francis try to kill

Ellen. Mic also knew he was there. Then Bill heard the boy's voice calling Max.

Bill found out the boy was standing right where he was. They watched Mic and Angel kiss. As they try to hold on to each other. The time-warp was pulling Mic back. The last words to each other was I love you. Bill then heard the voice of Max. He was calling for the boy. His name was Stephen.

Stephen felt bad for the two of them. He saw it was pulling on them to let go of each other. To see them older was wonderful. He will remember this man who works out. He smiled at the two of them. When Mic took one last kiss. He didn't know where Mic had gone. Just knew he was sent back. The two of them was safe.

Bill heard Stephen say. "*Fairy magic is very strong. Yes, there is magic in Scotland. Could that be where Mic came from? Ellen said she was going to school in Scotland.*"

Bill understood that Stephen knew he was there also. When the two of them are back in America Stephen will watch over Ellen.

Bill saw Stephen go into the tac-room. "*Ellen are you, all right? Don't say anything just listen to me. You heard something in the tac-room. You went to grab the pipe. Ellen you were the one to stop him. Let Francis tell his story. If I'm right he's going to be locked up.*"

On the floor was the metal pipe. Stephen called for Max.

"Where in the barn. Call my father. Francis try to kill Ellen."

Max came running. Maryann was running to the house. She was calling Stephen's dad. Max had left Francis where he was until the police came.

Stephen said. "*I saw Francis swing a heavy log at Ellen. He just missed her head. If he hit Ellen, he would have killed her. I believe he would have had his way with her. He didn't care if she was dead. He's been that crazy to get her alone with him. She told me that she picked the pipe up before she went into the tac-room. She blocked the blow. Before he tried to hit her again. Ellen hit the log out of his hands. Then she kicked him in the stomach. He hit his head on the boards and went down. Ellen checked him to make sure he was breathing. Then she tied him up and she took off the mass he had over his face.*"

The ones that did come was Stephen father and Francis uncle. An ambulance showed up for Francis. Stephen never told Max of the bright light or the two other men.

'So, Max, was the one watching over Ellen at the ranch. I wonder if Mic would remember what happen here with Ellen? This magic the two of them have. It must call to the other when the one is in danger. The magic rose can bring Mic or Angel to where ever the other maybe. Stephen must know about Ellen's having magic. He just saved her by telling a different story.'

In the vision, Bill saw and heard what everyone said and did. He had a photograph memory. What had happened to Ellen made everyone scramble. How did Francis cut the fence and scare the horses? No one seen him do it? Bill knew what happen. It was Marcuse that did everything. Stephen never said anything about what he had seen. Francis was sent away to try to control his demons. The story he told got him placed in a hospital.

Bill talked to Mic and found out he couldn't remember anything that happen. He didn't know if he should tell their parents what he knew. Soon Ellen will be coming here to Scotland. Would it be better just to let it go for now? One thing Bill knew. Mic would go anywhere to save Angel. He wondered who will be with Angel after this. He knew of one woman. Angelica McKinnon, the daughter of Murdock McKinnon. Murdock had pulled Bill after most of his training for the Navy Seal. This is what happen to Raymond. Could he pull his daughter for this job? Angelica was the best woman to protect Ellen.

When Mic was in school. Bill asked if he could live here on the ranch. The Macgregor's like that idea. In the barn there was a small apartment. With heat and a place to cook and sleep. They haven't heard yet on what happen to Angel. When Mic is at the ranch there would be someone keeping an eye on him. Today Bill needed to speak to Raymond. He knew that Raymond was in the Highlands. He was claiming the family land. Raymond had to pay the back taxes on the land first. He told the town he would like to raise horses. The MacGregor family was helping Raymond to get started. They gave him the paper work on a few of their horses. This was to be shown to the town.

It was time Bill talk with Raymond. The incident was too much for one person to handle by himself. Bill had to tell someone what he saw. The incident at the ranch had brought in Angelica. She will stay with Ellen intel she safc at the school in Scotland. Raymond had to help his father take Ellen's name from her memory. Now she became Angel. It was set up that Ellen only remember the name Angel. Anyone that new the legend of the MacGregor or saw the painting. The spell also made sure that the people of the Highlands. Wouldn't think they were the next Thomas and Eleanor MacGregor. Bill and Angelica could take them diving and camping in the summer.

"Hello Raymond. Thanks for coming over so quickly."

"That's okay. Anything about my sister, my wife and her brother. This is very important to me. Tell me what you know. Did you see what had happen on that day?"

Bill told him what he saw. To save Angel. Mic went all the way to Vermont. Marcuse was there in the tac-room. The two of them have their own magic. Mic told Marcuse that he has Garret's magic. I think it's in the dream world and any kind of time-warp.

"Bill did Mic remember anything about what happen?"

"No. However, Stephen O'Connell saw everything with Mic being there. He knew it was fairy magic. When Max came into the barn. I heard Stephen telling what Francis try to do to Ellen."

"Marcuse is trying everything to kill Mic and Angel. The first time he tried to kill Mic in his sleep. Angel called to grandfather Garret. She knew if she was older, she would have her magic. This time round both will need magic. So, Marcuse tried to kill Angel. Mic had me make something for them. Both has a piece of each other's hair with them. There is strong fairy magic with the rose. Now tell me how they were standing. When they let their magic flow."

"Angel was to his right. When he took her hand. They lifted their hands together. Mic said the words Satan begone. Bright light bored into Marcuse's chest. It cut Marcuse in pieces."

"Wow! I would have loved to have seen that. I knew those two would have magic this time around. I guess that I helped that a bit. It was my magic that made her hair into a cross. Mic hair is in Angel's locket. In the dream world. Mic came here to the Highland's for the magic fairy rose. He gave Angel the locket that is handed down. It has a lot of magic inside it. The locket in the dream world is very strong. In the dream world Mic had mated with Angel. Now she has two lockets to keep her safe."

The two men had walked to Raymond's land. He was doing what his grandfather had told him to do. Raymond had told the family. He had to claim the land, so Angel and Angelica had a place to stay. Each time, Raymond's blood touch the land it boiled. When all four corners were done. Raymond cleared the meadow where the house was to go. He also put a drop of blood there and waved his hands over the land.

"Bill what you saw happen with Mic and Angel will stay between us for now. Angelica McKinnon will stay here with my wife and sister. I will come back to start my new home. My father gave me money to do all this with the help of Garret.

What Mic had done wasn't the first time. Mic would do anything to save his Angel. When he was just a year old. He had a fight with Marcuse the day Angel was to be born. Two months before she came. Mic was talking with Angel. At the hospital. Marcuse was trying to scare Angel. Enough that he thought she would die. Mic kept talking to her. He told her that her daddy wouldn't let that happen. Our grate grandfathers had come to help us. They save Mic from a tree lim. It was Mic who stop Marcuse. There was a piece of glass that could have kill Mic. He used that glass and through it like a knife. It went into Marcuse. We saw the blood. I had to push it in deeper with my magic. I was only thirteen at the time. Marcuse try to kill my sister and my little brother. The two of us believe the same way. No one will hurt Angel or Mic. This is how my sister feels. He's my brother.

"Soon Angel will be going to school here in the lowlands. I must have the house ready for them. Angel will stay here in the Highlands on weekends and holidays."

The two men were back at the piece of land that Raymond now owns. It was good to see the grass growing. With a wave of his hand a house appeared.

"Raymond, isn't this taking a chance? Don't you think they will know you have magic?"

"Bill, I have already thought of this. If anyone comes here, they will see a part of a building. Every day will show a little more. If anyone stay here all they will see is men building. When the sun goes down. There will be no-one working. When the sun comes up. The men will start working on my home."

"Bill do you know Angelica McKinnon?"

"No. I have heard of her, she is the best. I believe the school will ask her to help teach the girl's diving. I work with the boys. When the girls heard about diving. They wanted to learn."

"That will be good. Angel will be diving with the other girls. Bill, I don't know how you could see what Mic and Angel were able to do. When Marcuse made his move with Francis. He thought Francis could kill Ellen. We have a little breathing room. We made are move and brought in Angelica to the ranch. She can go any where's Angel may go. My father and I had to slowly take away things from her memory. All her things that was going to Scotland I now have. Come on Bill we got other things to do. Angel will be here before we know it."

Chapter Eight: Francis and Marcos

AFTER SHE HAD HER LAST DANCE RECITAL. Ellen had for gotten her birth name. She became Angel. Angelica was teaching Angel everything she needed to know about diving. There was a lot of classroom homework to do. Angel two friends liked the idea of knowing how to dive. The three of them got through all the classroom work together. The pond out back was just what Angelica needed. She had to get Angel use to the tanks, mask, and her fins. Angel's grandfather gave her friends each a mask and fins. This pond had a deep spot to dive in. Angel worked hard. She knew a lot about diving when she left her grandparents ranch.

At the end of the month Angel and Angelica was taken to Arthur's private jet. He learned not to go overboard with Angel. Her past port, Arthur also had. Anything she needed the school will take care of it. Angel found herself looking out a small window. The sun was out. She could see the land below. Then she was up in the clouds. From here out. She won't be able to see much. Angelica gave her some books to read on diving. She also did some drawing and work on her story. After a while she started to get sleepy. They had just flown over the World Clock time zone. Then they were landing in Scotland. Arthur had two rooms for them. Angelica and Angel were going to share a room.

The next day they were going to her new school. Angel will take another test for college. She didn't remember much of the landing.

Nor did she remember being help to her room. The next morning Angel remember smelling coffee and something sweet. When she opened her eyes, she was in a big room. Angelica was sitting at a table drinking the coffee.

"Good morning Angel. I have some food and a hot chocolate with a little coffee in it. You will need it to take a test today."

"Angelica, where are we?"

"Where in Scotland. I will be taking you to your new school. So, get up and come and get something to eat."

Angel got out of a soft bed. "Okay where is this hot chocolate with coffee in it?"

She took a sip. Angel was remembering her dream. "Angelica, I had a dream of a castle."

As she took a bit of food. She was drawing what she remembered. Angel saw different ages of children. On one side of the castle there were many colors of rose bushes. However, there was one rose bush that was redder than any other color red there. Every time she dreamt, it meant something. Angel had this dream once before. She draws the castle with the deepest red roses. Next, she drawn a man sitting on a Clydesdale. The man had a white baseball hat on.

Angelica came over to stand behind Angel. "That's beautiful Angel. Did you see anything in front of the man?"

Angel thought about it. She started to draw the pond. What did she see near that pond? A path leading down to it. Then Angel remembered there was two people walking with tanks. From that moment she felt a presence. It was coming from her drawing. How can that be she thought? In her mine eye she was on that path with him. Whatever had happened. He knew she was there with him. Angel stopped drawing and quickly closed the book. She moved fast to stand up. Angelica was watching Angel draw. She had to move quickly to get out of the way of her chair.

'Something spooked Angel. She knew it had to be something with her drawing.'

"Angel are you okay?"

"I'm find. I thought it was getting late. Don't we have that meeting?"

"Your right Angel. We better get dress. Ware something comfortable."

The two of them were off to the school. Angel was thinking about what she had felt. Angelica pulled into a driveway to a check station. The man told them to park outside the gate.

In Angel's mind she was screaming. *'No... no...no! I'm not a bad girl. Please don't lock me up.'*

In the Highland's. A teenage boy was learning more about diving. Mic stood up fast. He had just swallowed a lot of water. Quickly, he went on land. In his mind he heard a girl screaming. All he could do was scream back.

'STOP...! It's not that bad. The school is not a jail. You'll be just fine at Deilondolay for girls. I'm at Deilondotay for boys.'

'I'm sorry I screamed. You can hear me? Who are you? How do you know I'm at Deilondolay?'

'Because I felt the same way when I saw the big gates.'

Once the car came to a stop. Angelica turn to look at Angel.

"Angel, I hope this fence is not scaring you. One minute you looked scared to death. You came out of it very quickly. I thought I was the only one that could do that. I think you can take the prize this time. Now that were stop, you're okay about it. What changed your mine?"

Angel was biting her bottom lip. She was wondering how much she should tell her. When she didn't understand it herself.

"Angelica there is a lot of things happening to me. Give me some time to figure it out."

"Alright I understand, you don't trust me yet."

Angel didn't know what to say. "Angelica what would you do if your memory had been mess with. Would you have the answers?"

"At your age. Maybe not. Angel, you and I have been thrown into this together. There are things you have been doing scare me. Because you are blocking me out. I was told to protect you at all cost. This is not a jail. You can come and go. The grounds are like a city. Yes, it has a big fence around both schools. The schools are on 150 acres. The information that I give you didn't tell you much. This school takes in all kind of children. Some are kids that keep running away from home. Others are trouble makers. They all have their memories taken from them. Now there is children like yourself. Your father is looking for a bad man. You're a very talented young woman. Someone would love to use your ability's.

"That's where I came in to the picture. I had tried out for the Navy Seal. I almost made it. You could say my body told me. NO way in hell are you going to make it. I'm a strong woman. Not that strong to fight all kinds of weather. I tried... It almost took my life. I'm part of this team. You don't remember your family and I don't know them. I was told to protect you at all cost. Do you know what that means?"

"Yes, I know what it means. To give your life to save mine."

"Alright Angel, we can talk more about this later. I want to be your friend. I hope you can come to trust me. Right now, we got to get inside. You have a test to take. Think about what I said."

Angel grabbed one of her bags. While Angelica grabbed the other one. At the gate, she took a deep breath. With her eyes only on the opening she walked through the gate. Happy with herself she called to her mystery man.

'I'm went through that gate. I hope, I can meet you.'

In the Highlands a young man was walking with his friend. A big smile came over his face. Mic looked at Bill and smile.

'Maybe.'

"Okay Bill. Let's get the horses. It's time for your lesson. I like to see how fast you can ride to the castle."

Angelica place a hand on Angel shoulder. The two of them went through the office door. After Angel took her test. They asked her what she like to take for activities. They were very happy with what she chose to take. Mrs. McPike smiled at Angel. She took Angel to the building where she was going to sleep. Mrs. McPike was the freshman house mother.

"Your roommate is called Bunny. She will be here next week. This is when you must be back here."

Raymond and Emily took Angelica and Angel to see some of the sights. They stop at the Fair. They saw men fighting with heavy swords. Many things were going on. They heard the bagpipes and saw the girl's dancing.

"Oh yes, I like to learn those dances. Can I get a kilt? Please Angelica could you buy me a kilt."

"Alright I'll get you a kilt."

"You have no need to do that. Here look in the bag."

Angel squeal with delight. She through her arms around his neck. "Think you. I just love it." She went to put the kilt on.

"How do I look?"

"Like a true Scottish woman. Which I believe you are. I think it was Arthur who told me this."

There were young men going around looking for girls to dance with. A tall young man came over to them. Raymond knew this young man. It was Mic from the school Deilondotay. Bill was with him making sure he stayed safe.

"Hello young lassie. Would you like to dance with me?"

"I would love it. I don't know any of those moves."

"I would love to show you. If it's all right with your family?"

Out of all the girls around them. Mic found Angel. Angelica looked at Raymond for help. He nodded his head for okay.

"Alright Angel. You can go and dance. Young man what is your name?"

"They call me Mic. This is my cousin Bill Colman."

"Hello, I am Angelica. This is my cousin Angel McKinnon."

Before Mic took Angel up on stage. He showed her all the moves they were going to use. Angel caught on quickly.

Bill came over to Raymond. "I had nothing to do with this. When Mic saw her, he made a beeline right to her?"

"It's all right Bill. I had a feeling this was going to happen. Come on let's get closer to them. There is a lot of people here today."

"Raymond is that who I think it is?"

"Yes Angelica."

"Wow! She is very beautiful isn't she.' It didn't take Angel long to learn the moves. It's as if she had done it all her life.

"Angelica, she has."

Raymond could feel the spell trying to work. Will it be the same with Angel? She stronger them we thought. If she is that strong in her mind. The spell won't last long.

'Could Mic be the same way? The moment Marcuse tried to kill her. Mic went right to Angel. Right now, Raymond will have to watch himself. He cannot call Angel his sister. Today is there day. How it turns out is all up to them. We four will be on guard to keep them safe.'

※

Angel had to get back to school. She enjoyed dancing with Mic. When he came over to her, she thought she knew him. Was he the one she had felt? He said he went to the school for boys. It was on the other side from her school. She hoped to meet him again. Today was the day she was to meet her roommate. When she went through the gate. It wasn't as bad this time around. At the gate she said goodbye to Angelica. Angel knew she see her next week. This week was for all the students to come back to school. Freshman were the first ones to come to school.

"I'll see you next week for my diving lesson Angelica."

"Angel are you going to your room."

"No not yet. I thought I do some running. I like to look around first. Is that okay. I have my room already set-up."

"Yes, you will have to go there soon. Don't forget to sign up for things you like to do."

"That's why I'm going around looking at all of the different buildings."

"I'll see you next week. Have fun and stay out of trouble."

"Angelica don't worry. Mary told me who to stay away from. Misty was one of them. I have a bad feeling we are going to tangle for dancing. She is not going to like me. Because I'm in college. Don't worry. I'll be good."

Angel ran off to look around the campus. She thought about the handsome young man. She loved dancing with him. Why would it feel so right being with him? What was it about his name Mic?

"Mic…, Micky…, Micky Mouse."

Angel stopped running. The name Micky Mouse was from her childhood. She used to sit with a boy watching the show Micky Mouse. He is a part of my life. It felt right when Mic took her hand. Is Mic from her pass?

Angel was close to a building. This must be where they would do there dancing. She when over to the steps. As she climbed.

Angel was wondering about Mic. Since she been here in Scotland. A young man has been helping her. I can hear his thoughts. I know he hears mine. If Mic is a part of my passed. He may like to do a lot of things that I like to do. If he comes to this building I will be here.'

Angel went up some stairs. She tried the doorknob. The building was open to the students. In the corridor was a bulletin board. There were papers to sign up for dancing. Another one for becoming a team leader. This was only for the senior's and upper-class men. Down one of the halls came a teacher.

"Hello. Welcome to the building of arts. Here we have three things. Dancing, painting, photography. We will work with you on what you pick."

"I know just what I want to do. Can I pick all of them?"

"Yes, if you like."

"Thank you. This is just what I'm going to do."

Angel put all three activities. *"If it's too much for me. I will drop one. I have my camera with me. I can always show the teacher my pictures. It will be photography."*

The teacher watched her write her name. Angel E.H.

"So, you are the one Principal Tensaw was talking about. I hope you can help this school win this year. My initials must go next to your name. Make sure that each teacher does the same. You have these papers in your dorm. Sign up there too. Last year some of the papers got lost. I'm going to make a copy and send it to Principal Tensaw. Good luck, Angel."

Angel went to all the buildings. She signed up on what she like to take. In the afternoon she checkout the horses and sign up for the competition. It was time to go to her dorm. There was papers she had to sign there also. Angel went in the building at the back door. She could hear girls laughing.

"*Wow!*" If it stays this loud, she will have to study at the library. Then she saw the house mother.

"*Hello Angel. I heard you been going all around. They said you signed up for things you like to take. Here, I will place my name next to yours. Then you can go meet the girls.*"

"*Alright, I have three more places to sign up. I think I will do it after lunch. Mrs. McPike. Thank you for your help.*"

It's was time to meet her roommate. On the way down the hall she said hi to some of the girls. Bunny wasn't in the room. The gym was downstairs from the lunch room. Angel got her gym bag. Before she eats, she like to do some dancing. She saw one of the girls bouncing around. She couldn't stay still.

'*That must be Bunny my roommate.*'

Angel smiled at her roommate. "*Hello Bunny. I hope I got that right?*"

"*Yes. Then you must be Angel?*"

"*Yes, hello roommate. It's nice to meet you, Bunny.*"

"*It was easy to pick me out from everyone. I don't know why I do this. I just seem to hop.*"

"*Bunny could you be nervous?*"

"*Maybe I am. I never thought of it before.*"

"*Bunny how about you get change and come down to the gym?*"

"*Angel what are you going to do?*"

"*I'm going to work on my ballet. I have sign up to be a team leader.*"

"*Angel how can you be a leader? I was told that you have to be a senior or higher.*"

Angel just smiled and walk down the hall. What better way to get people down to the gym? She also felt that Bunny loved to talk. She turned the corner to go outside. Angel saw a few girls coming down the hall. Mrs. McPike smile at Angel. She had put up another paper for any girl who like to be on Angel's team. Bunny was at the bulletin board.

She cried out. "*My roommate is a freshman in college.*"

Angel went through the door and smiled. She saw the sign for the gym it was down stairs. The lunch room was straight ahead. Down stairs she saw were the showers were and were to play her music. With her music on one sung to warm up by. The other sung to dance with. Angel went through her warm up. When her music change. She went into her dance and did her leaps and spins. When she saw the girls come in. Angel did a little more before stopping. She smiled when she saw Bunny was leading the girls. All the questions came from Bunny.

"Angel, that was beautiful. Could you tell us how long you been dancing?"

"Since I was four. I love to dance. When I went on stage for the first time. I did my spins just right. My leaps were higher than before. I knew then dancing will always be a part of me.

"I became the youngest ballet teacher aid. I showed the girls and boys of all ages. They learn how to do better spins and leaps. Does anyone know what classical means?"

No one could answer her. "It is a standards style of ballet. A force that is influence by a teacher. The words I'm going to tell you. Is the history what the judges of the competition could ask us.

"Classical Ballet: a traditional style of ballet. Which stresses the academic technique. This was developed through the centuries. For the existence of ballet.

"Ballerina: a female dancer in a ballet company. This is what we will be.

Danseur: a male dancer in a ballet company. We will be dancing with the boys. You must learn these words and much more. The judges may ask us these words. We are going up against other schools.

"I've been told. Deilondolay and Deilondotay haven't won the ballet competition, for three years. Now, how many of you have done ballet before?"

Three hands went up. "How many like to learn how to dance?"

Four hands went up. "If you want me to be your team leader. You must sign up on more than one sheet. Tell the others about this. We have a little time before we eat. The ones that have their dancing clothes and ballet shoes go get change."

A teacher came from out back. She had ballet shoes for the others.

"I have shoes you can borrow tell you can buy some. If you don't make the cut. There are classes you can take. There is next year you will be able to try again."

All the girls were able to get a pare for today. The teacher took their names to order them some ballet shoes.

"We will go over the positions. The firsts position who knows them. I like for you to show me. The others watch them. Then if you think you have it. Go try it for yourself."

Angel went over to look at each of the three girls' position. She was pleased to see two of them had it.

"Bunny you did the first position exceptional."

The next girl. "You almost have it. Put your heels closer together. Like this." Angel went and showed her.

"Yes, that's right. They must touch. It will make your toes turned out. Better!"

The last girl did the movement skillfully. Angel went over and looked at the other four girls. She saw that their feet needed work.

"Keep trying you'll get it. You four are doing well for your first time. You can watch the others work on their feet positions. I like for you three to hold your arms in front of you in an oval shape. Then we will put it all together. This is all we are going to do for today. Do it again."

Angel did it with them. "It will take time. Work on how you place your feet. Now rest and watch me as I go through the positions.

"1st Position: Your heels should be touching with your toes turned out. Hold your arms in front of you in an oval shape, like this.

"2en Position: Move your feet apart. Open your arms wide but don't stretch them back. They should be slightly rounded and slightly in front of you.

"3rd Position: Cross one foot in front of the other. Bring one arm curved in towards you and the other arm out to the side.

"4th Position: Put one foot in front of the other with a space between. Raise your arm and curved it above your head. The other arm out to the side.

"5th Position: Finally, have one-foot exactly in front of the other. This time close together. Raise both arms up in a beautiful ballerina oval."

"Before we leave here is three more words to know. Pointes Shoes: The satin ballet shoes used by dancers. When dancing on their points of their toes. Pointes shoes used are reinforced with a box. Constructed of *many layers of strong glue in between layers of material. These shoes are not made of cement or wood.*

"*Tutu: the short classical ballet skirt made of many layers of net. A romantic tutu: is a long net skirt reaching below the calf.*

Chapter Nine: Nightmare was Safed

ANGEL HAD LUNCH WITH THE GIRLS SHE MET. After lunch she went to see the horses. She had to sign-up for the races in this competition. She found the sign-up sheet. Now she had to pick a horse to ride. Laron was the one who ran the stables. Angel could see no one was around. The first horse she saw was too old for this competition. Off in the distance she heard a horse that was upset. Angel turned quickly. She saw men trying to get that horse into a trailer. When the horse broke away from the men. Laron hollered for me to get out of the way. Angel wasn't scared of the horse. This must be the horse that one of the girl's tormented. She knew of his name, it was Nightmare. He was coming very close to her. Angel knew how to get on a horse that was scared. She grabbed his mane and swung her leg over his back. She had to get closer to his head. He had to hear her voice.

"Nightmare it's just you and me. Let's see what you can do."

He had to know she wouldn't hurt him. She kept him running full out. Angel brought him around. She took him over the jump's then down the home stretch. As she slowed Nightmare down. She saw a man coming torte her. This must be Laron. He didn't look happy with her. Angel knew she must be in big trouble. She brought Nightmare to a stop and quickly spoke.

"Are you Mr. Laron? I'm sorry sir. I know I'm in trouble. You see sir I've done this many of times. I know when a horse is scared. My grandfather showed me how to get onto a horse when I was ten."

"Tell me lass who are ye?"

She walked Nightmare around as she spoke to Laron.

"They call me Angel. My family has worked with horses for a long time. This horse someone had tormented him. I don't know how she or he did it. Not yet."

"Aye, ye are right about that."

"Where were you taking him?"

"Well to a place where…"

Angel turned and looked at him. "You were going to have him killed."

"Aye! That was my orders. You know if Nightmare will trust ye. I will tell them that he is responding to you."

"Nightmare is a fine horse. I know someone who will take him. Give me a bit of time. Just don't kill him. Laron has Nightmare always had a limp."

"Let me think. No. I never thought of his hoofs. Do ye think this is what making him act crazy?"

"Can I have something to clean his hoofs. He's not walking right. I'll let you know in a minute."

Angel knew there must be something in Nightmare's hoofs. All four of his legs, were given him trouble.

"With him acting up all the time. I never thought to check his hoofs. A man was called in to put new shoes on Nightmare. It was someone that Misty's father called."

When Angel bent Nightmares leg. There was something between the shoe and hoof. Angel had to dig it out. She handed it to Laron and preceded to check all four hoofs. Whatever it was. He had a feeling Misty had something to do with it. Angel looked at the last one. To her it was a device that could shock him.

Bunny was coming toured them. Angel saw her and made the sign to slow down.

"Is there anything wrong Angel?"

"Have you ridden before Bunny?"

"Yes, I have. I came down here to sign-up for the competition. He is beautiful. May I ride him?"

Laron stepped away from them. This young lass knows what she is doing.

"Not yet. What I like for you to do. Is talk to him and slowly come toured him."

Bunny spoke softly. *"You're a beautiful boy Nightmare. Can I get on you?"*

"Okay Bunny. Take him for a little walk. Now turn around and bring him back to me."

There were no limps. Angel looked into Nightmares eyes. She could see he was a lot happier. Laron watched as the girls did the magic on Nightmare.

"Bunny can you ride bare back?"

"Yes! Like dancing I have five years on both."

"First, run your hand over his back. Then get yourself on him."

Bunny swung her leg over and got on Nightmare. Angel led them around. She told Bunny to walk him. Then slowly pick up speed. Laron was pleased with what Angel and Bunny was doing. He knew that Nightmare wasn't a bad horse. He needed more than one person to ride him with no trouble. Off in the distant Laron saw another girl coming toured them. She went over to the sign-up sheet. Now Laron had three girls that signed-up for the competition. Can this girl ride Nightmare also? Angel waved at Mary to come over to her.

"Mary how long have you been riding?"

"Seven years. For ballet dancing only two years."

"Have you ever been in a competition before?"

"Yes, I even won in the jumping competition. I can show you what I can do. If you like."

Bunny was now running Nightmare. She took him over the jumps. Nightmare flew over each jump with ease. Then Angel waved Bunny in.

"Well done Bunny. Bring him in."

She walked him slowly. Bunny was giving Nightmare a lot of love and praise.

"He is wonderful. Nightmare is the best. I never had a horse that fit me. He knew what I wanted from him. Mary are you here to pick out a horse to ride?"

"Yes. I saw you do the jumps. Bunny I'm glad you're on my team. You would give me a run for the money."

Angel had Mary come over to them. She had to see if Nightmare would react to her. Mary walked slowly to him. She had let him smell her before she touched him. Nightmare was in seventh heaven with the girls making over him.

"Yes! I also signed-up for the competition."

"All right Mary you're up. First walk him then slowly go faster. When you're ready take him through the jumps."

'Angel had two girls for the competition. She didn't understand why a person would do that. Now Laron must find that person with that device. They said Nightmare would throw the ones that try to ride him. If I was a horse and was shocked with that device. I too would throw them off. There was some-one with the other part of the device. Who would have it? It had to be someone that was here all the time.'

One of the men called to Tyler. "Your late! Laron's been looking for you."

Angel was watching Mary. Like Bunny. The two of them did wonderful. She waved in Mary. She heard the men call him Tyler.

"I like for the two of you rub Nightmare down. Don't forget to make over him. Someone been trying to get him killed."

Angel had turned around to see who was late. She saw that he had a box of some kind in his hand. Tyler was pointing the box at Nightmare. He's trying to get Nightmare to act up. Laron also saw it and felt it.

'Oh no poor Laron. He had those shock devices in his pocket.'

Each time Tyler kept pushing the button. Laron was getting madder. He had felt the jolts, on each of his sides. Now he was going after Tyler. Laron didn't like to be shocked. At the time he was talking to Principal Tensaw. When the devices shocked him, he swore. It was hard not to swear into the phone.

All he could say is *"Get the guards to come down to the stables right away."*

Laron had the men to surround Tyler and close in on him.

Angel knew which way Tyler was heading. She ran ahead of them and picked up a stick that had fallen. When Tyler came running up, she swung as hard as she could. Tyler went down hard. Laron got to him and placed a foot on his chest. *"No Tyler, you're not going any where's."*

Laron had the box Tyler was using. *"All right who put ye up to this?"*

Tyler didn't say anything. *"We have the shock devices. I know you were the one pushing that button. I saw you and felt the devices. Boys pick him up."*

Laron put two of the devices in Tyler's back pockets. Then he pushed the buttons. It was a good thing Laron only place one in each pocket. Principal Tensaw and the guards had showed up.

Tyler cried out. *"Misty said her father would pay me to get rid of Nightmare. Stop shocking me Laron."*

"Now ye know how Nightmare felt. Mrs. Tensaw he is all yours."

Angel was out for her run. She had just got to the fence that was on the boy's side. She could see cars pulling up and the boys getting out of the cars. When she turned the corner, she felt a presence. The same presence she felt at the fairgrounds.

'Could it be Mic? Should she say something. No, I would want to go and meet him. Is this the person that talks to me when I'm scared? Even her dreams were mixed up. I keep getting little things. His name Mic. Then a flash back. Angel saw a stuff Mickey Mouse. What does it mean to me? She had to get back to the dorm.'

After her five-mile run. She went down the hallway of her dorm. Angel could see a few of the sophomores were already here. Bunny and Mary was near her room. Some of the sophomores were also waiting for Angel.

"Good morning Angel. We have some more girls for the two competitions. They heard that we be running in the first competition. They like to run with you in the morning. This is Eva and Joy they have the rooms across from us."

"Hello girls. You're in early. You must be glad to be back at school."

"No not really. I'm called Eva. We felt that we needed to warn the freshman about Misty. Bunny told us that you are going to be a team leader for ballet and for the competition. How could this be when your younger than us."

"Angel they didn't believe me that you're a freshman in college. They said Misty will get it changed."

"I been getting that a lot. Thank you, Bunny, for trying. Things have changed this year. If you like to be part of my group. Go and sign-up, on every paper you can fine. The teachers will be taking copies of the sign-up sheets. If they come up missing. If only Misty's girls are on the sign-up sheets. Principal Tensaw is going to have a fit. She was the one who told me to sign-up as a leader."

"I like doing some dancing before lunch. If you like to dance with me. Come down and see what I can do. I run five miles in the morning. You can run with me if you like. It will help if you make it in the competition. Eva and Joy thank you for telling me about Misty. I've heard a lot about her and her father. I'm not going to play games with her. I love dancing and teaching girls much older than me. I have a Hi IQ. If anyone needs help with homework. You must let me know. The judges, for the ballet competition will be professional ballet dancers. We will make them think of us as a professional dancer. We will work hard. I will make you do the dances repeatedly. I won't have you do anything that I haven't already done. Many times, I will be doing it with you. If this is not what you want. Don't sign-up for my class. You can go into other classes for ballet. We will be doing a Pas de Deux: a dance for two. The boys will be dancing with us. Also, this year. We will have two girls from each grade. After two weeks I will choose one or two girls out of my group. Bunny just because you're my roommate. It doesn't mean your safe. Do you understand?"

"Angel I knew that from the start. I saw it when you dance for us. You are a teacher."

"Thank you, Bunny. One thing. I don't yell. However, there is always the first time for everything. Take care of yourself, don't be late for classes. If you are late and you don't have a good answer. Then you could be taken out of the group. I've been hearing that Misty is evil. I'll let you know if she is or not. I don't want to hear any of my girls bad-mouthing anyone."

"Angel do you know if Mic is going to teach this year?"

"Who is Mic?"

"He's taller then you are. Maybe a year older them you. He's very strong. Mic had to be strong to lift Misty. He has black hair and golden-brown eyes. Mic has a Hi IQ and is in his second year of college."

"Eva, I don't know. Did he teach last year?"

"Yes and no. Misty brother didn't want him to teach."

"Eva that wasn't it. You and I know that Misty didn't want him to teach. She made Hawkeye say Mic got his sister hurt. It was a lie. Misty has this hair that is long and thick. He had to pick her up and place her on his shoulders. He asked her to put it up in a bun. She didn't want to. She stepped on her hair and lost her balance. Misty fell and broke her arm."

"You're right about that Joy. Mic still help the guys when they came to him. Some of the girls and guys meant with him in another building."

※

Bill was driving Mic back to school. "Mic are you, all right? You look like something just happen."

"Maybe! I've been thinking of Angel. There was something special about her. You see I've been hearing this girl's voice. It's always happens when she's scared. The day when you and I went diving at the lake. She was at the school gate it had scared her. I heard her scream saying. She didn't want to be locked up. Why does it look like a jail?

"Bill, I don't know why I picked Angel to dance with. All I know it felt right when I took her hand. Just now. I think she was near the boy's gate. She is running. I know she does it a lot like I do. I don't want Angel hurt. You know Misty will be here in two days."

"Mic it will be alright. Come on let's get you sign in. I must find out when I'm teaching this year."

The two of them went into the office. Everyone was happy to see them. "Hello Mic, it's good to see you. We have a new girl that's going to be a team leader. She's been holding ballet classes. This is not all. She found out that someone had put shock devices on Nightmares hoofs."

"Anna! That is enough of that. Laron wanted to tell Mic himself. Angel had saved Nightmare."

"Hello Bill. Your class start next week on Friday. We are adding the girls this year. Their teacher will be Angelica."

Mic looked at Bill. Mic could see it had made his's day.

"Bill there maybe another class opening up. It's an engineer class."

"Yes. If something comes up let me know."

"Sally, I didn't tell them what she had done. Angel is quite a young woman." Bill looked at Mic. He saw that it had please Mic to hear that.

In Mic thoughts he said. *'Well done.'* In Angel's room she heard the praise.

All she could say was *'Think you.'*

Outside Bill help Mic to take in all his clothes. "Mic are you going to become a team leader this year?"

"That's a good question. Angel is in everything, ballet and endurance competition. You know being told that. I was proud of her. Bill there's little things that pop in my mind. I ask myself. Did I know her before they took my memory from me? If Misty fines out that she was the one that fix Nightmare."

"Mic do what you think is right. Think about this. Is it being proud for a friend sister or a childhood love? Don't tell me. It's for you to find out. I will tell you this. I like to get to know Angelica."

"Bill would it be all right if I get to know Angel?"

"All I can say to that is. No one can tell you who she is. We have only one life. Live your life to the fullest way you know how."

"Then I'm going to be a team leader. I think I'm going to talk to Laron after I sign-up. I'll see you this weekend."

Mic made the rounds to fine all the sign-up sheets. He will see if any of the guys will sign-up now that he has. Mic ran to the next building. Every teacher took copies. They told him to go see Laron. With the last building done. Mic headed to the stables.

※※※

"Hello Laron. I heard that you found out what was wrong with Nightmare."

"Mic, it's good to see you. Wow Mic! You sure have filled out a lot this year. Have you decided to be a team leader?"

"Yes Laron. Now to just wait to see if the other guys will sign-up also. Tell me about the girl's team leader. Ann started to tell me until Sally came in."

"She did! I told everyone not to tell you anything. So, what do you know?"

"Only she found out what was wrong with Nightmare. Laron what did Angel do?"

"First of all. I'm sorry Mic that I didn't believe you last year. You told me there was something wrong with Nightmare. Now we know why he was doing those things."

"Laron how did Angel get to help Nightmare?"

"Mic I was just thinking about that. I guess by overwhelming me. You see Nightmare was to be put down."

"Say what!!! Misty almost got her way, damn that girl. She is a lot of trouble."

"Mic settle down! I like to tell this story to you. Nightmare must have known what we were going to do. He was heading for Angel. She was right in his way. What she did was side step him and grabbed his mane. Then swung her leg over his bare back. How Angel did it. I don't no. Nightmare was running full out."

'Angel what the hell were you thinking of? That horse could have killed you. You feared that gate. Why not the horse coming at you?'

'Mic I like those pants on you. It makes your butt look hot. At the fair that shirt didn't show me that you have muscles. A part of me don't remember how we looked. We are both older. I think I've missed a year.

Mic at times things scare me. It shows that I'm still young. I don't like to be locked up. I been remembering little things. Like a stuff mouse. It's Mickey Mouse. Mic does that mean anything to you? I gave you Mickey the day after you kissed me. Will you kiss me again? If only I could remember our names. Why does my head hurt?'

'Angel stop trying to remember our damn names. You will lose everything you have remembered.'

'Mic I'm sorry about being scared at the gate. I don't know why your voice makes everything better. I got to get out of here. I'll be back.'

'No… Angel don't go. Please!!! Damn it… stop trying to think of our names.'

Mic needed to go after her. He knew what she was talking about. He had started to remember things about Angel. When he tried to remember their names. He lost everything. The spell that was put on him. It restarts as if it was the first day.

"Earth to Mic are you listening to me? Angel is quite a young woman. She kept Nightmare running using her legs to steer him. I think all she saw was a horse that needed her help. Did they tell you it was Tyler who had a device to shock him?"

"No Laron, they didn't tell me anything like that."

"Mic, Mic you should have seen Angel run. She had the girls take care of Nightmare. She ran ahead of Tyler and found a big stick. When he came past the tree. Angel swung the stick and down he went. I had those devices in my pocket. Every time Tyler push the button it shocked me. Of all things I was talking to Mrs. Tensaw. I swore every time he pushed that damn button. I paid him back. By putting two of the devices in his back pocket. Tyler told us that it was Misty. She said her father would pay him to get rid of Nightmare. Angel is with Nightmare right now. She said she was going to take him for a run. I like you to meet her."

"Laron, I've met her at the fairgrounds. We dance together."

When she heard Mic. She asked him. *'Mic do you know me from a year ago? Or is it just at the fairgrounds? That day was wonderful. It felt right when you took my hand. I felt that you couldn't be my brother. You're no part of my family. I know that much. Mic, I saddle Lightning for you. You can follow me or stay there.'*

Chapter Ten: Misty Falls in the Pool

ANGEL HAD OPENED THE GATE AND LED NIGHTMARE OUT. She called out and said. *"Laron, I sign out Nightmare, see you in a bit."*

"Angel, I have someone I like for you to meet. Don't go."

"Laron, that's okay I'll go after Angel. I'm signing out Lightning."

Mic ran to get Lightning. He could feel that she was still trying to remember their names.

'*Angel, you got to stop trying to remember our names. Yes! I remember Mickey Mouse and that kiss. On that night. I would have touched you. It was too soon for us. I gave you that locket.*'

Mic opened the gate and closed it behind him. He took off as fast as Lightning could go. Something was wrong. Angel stop talking to him.

'*Angel I would do anything for you. Do you really like my pants? I love everything about you. Your breasts are bigger than before. Those pants you have on make you look sexy. Angel talk to me.*'

It was scaring Mic. She can't hear me. '*Why do we have to go through this?*' He just got her back and now he might lose her again.

'*Angel where are you. Please tell me where you're at. You're scaring me. Angel!!!*'

She was setting on a rock near a stream. He got off Lightning and went over to her. She was crying. Now he was panicking. Did the spell restart on her?

"Hello Angel." Angel got up and ran right into Mic's arms. Mic wrapped his arms around her. She trusts him. He had to tell himself to relax and just go with it.

"Angel are you, all right?"

"I don't know. Where am I?"

She looked up at Mic. Her eye's looked lost. She didn't step away from him.

"Angel, do you know me?"

"Yes, you are Mic. I dance with you at the fairgrounds. We had something to eat together. You took me on some rides there."

"Is that all you remember?" Angel was still holding on to him.

"What I remember, I had a headache. It was getting worse. As I tried to remember something. Until I heard that voice. It was telling me to stop trying to remember our real names. Mic, what was the voice talking about."

Angel laid her head back on his shoulder. His hand brushed over her hair. He swallowed hard.

Angel looked up. *"Mic thank you for being here for me. Mic, Mi-ck Mickey. I remember this was from my childhood. There was someone very close to me. I called him Mic. I loved the show Mickey Mouse. I think I loved this Mic. I don't know why I said that. Are you my Mic?"*

"Angel, stop. Yes, I'm your Mic. Listen to me. If you try thinking of the names of love ones. The spell will restart your memory. Anything you remembered will be wipe clean. Your mine will have to restart."

"I believe we had enough thinking for now. Did you know that Bill was taken with your cousin?"

"He was? I believe she was also."

"He like to take her out. Angel would you go out with me?"

"I would like that Mic. I enjoy being with you."

"Angel I'll tell Laron we can do the test tomorrow. Around the same time today. How does that sound?"

"I like that idea Mic!"

Angel was still in his arms. She looked up at him. She gave him a sweet kiss on his lips. Then quickly got on her horse. Mic thought it would be better like this. He could date her.

'We been together for a long time.'

'Wow! How long have we known each other?' I'll let that knowledge set aside for now. I still must find a way to get her to dream about him.

Angel road down the path. She wonders if he was her Mic?

'Why else would she have kissed him? I can think of things that I have done. I cannot think of our names. I believe I could do that.'

"Laron, Angel and I decided to do it tomorrow. Around the same time that we had come here today."

"Mic are you going to be Angel's partner?"

"Yes. I'm going to be a team leader for dancing. I still have to find out if the guys want me."

"Mic what are the two of you going to do now?"

"Angel asked me to teach her more of the Scottish dances."

"I'll see the two of you tomorrow."

"Mic why is Laron running to his office."

"I believe he is going to call our dorms. The den mothers will pass the word to the others. If they like to see the new team leaders dancing together."

"I thought that's what he was doing. Mic do you think we should get there before anyone else?"

"No, I have all my things there for dancing."

"I did the same thing. When the junior's gets here. I'm going to have classes over here. I've been told that Misty likes the gym near the dorm."

"Misty don't like to do anything that takes work."

"Mic don't do that. I don't want you to go down to her level. You're better than that. Mic where do you live when you're not here."

"In the Highland's. Bill will set it up with Angelica. I will tell him Friday when he comes to pick me up. Is it a date for you and me this Saturday?"

"Yes. Its sound's wonderful. We're going on a date. I also live in the Highland's."

The two of them ran to the building. Sitting on the steps were eight boys and eight girls. They watched Angel and Mic. The two of them was in sync with each other. Angel could see they were talking about them. At the same time, Mic and Angel slowed to a walk. He wondered if the group were talking about them.

"Mic, the group has been watching us. One of them asked. If we have done things together before. It's as if we move as one person."

"Angel, you can read lips?"

"Yes, I had this person giving be trouble. Before school was out, I could read his lips. They think we know each other before school."

Angel stopped and looked at him. "Mic… you said that you were from my childhood?"

"Angel I believe that I am. I need your help. Tonight, when you go to sleep. Picture me sitting on a rock near a waterfall. Don't try to find out who we are."

At the steps Angel and Mic stopped.

"Hello everyone. Bunny is this group waiting for us?"

"Yes, Angel we are. We were told that Mic was going to teach you more of the Scottish dances. Could you show us more of the ballet dance? Before Scottish dances, please?"

"Mic this is Bunny. She is my roommate. Do you think we should?"

"Why should we. Damn it… What's with all of you guys doing? Can't you take the girls word for it. You think their lying to you. Angel is not Misty."

Jim looked at Mic then at Angel. "Mic I'm not going through that again."

"Jim… What the hell are you talking about?"

"You know what I'm talking about. When Misty gets here, she will change everything. Mic you know this is true."

Bunny yelled at Jim. "Jim, I told you to talk to them. Not to demand things."

Angel then raced her voice. "Enough you two. Your acting like baby's. Just remember I have a say who stays and who goes. I don't care if it's a boy or a girl. I've have taught many groups before. I have never yelled at anyone. Well this is the first time I yelled? Is this what I'm going to have to do every time?"

Bunny was going to say something. When Angel turn quickly to look at her. Bunny quickly sat back down. Jim thought he would try. This time both Mic and Angel gave that look. Jim sat down and bent his head.

"*Angel shell we go in.*"

She looked at both groups. "*I don't know anything about Misty. To tell the truth. I don't care who she is. I was told to try out for team leader. I love teaching, I had all ages. Even girl's older than me. I've been dancing since I was four years old. I have never been questioned about my ability to dance. You are letting Misty run you. What she almost done to a beautiful horse is sinful in my book. I'll let Bunny and Mary tell you about Nightmare.*"

The boys looked at the two girls. "*Is this true Mary?*" Mary just nodded her head.

"*This is what's going to happen. Mic and I will go and change. What we decide is what you will get. Misty may try. I believe she's not going to get what she wants. I don't care about her. I care about the once in my class room. If you do this in class, you will be the one to leave. Mic what do you think?*"

Mic was upset with the guys. "*It sounds like a very good idea. This will be for the upper classmen also. Let the other classmates know. One, school work must be kept up. Two, your grades must be at least a low C. Three, being late, without a note. You get three tries. If you're sick go to the nurse. She can let us know. You will have to make the class up. Your partner can show you and the two of you work together on it. Four, bad mouthing classmates. If you are caught doing this. You could be kick out of ballet. If you are one that has been pick. The group can vote to keep you or kick you out. We will have a paper for you to sign with what we have said on it. No more games. If you need help in classwork, ask us.*"

A door opened behind them. The teacher came out. "*I heard the rules and thought it was a good idea. You must have both Principal's okay on it. Now I can't stay. It's time for me to go and help the cook. This building is open just until 4:30. I think you will have to wait until everyone is back in school. Mrs. Tensaw is going to have the group choose the team leader.*"

"*I don't understand. I was told to sign-up if I like to become a team leader. I even was holding classes for the girls that like to learn how to dance.*"

"Angel there are the other grades. Right now, you have two grades that voted. They want you to teach them. They signed up for you. We must wait to see if any other girls would like to be a teacher. Once everyone is back and the girls see how you dance. The Principal's will call in the winners.

I'm sorry that Laron went overboard. The endurance competition is also a race. We will have this before we get snow. Before November we will start the ballet competition. There is a new competition we are adding. It will be the Scottish dances near the end of the school year. It's time to go and eat. You don't have to worry about the endurance competition. Misty cannot go near the horses. Now go and get some food all of you. You kids are thinking too far ahead."

In the background of Mic and Angel. Three boys were listening to what they were saying. They went off after the group brook up. They had to call Misty to tell her what they heard.

The food taste good when you're with someone you like to be with. Angel still wanted to get something done before Misty came.

"Mic do you think the library is open now?"

"I don't really know Angel. If you like we can walk over."

"Mic tell me more about this place by the waterfall. You said the two of us can go there to dream?"

"What I remember Angel. It's a place where I can be twenty-one. It was always sunny there. Yes, there was a waterfall. Next to it there was green grass. This is all I remember. Now what do you need from the library?"

"Mic... what we need is the names of the ballet positions. Could you do that for me please. I'm going to write up what we talked about. Then I will see if Mrs. Tensaw will sign it. If it's ago then I will give you one."

"It sounds like a plan Angel. Are you still going to try out tomorrow?"

"Yes Mic. We can go there in the morning. I don't want to be at the dorm when the junior start coming in."

"That's a great idea Angel."

Angel got everything ready that night. She took her shower and went to bed. In the morning she was up before anyone got up. She met Mic for breakfast.

"Hello Angel. Did you sleep alright last night?"

"No…! I don't remember if I even dreamed. I'm sorry about that. Maybe I was trying too hard. Mic I don't know why I'm so upset about things."

"It's all right Angel. Come on we can get some food."

"Just remember. It should be a lite breakfast. We're going to be running and swimming."

"Angel we can go there after an hour. I just didn't want to be around the juniors. All of Misty's friends will be coming in."

"I know how you feel. I too… Don't want to be there right now. Just great! I left my riding boots in with my ballet shoes. After we eat, I'll have to go get them. I'll meet you there Mic."

"That's okay Angel. Please don't be too long. You do know he's going to tell me everything about what you had done. He hasn't even had a chance to tell me how beautiful you are. I already know that."

It wasn't Laron who talked about Angel. "Laron to tell the truth. Angel is a wondaful young woman. She's beautiful and not bossy. With long legs and a nice shape to go along with the package. They said she has a heart of gold and goes out of her way to help anyone."

Laron gave a little giggle. "No, she is nothing like Misty. She puts a horse before her own safety. Angel didn't use her arms to control him. Those legs made him do just what she wanted him to do. Now if she had got her legs around a man. I believe he would let her do anything she wanted him to do."

Laron started to laugh. "Laron thanks a lot. Now I have that picture in my mine. What are you trying to do to me?"

Laron couldn't help himself. He burst out laughing. He knew Angel had been listening. He didn't tell Mic she could hear him. Mic gave Laron a dirty look. He didn't think anything was funny.

"All right Laron yes. What a way to go. Angel is quite a woman. A beautiful mind and slender body. Her height matches quite nicely with me. Her face is of an Angel. With rosy lips and beautiful eyes. Those eyes. A man could drown in those bluish green eyes. To top her looks off she has long golden-brown hair. I love her ponytail."

Then Mic felt Angel watching him. *"Laron you set me up. I thought men stick together. I guess just the same age would do it. Thanks Laron. Thanks a lot. You know, I'm not looking forward to seeing Misty. I'm glad Angel is not in the same dorm. I think I'm going to get the horses saddle."*

Mic's face was red as a beat. These feelings for Angel have been getting stronger.

'I'm sorry Angel. I don't know if what I've been feeling is right. One moment I think I knew you from a while back. Another time. It was from our childhood. We grew up together.'

She watched Mic heading for the horses. Angel knew how Mic felt. She had the same feelings.

Laron was laughing so hard. How could she stay mad at this old man? His laughter was getting out of hand. He started coughing to the point Angel went for a bottle of water.

"Laron, you got Mic really good. I think your coughing paid you back."

It didn't take Mic long before he came back with the horses. She watched him coming toward them. There was something about Mic which took her breath away. Angel told Laron how she felt about Mic.

"I understand how Mic maybe feeling. To tell the truth. Misty and I are destined to bump heads. I'm one grade higher than her. There is no way that I will be able to avoid Misty. I'm younger than her. I'm closer to Mic's age. He's two grades higher them Misty. No woman likes to be shown up by another woman. She will fight back some way or another.

"I love the way the jeans look on him. I would love to see him with his shirt off. Mic is easy to talk too. He makes me feel save when I'm with him. When were face to face? I love to gaze into his golden-brown eyes. Back home when I dance. It was hard to find a boy that was my height. I can't wait to see him in tights. Mic should look hot in them. There Laron. I told Mic what I like about him."

"I'm sorry you two. I went overboard this time. What you did to make Mic feel better. It took guts to tell him that. I'm telling you this. The *seniors will be here today at 1:00. Juniors are coming in this morning. If you two would like to run through the whole race. I will call all the teachers to stand by."*

Mic had heard everything Angel said. He had both horses and stopped to listen. When Angel said now Mic knew what she thought about him. Laron was the one turning red. He had turned to see Mic standing there. Mic just smiled and came up to Angel with their horses. Once Laron was out of sight. He pulled one of the horses up to block anyone from seeing them. Mic's hand came around her neck. He looked into her eyes. As he brushed a kiss over her lips.

"Angel you are quite a woman. We're going to do well together."

Mic had left his words hanging. He held Nightmare, so she could get on his back. Mic didn't like that Misty was coming to school a day early.

'Angel wonder what was happening to her? Why did she wish Mic had deepen that kiss? Mic knows something about her. Tonight, she will try to dream of the man name Mic.'

Then Angel saw Bunny and Mary. There were some juniors with them. She rode Nightmare over.

"Hello Bunny, Mary. Who's your friends?"

"Angel, this is Rosy and Katy. They signed-up for ballet with you. There also going to try this race also."

Mic came over to them.

"Hello Mic. It's nice to talk freely to you. You're going to team up with Angel?"

"Hello Katy, Rosy. It's good to see you. Yes, I will be with her also in dancing."

"Mic, I hear Angel can really ride."

"Yes, she knows a lot about horses."

"Mary told us that Angel teaches ballet. Bunny said that she also saved Nightmare. We're going to help Angel with the senior's classmates. We will be talking to are friends. I'll tell them they can try out for both competitions now. Let the guys know that it's okay on their side also. I know it wasn't fun for a few of the guys. Misty's brother wasn't nice to them. Can you tell Bill I'm trying out for everything this year?"

Mic replied. *"I'll be happy too, and I'll tell John also for you Rosy."*

Laron sent the word out. Mic and Angel was doing the endurance competition. The boys that would like to signed-up was there. More of the girls came out. Same with the boys. The two riders rode side by side. The girls and boys yelled.

"Angel and Mic can do this."

Then they heard Laron say. *"Back up kids. The race is going to start. Angel and Mic, you will end up at the swimming pool. My men will be timing you two.*

"Listen up everyone. As soon as they are ready, we will start. From this point on. The teachers are the only ones to talk to them. They will give them water. This is an endurance competition. They are going through to the end."

Angel closed her eyes. She felt Mic focusing. Then there was energy flowing between them. They were as one.

Her thought drifted to him. 'How are we doing this.'

'I don't know. Just go with its Angel.'

Laron walked over to where they could see him. "Good Luck. Are you both ready?"

They looked at each other and nodded. "On your mark, get set, GO!!!"

The horses were off in a flash. Laron watched the two of them go quickly around the court together. When they came to the gates. Laron never saw two teammates in sync with each other. The horse's hoofs flew over the gates without touching. One after another. Once they cleared the gates. The horses flew like the wind to the finish line.

The schoolmates yelled. *"They did it. Angel and Mic did it."*

Mic and Angel had fifteen minutes to rest and get changed. The next run was bicycling. Angel put her hat on. She wore a light-yellow top and a navy-blue pair of shorts. She had her hair in a long braid. It went down the middle of her back. When Mic looked up from putting his shoes on. He stopped and stared at Angel.

'Wow!!! How long has it been? Did Angel look like she does now? Is she acting older? My God she is. Wow! What a woman.'

Then he heard. *'Thank you, Mic.'*

There was no time to think. When Mic heard.

"*10, 9, 8, 7, 6, 5, 4, 3, 2, 1.*" All the schoolmates chime in.

"*Get to your bicycles. Ready set. GO!!!*"

The two of them where off. They were on the path to the racetrack. The next run would be the Relay Race. Mic was in the back of Angel. He just couldn't help himself. In his thoughts all he said was.

"*Wow!!!*"

Mic understood why Laron comment about her legs. Being in the back of her. Mic could look her hold body over.

'One day I will have those legs around me. On that day. We will be lovers and I will have my hands on her sweet derriere.

Then he saw Angel look back at him. She motioned him to come up beside her.

Mic didn't know if she heard Him. *'Oh boy. Did she hear me???'*

He saw that the path was wide enough for the two of them.

'Angel wondered if she heard Mic thoughts. She remembered he said they would do well together. He doesn't know me that well. Or does he?'

She tried to remember what he said. *'One day I will have those legs around me. On that day. We will be lovers and I will have my hands on her sweet derriere.'*

Then she heard Mic's voice. "*Angel your slowing down. We have no time to think. Just do what we set out to do.*"

They made it to the track. The teacher was Scott Friedrich. Once Mic and Angel sat down. Scott handed them both a bottle of water.

"*You have fifteen minutes. Change your shoes and catch your breath.*"

"*Mic you go first. I think you could past the baton better to me then I could to you. Where going to be pushing to get a head. I don't think they could knock the baton out of your hand.*"

Mic understood what she meant. He hasn't seen Angel run in over a year. He knew she was fast. I'm remembering things. A nice slim body and long legs. Yes, she was right for him to go first. Everyone was in the band stands. Both sides of the schools were there to cheer them on. The two schools new Mic was fast. They were hoping that Angel was just as fast. Mic gave her a smile.

"*Times up. Who goes first?*"

"*I'm first.*" In Mic's mine he said.

'*Angel when the time comes. I'll get that baton into your hand. No one. Will knock it out of my hand.*'

He was ready and nodded his head to go. In Angel's mine she said. '*Good luck Mic.*'

The teacher asked him. "*Mic are you ready?*"

He nodded his head. "*All right get set. GO!!!*"

Angel watched Mic take off. He was a tiger running down his prey. She could feel her whole body getting in tune with his. Her mine focused on his hand. All she could see was his hand and the baton. Angel could mentally picture herself taking the baton. She felt the power between them. They were as one. Mic saw her hand. The pass went flawless. As they had yelled for Mic. Angel heard their classmates yelling

"*Go Angel Go!!!*"

It was in her hand and she was running at top speed in seconds. Mic was gasping for air. It didn't matter. He had to watch Angel run. The power in her legs made him think of a cheetah. Angel moved gracefully through the air. In a blink of an eye. She had run past Mic. She turned and walked slowly over to him. Angel dropped to her knees beside him. Scott brought them each a bottle of water. He watched Angel breathing slowly and smiled. The two of them drunk deeply of their water. They had twenty minutes to change their shoes. Their time was a head of the school that had won last year. They didn't have to say anything to each other. It was and easy jog to the swimming pool.

Mic was remembering more as the two of them jog together. Last year was hell for him. He hoped that Misty will stay out of their lives. He knew at the end of school. He had felt the cross get a little hot. No time to think about it. They were at the building.

Miss Rosemary Stover was waiting for them. She ran this building for both schools. A bottle of water was place in their hand. As they ran up the stairs. Angel watched Mic as he took off his shirt. In her thoughts all she could come up with was.

'*Wow!!! Your stronger now.*'

She had to stop thinking. Angel slipped off her shorts and top. She had on her swimsuit under her clothes. Mic had a hard time when he saw Angel slender body. He couldn't say or do anything with their classmate watching. Only Angel saw his mouth drop open.

She did hear him say. '*Wow!!! You have blossomed in to a beautiful woman.*'

Mic couldn't remember when he saw such a beautiful woman before.

'*Mic are you okay with this. You know when I take my shorts off.*'

He shook his head. Angel saw his cheeks turn pink. As he fought with his shoe laces.

'*Mic, you and I will have to talk this weekend.*'

'*Yes, I think that would be a good idea.*'

Angel walked over to the edge of the pool. She had to focus on her breathing. She was trying to get herself ready. She dipped her hand into the cool water. Angel wet her neck and under her arms. Mic was doing the same. Each time the two of them could feel the power between them. With her eyes close she felt her body was mentally and fiscally in tune with Mic. There was no time to ask Mic what was happening to them.

Rosemary had called out. "*Times up.*"

The two of them stood up. They walked over to take their positions. The other teachers had their scores.

"*The rules are as follow. First the two of you will swim under water. When you push off the wall. You will be swimming on top of the surface. Angel and Mic good luck. On your mark. Get set. GO!*"

Together they dove into the water. Angel was moving the fastest. She was the first to push off the wall. She knew Mic would be coming fast. His power was in his arms. Angel's lead was going fast. She had to hold this small lead. At the last minute. They were neck to neck. It felt like magic. The moment their hand reached out at the same time. Rosemary called out the time. In swimming they beat the other school's time. Both principals were there to wetness their win.

All their classmates were yelling *"They're the best."*

When each teacher called there times out. The classmate found out that Angel and Mic beat all the other school scores.

Mic had swum over to Angel. He knew that Misty wouldn't be able to take Angel's place now.

"Come on. We need the hot tub. Then you can take a shower to wash up."

The hot tub felt so good on her sore body. *"Mic that was a work out. I run five miles daily. I don't miss a day most of the time. This hot tub feels so good."*

"Angel come over here. I'll rub your shoulders then send you to the showers. Then you can go back to your room and take a nap."

"Your turn for a shoulder rub Mic. We pushed are self-hard. Next time we will have everything down pat. Thank you Angel for being my partner. It's time for you to get to the showers."

Mic got to his feet. He helped Angel out of the tub. *"I feel like a rag doll."*

"Angel thank you for being my partner. We have just two months to get ready. We also must get four more teams together. Are you going to be up to it?"

"Yes Mic… With your help. I think our showers are calling us. Hot water hear I come."

"Be careful Angel. Something is going on with Misty. Before school ended. I felt she was getting on the wrong side of good and evil. Go get your shower we will talk on are date."

"That sounds good. Thank you, Mic, for everything."

⁂

The shower felt so good. Angel had stayed under the water to long. Then her cross started to get hot. She had to get dress quickly. She heard yelling from the pool area. The voice sound like Mic. The other voice sound gruff like a man. Mic wasn't happy with what was going on. Why was a man yelling at Mic? Angel peeked around the corner. There in front of Mic was a big boy. He had a short haircut. The haircut was cut like an old man. Then Angel saw that he was a she. An evil woman who talks like a man. Angel saw Mic. He was as tired as she was.

"Mic you will tell the principals you won't run without me."

Mic started to laugh. *"Misty why would I do that? You can't run or ride a horse. For you and me to win. This is a big joke. You are so out of shape. I believe you put on a lot of weight this summer. Now you look more like a man."*

Mic started to laugh even harder. *"Mic stop laughing at me. There is nothing funny about what I said."*

"Misty, I don't like you. I've had enough. It's a joke if you think we could win. Your too heavy to run. You're not a good enough of a swimmer. You're blind as a bat. I have never thought of you as a woman. You were never my girlfriend. I don't like working with you. I won't be your boyfriend or partner. Leave me alone."

Angel could see that Mic was making Misty back up. He was getting her closer to the edge of the pool. At that moment Mic saw Angel.

Mic yelled in his mine. *'Angel get out of here. I don't want Misty to see you.'*

In a demanding voice Misty said. *"YOU WILL BE MY PARTNER THIS YEAR. Look into my eyes."*

Mic and Angel felt their cross go even hotter.

'Mic she has evil with her. Be careful of her eyes.'

'Angel get out of here. I can't have her going after you.'

'Mic she will go after you and not in a good way.'

'Better me then you. Get out of here.'

Mic burst out laughing and took another step. *"I will not be your partner. You are so full of yourself. BOSSY!!! I told everyone. This year you're not going to boss me around. I'm not going to do your homework any longer. Besides, for a woman. You have a filthy mouth. Now you look the part of a man. Your evil eyes don't work on me. I know your evil. Your face has turn red. I believe you should cool off. I don't want to be part of anything that involves you. Your evil Misty. Evil!!! I am through with you."*

Mic took another step and Misty fell into the water. When she came up.

"Damn it! Mic if you don't become my partner. No one will have you. It's up to you Mic. You can live and be my partner. Or you will die."

Rosemary was talking to the principal. She heard the swearing and let the principal know. She also told her the Mic didn't touch Misty. He just back her into the pool. Angel also saw it and heard Misty.

"Misty just threaten Mic. I must get Angel out of here. I think you should have the guards come and get her. Just telling Misty to go and see you. I don't think she will."

Rosemary grabbed Angel's hand.

"I'm okay Rosemary. Did you hear what Misty said? She's going to have someone to…hurt Mic or killed him."

"I heard, and the principal knows. Angel you must get out of here. The principal doesn't want Misty or her friends to see you. Don't tell anyone what happen here. Go back to your dorm and rest."

Quickly Rosemary took Angel to the side door.

"Angel is that any of your friends?" "Yes, that is my roommate Bunny, Mary. Her room is across from ours."

All the girls came around Angel. "Get her back to the dorm now. If you could watch over her. Things my get out of hand before the day is out."

"Will look out for her. We heard that Misty was coming down here. We're here to make sure Misty don't try anything."

Angel saw Mic coming out. 'Be careful Mic. Evil is with her, she acted like she wants you dead.'

'I'll be careful Angel. Misty eyes has no power over me. I see Bunny has you in safe hands. See you tomorrow partner.'

Angel started to walk with the girls. 'Mic please be careful. Her eyes may not work on you. What about the once they do work on? She can have someone do her dirt work for her. You're not going to be safe. I have a bad feeling. Please don't take this lightly. It scares me Mic.'

'Angel I understand don't worry. I'll be careful.'

Angel felt a strong bond between them. Tonight, she will try to dream of him at the waterfall. The girls saw a car coming down the road.

'Mic their coming to get Misty. I don't think they're going to fine her.'

All the girls wanted to talk. Seniors and juniors came over to her dorm. They heard what happen to Misty. They wouldn't let Angel get a nap. One girl said Mic push her in the pool. The other said No.

Angel had to say something. "Hold on. I don't know too much about Mic. However, when you ride hard and run with someone. You get a sense of who he is. To me that's not Mic stile. What happen to Misty. I think her mouth got her in trouble. What you girls told me he went through hell with her. Mic's not the type to get in trouble. If I was Mic. I would step closer to her. He's a tall guy. It could have made Misty taken a step backwards. I know that's just what I would do. This way it would shut her up." A lot of the girls agreed with her.

"Come on girls' last year did he get in trouble at any time?"

The girls looked at each other. Some shook their head No.

"Mic could have just kept stepping closer to her. While she ranted about him being her partner. He wouldn't get in trouble doing that."

The den mother came over to them. She told them Rosemary said Mic didn't touch Misty. All the girls were happy to hear that. It made Angel happy, she didn't have to tell them she was there. She was able to keep her word to Rosemary.

Chapter Eleven: A Shield Around Mic

THAT NIGHT ANGEL TRIED TO DREAM OF MIC. He told her that he sets on a big rock at the waterfall. There will be green grass nearby. She couldn't get any picture of Mic. Angel only could see darkness. There was no sunlight any where's. Then she felt someone was in trouble. Who could be in trouble? How could I see when its pitch-black?

It kept popping up in her thoughts. She then felt evil through the darkness. She understood why she couldn't dream of Mic. Mic was in trouble. Angel took hold of her locket and thought of Mic. Misty sent demons after him. They were trying to stop me from helping him.

'Mic… Show me where you are. Trouble is coming after you. I need to know to be able to help you. Mic… hear me please. Show me where you are.'

Then Angel saw it. In her dream Mic was heading to the gym to lift some weights. The hallway he went down had a room to the right. Angel saw three men coming quickly behind him. They had evil inside them. Demons that would kill for money. They were using the senior's bodies to kill or main Mic. She woke up quickly. It was the first day for classes. The time was 5:00. Angel got dress and ran to the Principal's office. She rang the bell then pounded on the door.

"Please open the door I need help."

Principal Tensaw came to the door. *"Who is it?"*

"It's Angel. Principal Tensaw I need to speak to you. It's very important, it's about Mic."

Angel's voice sounded scared. *"All right Angel come on in."*

When the door open. She ran in to her arms. Principal Tensaw told her.

"Angel, breathe. Much better. Let's go into my office. Tell me why you're so scared."

"It's about Mic. I had a dream that three seniors were going to beat Mic up this morning. He was going down a hallway to the gym. There is a room off to the right. Two of them grabbed him. The other one punch him in his side. He had something on his knuckles. The third man grabbed him around the neck. He shoved something into Mic's mouth and tied it behind his head. All three men hit him and dragged him into the room. I felt that evil was with them. These men were enjoying hurting Mic. Please do something. My dreams are never wrong."

Principal Tensaw remembered when Arthur Stanley signed-up Angel.

He had said. *'If Angel ever say something bad is going to happen. Believe her. It's a gift Angel has.'*

Mrs. Tensaw also knew Angel never was in the other School. She was able to describe that hole hallway right down to the room.

She quickly called her husband. *"John, take three of the guards and go down the hallway to the gym. The room off the hallway. Someone is in trouble. Please hurry there is not much time left. Call me when you can."*

Angel had placed a magical shield around Mic. She had to use her own energy to make the shield. Mic couldn't help. He was fighting for his life, with his own energy.

Mr. Tensaw's wife found out that someone was in trouble. He grabbed three of the guards. The principal had his secretary call the police. The four men went quickly down the hall. The room off the hallway the door was locked. There was laughter inside. The principal told the men to break the door down. There were three seniors beating another boy up.

'Who was this young man?'

Two of them was holding him. There was a hood over the young man's face. The principal notice that the boys was going after his legs and ribs. It was a good thing they didn't have a long steel pipe. They were using brass knuckles. The young man was able to keep his legs moving. The guards had moved in quickly. They grabbed the three men. When they did. The young man had fallen to the floor. The principal went over quickly to him. He took the hood off. They even had a gag over his mouth.

Mr. Tensaw said. *"Tell the police. Book the three for attempted murder. Take the three brass knuckles with you."*

Mic started coughing up blood. He said. *"Misty paid them. They said this was the best job Misty has given them. She doesn't want me anymore. If she can't have me no one will."*

"Can you walk Mic?"

"No, it hurts to even breathe. They were trying to break my ribs and legs. This way I couldn't fight back."

"Mic they were trying to do more than just hurt you. You are lucky to have an Angel looking after you, lay down."

Mic laid on his back. He thought of what Mr. Tensaw had said. Who saved Me he wondered? The way those guys were punching him. He should be bleeding internally or dead. He didn't cough up much blood. Before they took the boys out of the room.

Mr. Tensaw said. *"It's not like you boys to do anything like this. Was Misty's brother in on this?"*

One of the boys said. *"Her brother wouldn't think of anything like this. I don't understand Mic should be dead. How could he stop us? We were going after every part of his body."*

The other boy said. *"Shut up you fool! Where going to jail."*

The last boy had a deep voice. Then the men laughed. *"Were not going to jail. These boys are. Mic you win this time. Misty still must kill you. The Master wants you dead. Watch your back when you get out of school."* Then all three boys fell to his knees.

"Get them out of here. I want test done on them. These boys never done anything like this."

When they were punching him, Mic didn't feel it as much. The Men from the hospital came to get Mic. As they picked him up, he could feel the pain. Whatever was around him was getting weaker.

The pain was getting more intense. Mic closed his eyes. It was Angel who saved him. Yes, he could feel her magic with in him. It was a shield put around his hold body.

'Angel can you hear me?'

'Mic are you all right'

Mic could hear it in her voice. What did she do to herself? She sounded so weak. Then he knew what she used. This was her energy. She had put a shield around him with her energy. Mrs. Tensaw had been watching Angel. She noticed that she was crying. Her face was getting very pale.

'Angel how did you know I was in trouble?'

'I had a dream about you. I saw three men beating you up. I ran to the office and Mrs. Tensaw was there. Arthur must have said something about me. Where are you?'

At the hospital on campus. *'Angel you're going to have to take this shield down. Let the doctor see what happen to me. Your body is in danger. I can feel the heat from you. You got to drop the shield. Don't worry. I know I'm going to black out. You save me. I don't want to lose you Angel. Save yourself. I'm too weak to help you.'*

'Mic who had them do this?'

'Misty... The police are on their way to pick her up.'

"Remember what Misty had said to you. She couldn't control you. She said you will die if you didn't become her partner. Mic there not going to fine Misty. One of the girls said they saw her going out of the gate yesterday."

Angel forgot that she was talking out loud.

'Mic I said it out loud.'

'It's all right Angel.'

Mrs. Tensaw called Misty's den-mother. She found out that Misty wasn't any where's to be found. The police went looking for her on campus. Mrs. Tensaw check their records. Yesterday, Misty had a pass to go home on. She called her husband office.

"Yes, tell the police Misty went home. Her uncle is not on campus ether."

'Angel it's all right. It's time to take the shield away. Your making yourself sick. I can't lose you. You have to do it now.'

'You're sure Mic. The pain is going to be very strong.'

'Yes, I can feel it now. We don't have a choice. You keep going like this and they will win.'

'Mic you know I would do this as long as I could.'

'I know that. Do it now Angel. I can feel your burning up.'

Angel could hear Mic scream. Tears rolled down her cheeks. She was so weak. It took a lot from her to keep that shield around Mic. Angel was having a hard time to stay awake. She had fallen off the chair onto the floor.

"Hello John. How is Mic? Could he tell you who put them up to this? Angel had said that also."

"The doctor is checking him over right now. If you didn't call me when you did. Those men were trying to break his ribs and legs. Mic was fighting them the best he could. I don't know how Mic was able to stand the pain. I asked the men if Misty's brother had something to do with it. They said No."

"My God is that Mic screaming?"

"Poor Mic. Whatever had saved him. Just had stopped blocking the pain. Mic just blacked out."

"John hold on. I heard something. John you better get someone over here. Angel just fallen off the chair. She is burning up. John, I believe that Angel is more involve. She was the one that dreamt Mic was in trouble. I believe she saved him. I have to go there here to get Angel."

"How could she do that?"

"I don't know. We have to keep this quiet for now."

When she hung up, she thought. 'I believe she was the one helping Mic stay alive. I'll try to keep Angel out of this. Misty hasn't seen her. All I know Scotland is full of Magic.'

Both Mic and Angel was at the hospital. She had a high fever. Angel was dehydrated and delirious. She was calling for Mic.

Brandon MacGregors and Bill Colman was called to the school hospital. When Angel collapsed.

Raymond Angel-Heart a long with Angelica McKinnon. Were also called to go to the school hospital. The doctor was with Brandon and Bill. The hospital front desk. Told Raymond the doctor will be with you as soon as he can. To wait for him in the waiting room. When Raymond went in the room, he saw Bill and Brandon.

"Raymond why are you here? Don't tell me Angel's in the hospital."

"Yes. What is going on? Who got hurt?"

"Mic was attacked. If you're here. Angel was the one who saved Mic."

"Misty had three seniors trying to kill him. The way the doctor spoke he should be dead. They worked on his ribs, stomach and legs."

※

The doctor came in and talked to Raymond.

"Angel has a dangers' high fever. As fast as we get her intravenous fluids into her. Her body is burning the fluids up just as fast. The fever keeps her dehydrated. She's delirious because of the fever. What I don't understand is her calling for Mic. There is something about the two of them. Mic should have been killed. Something put a shield around him. All his bones were saved. His muscle has some damage. Mic skin tells a different story. There're bruises he has. These bruises show me there should be internal bleeding. There wasn't any. We don't understand what could have save him.

"Now we have Angel. Her body with through a lot. She used up a good part of her fluids in her body. If we don't get the fluids back up. Her body will begin to shut down. If I didn't know better. I would say this had to be magic. I've never seen it before. My grandmother had spoken of it."

Raymond waved his hand. The doctor was paused.

"Do not say this to anyone else." He waved his hand again. "Thank you, doctor do, what you can for her."

※

Brandon was making himself a cup of coffee. When Raymond came back in. He waved his hand and the room became a safe place to talk or do magic.

"Angel is not good. Mic is not any better than Angel. If I don't stop this will lose them both."

"Angel was able to put a shield around Mic. The two of them have magic. Not magic like my own. They will get their powers when Mic and Angel become twenty-one. What they have now is energy. Powerful energy when they are together. Angel couldn't join her energy with Mic. She had to save him without his help. Mic was using his energy to fight the men off. Right now, Mic is waiting for Angel to come to him. She can't. Somehow her memory of their dream world has been blocked. She scared and can't hear Mic. I need your help Bill. I must help Angel get to Mic in the dream world. She's weak and too scared to fine Mic. Keep me anchored here. I'm going to try to help her find Mic."

"Raymond who mess with their memory?"

"Brandon, I wish I knew. Right now, I believe there is more to this.

"I believe your right. Remember when Mic came to Scotland, he was very sick that day?"

"Yes, dad said that Mic was taken to see that doctor that does hypnosis."

"At first Mic seem to be all right. One thing he did say that in the dream world he couldn't see any faces. Remember Mic has two things magic and hypnosis. Angel just has magic. What if Mic is the one blocking the dream world from Angel?"

"Brandon you may have hit the nail on the head. I must get Angel to Mic. Whatever is happening I will fix it in the dream world."

Bill had some magic. He could do what Raymond asked of him. Raymond had to prepare the room. He sat in a chair.

Then Bill waved his hand. *"Sleep my friend. Save the ones we love."*

In the dream world Raymond called upon the magic of Garret. 'Grandfather I need your help. Angel and Mic is too weak to call upon their magic. She's scared and don't know where to go to fine Mic. Her energy is very low. She has a very high fever. Mic's energy is also low. I must get her to him.'

'Raymond, you know the place. It can only be with the magic roses is. Not the roses here in Scotland. Go to your sister and call for her spirit.

Pick her up and take her to Mic. Show her the way there. Angel needs to go there. Together they can heal each other.'

Raymond knew what he had to do. Angel can't go to Mic because she has no memory of the place. Standing next to his sister he placed a hand on Angel's forehead.

'Sis hear me. I need to give your memory back to you. You will remember the place we grew up as children. You will have everything you need. One thing you will not have. If someone ask you who you are. All you will be able to say is Angel. You will remember me as your brother. Sorry about this part. You and I cannot say brother or sister to each other out loud. We can only say it in are mines. When you dream. Mic and you can be together in the dream world.'

He waved his hand and everything he said was done.

'It's time sis to bring you to Mic.'

Raymond place his hands under her shoulders and legs. He picked her up and pulled her to him. Angel was a strong young woman. To see her and feel his sister this weak scared him.

'Angel you have to tell me where to go. I know how hard this will be to talk to me.'

She opened her eyes and smiled at her brother. Raymond felt a little pull from his energy. Not much because he was her brother and not her mate.

'Do you feel better sis?'

'Yes, I can tell you to go to America. Then to Vermont. We lived on the land of the MacGregors. Take me to the waterfall. Where the magic roses are.'

Raymond waved his hand and they were at the waterfall. He could see Mic laying on the large rock in the sun.

'Mic it's Raymond. I have Angel with me. Can you stand by yourself?'

'Angel is here? I'm too weak. I can't stand.'

Raymond knew he had to do it the hard way. He placed Angel on her feet. Then waved his hand to pick Mic up and keep Angel standing. Raymond called to his grandfather.

'Grandfather, Mic and Angel needs their powers. This must be done now. Please grandfather we can't lose them now.'

Raymond stood holding them up with his magic. This time when Mic receive his powers. It came to Raymond first then to Mic. The power was grater then his own. Raymond was glowing with bright light. When he waved his hand, there was a beam of light that went to Mic. Now Mic was twenty-one. A strong looking young man. He could see Mic kept up with his weight lifting. Mic's eyes weren't on Raymond. They were on Angel. He remembered the day his sister was born. Mic had that same look. Even then Mic could talk to Angel.

Then Raymond pointed his finger toward his sister. There was another beam of light that went to Angel. She was twenty-one and Mic change to twenty-two. The powers left wasn't just his. He still had too much power. It was grater then Raymond's own powers. Could this be a test for himself? Raymond tried to give all the power to them.

'Grandfather I don't understand. Why do I feel my body has more magic then before? Am I to have this magic? Is there someone else I need to give it to?'

'Very good grandson. You will be giving some of the Magic to Bill. He will need more magic to keep Mic safe until he is twenty-one.'

'What about Angel shouldn't Angelica have some magic?'

Raymond waited until his grandfather said more. It never happened. What grandfather did. He had shown him that Angelica had received some magic. Then he saw Bill take Angelica as his wife. When he gave Angelica his mark. Some magic went to her. She could do the things Bill could do now. There will be trouble coming their way. Raymond didn't understand why they were trying to kill Mic. One thing was clear. Bill and Angelica must be on campus. This can't happen again.

'Grandson it's because of the magic rose. Mic has mated with Angel in the dream world. She wears the mark from the locket Thomas had made for Eleanor. She is stronger when she is with Mic.'

'I understand now Grandfather. Marcuse plans the attack with Mic. Angel can see what Marcuse is doing in her dreams. If he goes after Mic and keeps Angel busy. Angel won't see Marcuse trying to take down our fathers.'

'Yes, that's why he is sending people after Mic. The stakes are too high. Marcuse is trying to find ways to make people who is weak to do his bidding. Not only he has to bring Angel and Mic to his master. He must bring a lot of souls this time around. Angel can see what Marcuse is doing when she is with Mic. The two of them can stop him each time.'

Raymond looked to his sister. She was beautiful and had only eyes for Mic. How many times has Marcuse came after them? He tried to kill Mic while he slept. It was the night their fathers were also fighting in the dream world. Demons where attacking both Mic and their fathers. Also, that night Angel became Mic's mate. He had given his sister the Magic Fairy Rose that night.

'Mic can you come over here?'

'I'll be right there Raymond.'

Mic dove into the water and swam to the other side. When he got to shore Angel ran into Mic's arms. He wrapped his arms around her and kissed her deeply. Raymond watched them. The two of them were glowing with bright light. From a toddler on. Mic fought demons for Angel. Angel would put her life in danger and many more times to save him. He didn't say anything to them of what his grandfather had showed him. He knew they would have to do it again. These powers will help Bill and Angelica. If we do not keep Angel and Mic safe. It will mean the end of the Magic Fairy Rose, and the MacGregors family. Raymond felt he was missing something…but what?

Then Angel cried out. *'Raymond daddy is in trouble. Marcuse knew I would see what he was up too. He could only block one thing at a time from me.'*

'What are you talking about Angel.'

'When I felt the trouble. Part of the dream was in darkness. There should have been two dreams. Marcuse block the dream of daddy and James. There walking into a trap. They will be killed along with their men. In the building there is four Americans. The helicopter just set down. There moving out.'

'Damn it! That is what I was missing. When he goes after Mic. Marcuse also goes after our fathers every time. This is what grandfather mint. Angel how much time do we have?'

'I don't know. Where ever they are. The buildings are all in cement. There is sand everywhere. Raymond the building that there going into. When they open the door, it will blow up. Marcuse will not be in that

building. He's inside a mountain in another town. Raymond their guide is in on it.'

'Damn that Marcuse. Join hands we three will be like an antenna for Angel. Angel you are going to have to tell dad what is going on.'

They held hands and thought of Joseph.

'Daddy stop… you have to hear me. You're in danger. The building you're going to go in is a trap.'

'Angel is that you.'

'Yes, daddy it's me.'

'I can't talk now. I'm on a mission. Talk to me later.'

'I know you're on a mission. Daddy stop your men and listen to me now. Before it is too late to safe you. Do I ever call to you like this?'

'No! Give me a minute. I must stand down my men.'

Angel had waved her hand. Then the three of them could see what Joseph and James was doing. The waterfall became a TV with its own antenna.

'What is going on? How do you know it's a trap?'

'Daddy you never question my dreams before.'

'There is three of us here in the dream world. Mic and Raymond is here also.'

'You're in the dream world. What happen? It's not night there yet. Why is Raymond there with you? That's yours and Mic's dream world not Raymond's.'

'Daddy don't worry about that now. Hear what I have to say.'

'All right. Go ahead and tell me. James is able to hear you also.'

'I saw Tim opening the door. The building had blown up. In the back room. There are four American's that will be killed. Marcuse is not inside that building. He's inside a mountain not far from a small town. One of the buildings holds a tunnel to the mountain. Your guide is one of his men. There is a bomb on him. The detonator is in his pocket. You will die one way or another.'

'Dad let us handle this.'

'Raymond why are you in their dream world?'

'Long story, you better come home after this is done.'

'Understood. Do you three have a plan.'

'Yes dad. We're going to start a devil sand storm. Once the storm is over the building. Mic will get the American's out. Angel and I will keep *the storm over that building. When the American's are safe. I will grab the guide and slam him into the door. This should set off the bomb's inside the house along with his bomb. Where do you want the American's?'*

'Mic is there any way you can scope out the area for us?'

'Yes, Dad give me a minute to look inside these buildings.'

Mic waved his hand over the waterfall. He was changing the channels to look inside the building. The fifth building down looked to be empty.

'Dad the fifth building to your left is empty. Tell your guide you will take your men and circled around to the back. The guide knows there are bombs on the back door also. We're going to start the devil sand storm.'

James had moved his men out. Their guide didn't seem worried about anything. Once James was cleared. Joseph made sure his men was out of arms-way.

Raymond, Mic and Angel took their hands one on top of the other. With the other hand they made a circle. They started the storm. One of Joseph men saw a twister and pulled back were there was more cover.

Angel shouted. *'Mic you're up. Get those four people out.'*

Mic use the waterfall to see were the four men where. Not wasting any time. He grabbed the Americans and place them near bye.

The three watch the sand storm. They knew when the American's were safe.

'Dad the American's are out. You can move in. Don't bring them back this way.'

'Will done son thank you.'

'Any time Dad. Raymond you're up.'

Raymond made it look as if the guide was sucked up into the twister. There was a big explosion. The hole building went straight up into the sky. The twister took the building away.

'Dad it's done. The Americans are safe. James has them. Come home after you get done. Bring James with you. There is trouble at Mic and Angel schools.'

'All right be there as soon as we can. Will done you three.'

'Mic I have to go. The two of you did grate. This must be done now. I can't have Angel and you not able to fine each other.'

Raymond touch Mic's and Angel's forehead. *'From now on, you two will know each other always. If something happens to your memory. You will always have each other in the dream world. No one or thing and change this. I give everything back to you. However, you will not be able to say your full name. You can't tell anyone where the family is from or write your name on paper. You will be only Mic and Angel. They cannot get your name from you even with a machine. I have done what I could for you two. The two of you have the memories all the way back to when you were little. Take care of each other. You only have now to enjoy each other. For hard times will be coming are way.'*

After he left Mic and Angel. Raymond had to stay in the spirit world. Here is where the safe zone must be. Any work that is done to any love once or people he cares about. Raymond had to do it in the spirit world. Grandfather Garret told him just how to do it. Raymond wrote everyone's name down on a magical paper. He even wrote his own name. Then he made the bowl out of magic. Tearing the paper at each of the names. He dropped it into the bowl. When that was done. He added one magic fairy rose petals for every person. Then he took a piece of Angel and Mic's hair. He made a cross with their hair. The cross had to be dip in holy water. This was to bine them to Tom and Ellen. Raymond place a drop of his blood to make the spell strong. On another piece of magical paper. He wrote the spell. Then folded the paper and placed another drop of his blood. It was time to light everything in the magic bowl. With his magic he called for white lightning. When it was over it had brought Raymond back to his body.

"Raymond how did it go?"

"Mic and Angel is safe. Could you get me some water?"

"Yes, be happy to. Here I just got word that Mic is out of danger. Before I brought you the water, I checked on Angel. The nurse said she is doing well."

"That's good."

"Why were you gone so long?"

"Do you remember. When they told you about Marcuse tried to kill Mic in his sleep? At that same time James and dad also in their sleep."

"Yes, I do remember that."

"They try to do it again?"

"What do they think were stupid. To forget something like that?"

"I don't know Bill. Angel was to have two dreams. One of her dreams was nothing but darkness. She only saw the first one with Mic. I was able to get Angel to the dream world in time. When the two of them was able to hold each other. Angel saw the dream of our fathers. They tried to take out our fathers hold team. When the spell was place on Mic and Angel. Evil made my father forget. He had to place them in a safe zone. This was to be their dream world.

"I had to take care of those three men. I paid them a visit. They won't be used again for evil. I had placed the cross and rose on their chest. The three of them will have to do some time. They were place away from the other boys. They must go through therapy from the time they have left in school. This is three years of college."

"Raymond there is quite a few like them. Is there any way we can place the cross and rose on their chest? We have to try to save some of them?"

"You could place a cross on them with your magic. Bill you do have more magic now. Grandfather gave you more. It's to keep Mic safe until he is twenty-one."

※※※

That Saturday Mic and Angel were in the Highland's. The MacGregor's had Raymond Angel-Heart family over. At the ranch Mic and Angel had to rest. They were sitting on the couch watching TV. The news came on saying that four American's were saved by the Navy Seals. Only their guide was killed in a devil sand storm. Raymond had come in when the news was on. He watched Mic and Angel to see if they would remember what had happen.

'Why shouldn't they. They just looked at each other.'

'Angel we save the American's.'

'No Mic. You were the one that saved them. Raymond save the Navy Seals from that guide.'

'Angel, we three saved them all. If you didn't say something about our father's. No one would have been saved. I don't want you to think any other way.'

Raymond knew the two of them was talking to each other. He wondered when his father and James would get here. He saw Mic turn off the TV.

"Angel all I been doing is resting. Let's go outside and walk around. There's a hammock that two people can lay down on. If I must rest at least we will be outside. How does that sound?"

Angel knew Raymond was there watching them.

"Raymond will that be alright with you?"

"Like my mother always said. Be good."

Mic replied. "Raymond that will be no problem for me. My ribs are still sore."

Then Raymond looked at Angel. He knew better them that. "Do you know what I'm talking about?"

"Yes Raymond. I know what you mean. I'm thirteen. I'm not stupid. Why does everyone treat me like a child."

"Angel that's why I said what I said. You're not a child. You are too young to start making love."

"I know that Raymond. I'm too young to have my own child."

Then Raymond's wife came out. "Dear you're not going to stop anything. The two of them know it's not time for them to be like us. Angel knows her body isn't ready for a baby yet. Mic also knows this. We can't be with them all the time. I can say be good. Don't start anything that you will be sorry for. Come on dear. Come with me."

'Mic I do have strong feelings for you. Sometimes I don't understand when I wake-up with those feelings. I've been kiss three times. Health-class told me a lot. The love stories I read. I can picture in my mine. No one has showed me why I have these feelings. When I'm with you. These feelings are even stronger. Sometimes parts of my body aches.'

'Angel, do you trust me? In anything's that we might do?'

'That is a very stupid question to ask me. What do you think?'

"All right come with me. I think we should walk a bit."

They walked down the road until they came to a tree growing out of a rock. Mic led Angel down under the tree branches. Here they couldn't be seen from the road.

"Mic what are we doing here."

"What if I told you. I will let you touch me were every you like. It's okay Angel. Your eyes tell me that it scares you."

"Why is it everyone things somethings scared me. Mic I'm not scared. Just surprise of what you said. I just don't know what to do. Would you kiss me and touch me? You could show me what I could do to you."

"Will have to go slow. I can't have you until you are twenty-one. This is when we can get married."

"Mic why do I have to be twenty-one?"

"It's when I can give you my seed."

"Mic there are pills that I could take. Why twenty-one? How about eighteen? I believe there going to add two years of schooling. You would be nineteen and I be eighteen."

"Here in the Highlands. We could marry when I'm eighteen."

"Angel I would like to give you my real name."

"If we married. You can use the name MacGregor. I'll use the name Angel Heart. These names feel right to me. Mic if this happens. It's because we won't be together until I'm twenty-one."

"No Angel. I will be seventeen when I get out of school."

"Mic don't you remember what Bill said."

"Yes. To add two more years. Then that will work. Angel do you want to really know why you're having these feelings?"

"Yes, I do. Why is it when I just wake-up. There is an ache between my legs? Sometime my breast also feels this tingling. Why is that Mic?"

"I can show you. When were together we can touch each other?"

Right then Mic place himself against the rock. He guided Angel between his legs. He went slowly pulling her against him. His hands run over her back and bottom. He brought his hands to frame her face.

"Angel don't let me go too far. We can get to know each other's bodies. With our hands and fingers. Lips and tongue we will try things together."

Mic's hands framed her face. He was looking deeply into her eyes. Gently he kissed her lips. As he moved his arms around her.

His hands went to her bottom and push her into him. Mic held her tightly against him. So, she could feel what she was doing to him. His tongue brushed over her lips. Angel opened to all those feelings. They were making love with their tongues. He went under her blouse to touch her breast. Angel went under his shirt to feel his bear skin. Quickly Mic turned her. She was now against the rock. From her breast his hand slips down inside her pants. She felt something hard on her leg. A dream was coming back to her. She pictures them on green grass. A waterfall was nearby. Mic was on top of her. She remembered feeling something hard between her legs. It was like magic. Right then Mic push his finger deep inside Angel. An explosion went off inside her and Mic. She understood what that wonderful feeling was. As Angel held something long and hard in her hand. She had felt it pulse as her hand got wet. She understood what they were doing. This was one way of making love to each other.

On Sunday two teenagers came back to school. The principals didn't say anything to the students. The police and their mother were at the school. The boy and girl were let back into school.

Tuesday Mic and Angel went to the school hospital. They had to be cleared by the doctor to go back into school. The doctor told Mic. He had to take it slow until he knew he could do things without pain. Angel was clear to do most anything. She had to watch out for her breathing. If it was hot out, she was to take rest and drink water.

The school was told that Bill and Angelica had to be on school grounds. This was until Mic and Angel were out of school for good. Bill and Angelica took over Mic's and Angel's dorms. This was not to happen again. It was lunch time. Mic and Angel were with their teammates. Bill had come through the teacher's entrance. When he saw Hawkeye. They hadn't told Mic about Erica yet. Mic was about to stand up. Angel had placed her hand over Mic's.

Angel said. 'Mic you know this girl is not Misty. She looks more like Hawkeye. Her hair is a light brown. It's not at all like Misty's hair. Us girls were told before class. We knew Erica was coming back to school. They are triplets. She's not evil. She is Cal's girlfriend.'

Cal and Sunshine was with Hawkeye and Erica.

Hawkeye said. "Mic this is my sister Erica. We are triplets. I'm the oldest and Erica is after me. Misty is the youngest. We don't know where Misty is currently at. Erica was going to another school for the arts. Now that Misty is gone Erica can come back to this school. I'm sorry I didn't tell you about Misty. I'll let Erica tell you about her."

"Hello Mic. I'm sorry for what my sister tried to do to you. It's hard to tell someone about her sister."

Her voice sound choked up. Cal came over to her and took Erica's hand. She looked a Cal and went on with what she had to say.

"You see it's hard to tell you about someone who's been hurt by her own sister. Our first year here. The two of us would fight. I always had some boys around me. I tried to get my sister to take care of herself. She acted more of a boy then a girl. Misty never fixed herself up. The next year I saw her talking to this older boy. I didn't get to hear what he told her. All I knew after that day she was different. Misty called to one of the boys. When he came over to her. She had asked him to see what was in her eye. After that the young man would do anything for her.

"One day she tried the same thing with our brother. It made Hawkeye mad. He told her if she tries that again. He would kick her ass. Are third year here. Just before school started. We were at the park. The three of us were letting the dogs run around. You see I saw my sister talking to this man with the red eyes. I had a bad feeling about him. I got closer to them. He had told Misty. If you want to keep your powers. There is a young man called Mic. He's coming to your school. Get him under your power's. You have one year to do so. At the end of the year. If he is not under your power kill him. Misty thought that she had power's over me. It didn't work on me or our brother.

Misty has no willpower. To be part of anything. She would do what the kids said. She is weak and easy to control. She things she is a big deal now. In the past people picked on her. We were sent here because of that. The day in the park. I knew she had made a deal with a demon. I saw him disappear. Misty could make people do bad things. When her eyes went red. It hypnotizes that person. Then she can tell them what to do. They would do anything she tell them. Mic you must have a strong will. When you started telling her what to do. She lost it. My friend told me that she was losing it in dancing. Misty knew her hair was too long and thick. She believed that she could do anything with her powers. When she got hurt. She said it was you that did it. One of the guys had told Hawkeye that you made her fall Mic. This is how the story got to Hawkeye. He then heard it also from Misty. It was not until Cal talked to Hawkeye. The teacher who saw the two of you said Mic didn't do anything to Misty."

Hawkeye told the rest. "There is a story going around the two schools. They believed it was are father. To tell the truth. He is our uncle that worked here. He is my father's twin. Our father is in the Navy. They said he's missing. On top of that. Our uncle went missing the day Misty sent those guys after you. She was losing it the day of the fair. You went right by her. I think if she had a weapon on her. You would be dead. Those powers made her go crazy. Too top it off was the day at the pool. We heard that Mic had back her into the pool."

"Yes, I did. When her eyes went red. She was screaming at me. I heard her say you will die if you don't hear me. I laughed at her before she went in the water."

Hawkeye went on. "I didn't go back to school when Misty did. The way my sister told me that I better help her. If I don't, she would get someone to make me. The girl I like. She called me at home.

Now Sunshine was holding Hawkeye's hand. He looked at Sunshine and she nodded her head.

"Sunshine told me what had happened. Misty had told her that you pushed her in the pool. The teacher told everyone what really happened. Misty had no control over you. The man wanted you under her powers or dead. After the police took them away. Mic those guys I don't believe they will remember what they had done to you."

Then Cal said. "Mic when you left, I got up a little after you. I saw the guys with the guards. They were saying did something happen? Where are you taking us? The guards said. To a hospital off campus. They told them. They need to do some testing on the three of you. The three asked why. They had no memory of what they did to you."

Hawkeye then spoke. *"The police had talk to a lot of the guys. Cal was one of them. One of the boys in their dome he was outside for a run. He saw Misty talking to these guys the day that Misty got wet. She was telling them what to say. At the time he didn't think anything of it. When it came to Misty, he stayed clear of her. He thought she was evil, and he feared her. We believe that Misty had our uncle get her out. He knew what had happen. It was our uncle who brought Misty to this man. The police asked me a lot of questions about Misty. Mic my father is like me and my sister. Our uncle is like Misty weak. My father went in the Navy so he wouldn't be like him. They said the last boy died when he was fifteen, he was evil."*

Angel then spoke to Mic in her thoughts. *'Mic I had felt the evil with in them.'*

'Angel I believe they had demons inside them. That's the only way they wouldn't remember.'

Angel asked. *"So, Misty tried to control you Erica? What happen when you told her to get out of your face."*

Angel was watching Erica's face. She needed to see if she would get mad at Angel. What she saw was tiers in her eyes.

"Angel I told you she tried. When I didn't do what she said. She had three guys come after me. They almost rape me. Hawkeye had me watched. He had found out what Misty was up too. Him and my boyfriend Cal. He saved me from getting raped. Momma had taken me out of this school. Now that Misty is gone. I'm able to come back to go to college. Misty goes after simple mines. Our mines are stronger then hers. Misty couldn't get any girls under her powers. As far as we know of. Her powers are weak. She can only go after simple mines like hers."

Angel asked. *"How is it you know all this. I was told that are names are taken from us. All of us are not to be able to know our families. Here you are telling us your father is in the Navy. You said your mother is trying to hold everything together. Then you said your uncle worked here. How long have you known all of this?"*

Hawkeye added. *"Not long about two days Angel. All I want to say is be careful Mic. When you get out of school. She still must kill you Mic. The demon wants you dead. Misty is in love with the powers she has."*

"I know that Hawkeye. Because one of the guys who was trying to kill me. The demon that was inside him. He wanted me to know that

Misty still must kill me. Thank you for telling me this. You didn't have to say anything to me."

"Mic, we had too. You see we like to go out for the competition. Last year was a bus. Misty thought she was the best dancer. It Erica and I like to dance. We like to be able to work with you and Angel. If you two say no it's okay. We're trying to get through school. I know how you teach Mic. All the girls who talked to Sunshine loves the way Angel teaches. We like to give back to the school for what Misty has done."

Angel looked at Mic. *'What do you think Mic?'*

'We can work with them. Try to get to know them better.'

Then Angel said that they were looking at them. Angel looked at Mic. Turning her head Mic whispered. *"A lot of the girls like Erica."*

"The guys enjoyed being around Hawkeye. You know Sunshine and Cal. They want this for them and themselves."

"Yes, I know. So, we can say will see if you four will work out together."

"All right guys. So, you know Angel and I put in to be teachers."

The four of them looked at each other. Hawkeye spoke for the four of them.

"Yes, we know. That's why we are here. It will be up two you two. What say you."

It was a big table. Mic looked at Angel. She nodded her head yes.

"All right you four. Everyone must try out. We must put together four teams. Have you eaten?"

The four said no together. "Then go get your food and sit down with us."

Bill heard what they said. He knew what to do next. Once the four of them was sitting down he went over to them. Bill placed a hand on Hawkeye and Erica's left shoulder.

"So how is it going here you two?"

In his mind he told them. If you feel your shoulder go hot run. For evil is coming. This can give you a heads up. Bill had done the same to Cal and Sunshine.

Then Mic asked. *"Bill are you all set up in are dorm?"*

"Yes I am. I was making sure you were all right with all of this. It's too bad that you don't have something to tell you there is a demon *around. They say if you are good inside and you got away from evil. Here in Scotland there are fairies. They place a cross and magic rose to tell you evil is coming. If your left shoulder goes hot evil is around."*

Then Mic and Angel knew what Bill had done.

It was the end of the endurance competition. There two-schools had brought back with them over half of the awards. All their hard work paid off. The next competition will start next month. It was time to choose their leader. The girls already new who they wanted. Principal Tensaw had call Angel into her office.

"Hello Angel. Come on in. I've been told that all the girls want you to teach them ballet. For the boys there is two boys that they want to see you dance with. There is a young man. He asked to see you dance with Cal and Mic. Cal is a very good dancer. He is so-so in teaching. Mic was the one to teach the boys how to dance. They like how he work with them. Mic never had a chance to dance. Now that Misty is gone. They like to see the two men dance with you. Congratulation and good luck. You will go to the activity building. They will be there at 8:00. A teacher will be there at 7:00."

Angel has been working with the girls. On Monday the two groups will be dancing at the activity building. It was Monday and Angel had to get there before the two groups. With her backpack Angel jogged to the activity building. She found that she was very nervous. Angel was hoping the run would help. It didn't. Why would she be nervous? Angel knew why. On this day the two groups will watch her dance with Cal and Mic.

'What if the group went with Cal? I don't want to dance with him. He's not my partner.'

Her long hair was braided. When she got closer to the building. She knew she was being watched.

'No, they can't be here yet.'

At the steps Angel looked up to the second-floor windows. She couldn't see anyone. She just knew they were there.

'Grate, I know Mic is here.'

In the window stood two young men watching her. The second floor all the rooms were dark. When Angel looked toward the window. One of the men jumped back.

"What the hell! Mick you said she couldn't see us."

Mick gave a little laugh. He knew Angel would have known they were up here. She always knew where he was. Just as he knew she was jogging to the building. Something wasn't right.

'What was bothering him? Angel and I worked with Cal in the competition. Why is this any different. Ballet dance you can tell a story of love. So-what! He's going out with Erica. Could it be that Cal is a lady's man? He was tall like Mic. With blonde hair and bluest gray eyes. So-what! I have golden brown eyes and black hair. Cal wasn't as strong as Mic. They say women love older men. No! I don't think Angel would go for him.'

Last year Cal took Mic's place in dancing. Mic was the one to teach the guy's the dances. Even Cal, Mic had to teach. What is going on here. Cal is no threat to me with Angel. However, here he was upset. Someone is pulling strings to get me upset. No, I'm not going to let this.

'What would happen if the guys wanted Cal not him. When he came to this school. Cal befriended him.'

"Mic step back she can see you."

"Cal stop worrying. The lights are off and we're up high enough. Angel can't see us."

"Then tell me this why is she looking right at you?"

Mic just smiled and shrugged his shoulders.

"We better get in that surveillance room. Before Angel sees us."

"Cal, we have time. Remember I've worked with Angel before. I figure it will take her fifteen minutes. Think about this. She is to dance with you and me. Angel had jogged from her dorm. You and I took the bus here. I also would have jogged here then showered after would. You could see she wasn't ready."

"Mic they say she is thirteen. What I could see she is beautiful with a high IQ. Your fourteen am I right?"

"Yes Cal. I'm younger then you. I have a very high IQ. She's wonderful at everything she does. Anything else Cal?"

Mic headed to the surveillance room. Just as he predicted. Angel walked into the classroom. The two of them watched her rub her hair with the towel. She then brushed her long-wet hair over her breast. Angel placed her hair in a pony tail. Then braided the pony tail. There my hair will stay off my shoulders. She could feel strong emotion.

'So, I was right. Mic and Cal is here. Too soon?'

She smiled as she placed the last bobby-pin in her tight bun. 'You're giving yourself away Mic.'

Angel how can I not be turn on by this. I love watching you. Remember we touched each other.'

'I remember Mic. Now be good before Cal realize that we can talk to each other.'

She had on her ballet outfit. It was in the school colors. A one-piece pair of tights. It was all yellow with blue trim around the neckline. Tied around her waist was a short blue wrap around skirt. On her bare arms she placed long light blue scarves. These scarves were see-through. They were made to look like wings. Mic could see she was a beautiful woman. Not a thirteen-year-old girl. Angel walked over to put her music on. The sun was coming up. As she moved her scarves flowed like wings on an angel. Each time she moved past the window the sunlight danced over her. Mic kept on thinking.

Cal was way older them Mic. About two years. With his thin mustache and blond hair. He had every girl after him. Would Angel be one of them?

'My god Angel. You're so beautiful. A man can fall in love with you. When were not together for a while? Would you fall out of love with me?'

Angel had stopped dancing. She looked toured the mirror.

'Mic what is wrong? Why did you say that?'

She was trying to fix her scarves while looking at Mic.

'Angel will talk later. There is nothing wrong that I can't handle. Just dance for us.'

'If that is so. Why is Cal watching just you? This mirror if you look at it just right you can see the people inside.'

Mic glanced over at Cal. The two men were now eye to eye.

"Cal why are you watching me? You need to watch Angel dance."

"Mic she is not dancing any more. The word went out. They said you and Angel were in sync with each other. How do you two do that?"

Mic looked at Cal as if he had two heads.

"Cal what the hell are you talking about. Do you mean synchronize to be in harmony with her? We work good together. I had her back and she had mine. Wait one minute. You don't have a clue what you're talking about. What do you want from me?"

Cal could see anger in Mic's eyes. He thought of Mic as a friend. He didn't want him to get mad at him.

'Damn its Jim… What the hell did you get me into? That damn question he asked me.'

"Cal tell Hawkeye the plans I've been working on. It's no longer on school grounds. Also, I know that you're in Angel's programming class. Why did you change teachers? If Hawkeye is after Angel's work, tell him to leave her alone."

"Mic I don't know what you're talking about. The teacher has new ways of doing Programming. The guys what to see if Angel is anything like Misty. Remember they haven't seen you dance with anyone. Besides Hawkeye is trying out for dancing. You can tell him yourself."

All this time Angel was getting angry at the two guys. They didn't see her go out of the classroom. At the door she heard that Mic was getting upset with Cal. When the door open two heads spun around. She heard Cal say.

"Mic the guys want to win this year. They like the feeling of winning. They think your too much involve with Angel."

"Cal, I haven't heard anything like that. What it could also describe even you. You been in many of Erica's classes."

"I was told they think you won't have your mine on the job at hand."

"Who been saying that? I don't believe that the guys would want this. I think it was all Hawkeyes doing. So, stop insulting my intelligence. If you think you could. Go and try. She is her own person."

"Mic what are you talking about. I came here because Jim talk to the principal."

"Stop it you two. Cal I am my own person. If you think you can woo me think again. I've heard that the girls thought you're a lady's man. However, they say you have only eyes for Erica now. If you change classes to get what I'm working on. My teacher will not be happy with you. Cal, they said you're a strong dancer. I have been told you wasn't a good teacher. You guys was taught by Mic. Who is this Jim? Is he the one pulling these strings? The girls picked me as their teacher. The guys already know how Mic teaches."

Mic gave a big smile. Until he heard Angel say.

"Mic you're not out of the fire yet. Cal you're up. I like to see how you dance. Go do your warm ups. While you're doing that. Think of a greeting that the two of you would say to me. We are putting a love story on this year. The guys and girls will be here at 9:00. It also means you Mic. Move it. Go do your warm ups. Cal dances first."

"Wow! she sounds just like a teacher."

"Cal stop talking and do your warm ups. That's if you can remember what I showed you."

"Yes teach."

Then Angel understood why Mic was acting that way. 'He's jealous of Cal.'

In the room she watched the two men. When the girls and boys came to the room. Angel told them that she was going to watch all the boys. Then she will see who will dance with whom.

"No talking! I want you watching who is dancing. When it's Mic's turn to dance just watch him. For the moves he will be using maybe too hard."

"Angel is Mic going to be your partner?"

"I don't know. Someone is calling the shots."

"Angel are you, all right?"

"Bunny why did you say that?"

"Angel you look to be upset with someone. Your acting different."

"Am I? Wow. Like always Bunny. You been keeping and I on me. Sorry girls. If I find out who is doing this. This person better be the best dancer around."

Then she saw Hawkeye go into the room. Mic turn and started after him.

"Hawkeye what the hell are you doing here?"

"Have you forgot that we asked if the four of us could be on both teams."

"Yes, I remember now. Tell me this. Why does Cal have to dance with Angel? Did you do this?"

"Wow Mic! It's nice to see you two. No, it's one of the guys. I saw Jim talking with someone in the office."

Angel quickly went to the boy's side. "Who is Jim?"

It was the young man from the steps. "You again! Why did you put Cal in the middle of all this? Jim you better be good at dancing. For if you're not. You will be the first one off the team. When I work with someone, I try to get in sync with them. This is what you should do when your partners. By the way. We are putting a love story on. Come up with some line to say. All right no talking. Watch closely. You will be up next."

Angel then heard Cal, Mic and Hawkeye yelling at each other. The boys went over to the girl's side. Then she saw that Jim was the only one in the side room.

She called to Mic. 'Mic stop fighting now. We have evil with us. That's why we are at each other's throat. Mic ask Cal and Hawkeye if Jim stayed around Misty a lot? Why I'm asking is Jim has a big smile on his face. The other boys left the room. I have a bad feeling Misty is trying to stop all of us from dancing.'

Angel went to the boys and girls. "How many remember if Jim was around Misty?"

"Yes, I remember. We worked on are dance with Mic. Jim was always doing something for Misty. I believe through Jim she knew everything what Mic was doing. Cal and Hawkeye tried to teach ballet. The two of them went to Mic for help."

"What's your name?"

"They call me Don."

Angel looked at the camera. "Bill send someone to take Jim to the principal. He may know where Misty is hiding." Angel walked into the room with the three boys.

'Mic keep it going. Jim is the one working for Misty. Evil can use a person who is good. He may be under Misty's power. These people become their eyes and ears. He's not evil yet. Think back about this. Tell the guys to do their warm ups.'

'Understand, sorry about all of this.'

"Hay guys. I'm sorry. I just remember Jim was always around me. It seems that Misty knew what I was doing at all time. Can you remember if Jim dance last year? Think about it. It's time to do are worm ups."

"Gentlemen ones you are done. Cal you will show me how you dance."

Cal went and turn on his music. *"This is for you lovely lady."*

Mic had said Cal was a strong dancer. As he went through his reteam. Angel knew who she would put him with. Erica dances like Cal.

'Mic I think Erica would be a good match.'

'Angel if we can get through this. We will look at them together. That's if I'm your partner.'

"Thank you, Cal. Take a seat. Hawkeye it's your turn."

Before Hawkeye started. Sunshine and Erica came into the room.

'This is for a lady of sun shine.'

Sunshine watched Hawkeye with loving eyes. Angel knew he was dancing for her. When he was done. He went and sat with Cal, Erica, and Sunshine. It was Mic's turn to dance.

'Angel drink a lot of water. What we have to show them my take a lot out of you at first.'

'You're saying it's going to be over the top. I'll be ready.'

Angel walked back to the window. She retrieved her bottle of water and drank deeply. At the window she took off her blue scarves. She felt the warmth of the sunlight. She could see one of the buses pulling up.

It happened so fast. She felt a strong pull from her energy. Angel's hands started to shake. Quickly she placed her bottle on the window sill. She had to grab the sill to steady herself. With her eyes close she took deep breaths. She knew Mic was joining with her. Their energy was getting stronger each time they did this. Will there be a time when this won't overwhelm her body? Angel knew everyone was watching. She felt the energy slowly increasing. For a moment it overpowered her, she shook a little more. Then she heard music. Slowly she turned around. Angel still held the windowsill with one hand. There in the middle of the floor stood Mic. His body tall and masculine. He wore a tank top of blue with yellow around the neck. He looked hot in his tights of a darker blue. Mic smiled when their eyes met.

All she could say was 'Mic do you have something really big planned?'

He gave her a little nod and started his routine. Angel heard the tempo getting stronger. She could see the power he poured into his dance. Mic leaped higher into the air. His legs and arms were apart in front of him in a V shape. As he turned Mic landed with a step and with down on one knee. His arms one in front and the other in the back. The next part was a turn, turn then a leap with his arms and legs behind him. A turn in the air and landing with a step then down on one knee. His arms there one in back and there in front. Then Mic did a high leap and spins landing with his feet in a V repeatedly. He was using the energy to show them that he could dance. When the music stopped. Angel watched what Mic would do next. Slowly the tempo of the music softened. This time Mic walked closer to her. The two of them were a few steps away from each other. There before her he started to recite a poem.

"When I turn my music on. I felt a strong energy. Where was this coming from? I started dancing.

My mind only on the music. What is happening to me? The energy is running through me.

When I jumped, I went higher? My leaps into the air I went farther. Could this be magic.

When I came out of a long spin. The room was full of bright light. A sunbeam took shape.

There before me was a beautiful Angel. She stood near the window.

Beautiful Angel did you come down from the heavens?

Did you spread your wings and fly to earth for me?

Angel, please dance with this humble man?

Will you dance us to the clouds in the heavens?

Please beautiful Angel. Let me dance with you so I could have a taste of heaven."

A.E. Fortin 7/17/2018

The Fairy Rose in America

The closer Mic came to Angel the stronger the energy became.

'Angel take my hand. It's your time to fly to the heavens. Do what every you would like to show them.'

Mic reached out to her. When Angel took hold of his hand. She felt the energy pour into her. This was magic. Only the two of them could make this magic. As the music went to the next sung. Angel did a high leap. Her legs were straight in a line. Her head and back were bowed with her arms behind. When she landed, she was on tiptoes and her arms in front of her. Angel walked around Mic on her tiptoes.

'Mic get down on one knee. I'm going to lay over your shoulder. When I do pick me up.'

He did what she asked then he stood. Angel turned around on his shoulder. She slid down his body. As she led her head on his shoulder. Angel pushed herself up then touch his face. Mic had remembered these moves. She was going to do some spins in his arms.

On her tiptoes she did a spin in Mic's arms. She swung her leg out then brought it back to her knee, repeatedly. Her arms were close in front of her as she spun. Angel then dance around Mic on her tiptoes. The last part. The two of them moved as one. Angel ran and leaped into Mic's arms. She was in a sitting position. Mic through her up into the air as she turned. Her arms were on his shoulders. As her legs went into a straight line. Mic held her with one arm, the other arm straight out. Then he turns her to her back. He brought her down. Angel's legs were in a straight line as her arms.

When Bill saw this, he went right to the room where Mic and Angel was. By that time all the girls and boys were clapping.

Bill was also clapping then he said. "Will done you two. I think your practicing paid off."

Then Jim came out asking. "When did they practice? I don't think anyone saw them come here."

"Jim that was the idea. In the big room you can't see the lights."

Jim looked to be upset. *"No, she's not going to like this."*

Bill looked at Mic and Angel. *"Yes, thank you Bill for helping us. We knew that we had to show them something over the top. Jim who's not going to like this."*

"Misty's not going to like that you can dance with Mic."

Bill waved his hand. A cross appeared inside his pom. He went closer to Jim and place his hand on his left shoulder. The cross went through his clothes. In Bill's mine he said a prayer. Jim's eye's changed.

"Jim have you been working for Misty?"

"Yes. Misty gave me this number to call. It's on my hand."

"Do you know where Misty is at?"

"No."

"Jim can you dance?"

"No. Where am I? Who are you?"

Bill looked at Jim's hand. The number slowly disappeared. Not until Bill saw it. Right then someone came over to Bill. He had pointed out Jim.

"Take him to the hospital. Misty's powers over him is gone."

The man took hold of Jim's arm. *"Come with me young man."*

"Angel, do you remember I told you about my sister's first victim."

"Yes, Erica I remember why."

"The young man was Jim. He was the first one she got under her power. How could I forget that?"

"It's going to be all right Erica. It's over for now."

Chapter Twelve: Mic's last year of School

THERE WAS A BIG SURPRISE FOR THE MACGREGOR'S. Raymond had brought both grandparents to Scotland. Soon his wife would have their first child. Angel was feeling down. She was missing her parents and grandparents also.

"Mic I always have Thanksgiving with the family. This is my first year without them. I don't know how that will turn out this year."

Bill told Mic to take Angel riding. Mic and Angel had stop at the roses to cut some for the table. When they got to the ranch. Bill told them to go into the house. Inside they met their grandparents. However, Angel and Mic didn't know that. Both Mic and Angel was overwhelmed. Angel started to cry.

"I'm sorry! I'm just missing my own family. Please forgive me. I'll be right back." She ran outside to the barn. Mic started after her. A hand stopped him.

"Stay here Mic. My wife and I will go after her."

Without telling Mic that they were Angel's grandparents. He seems to understand. When they said.

"Today we are her grandparents. Mic your grandparents are inside."

Angel went to the barn to brush her horse down. Inside she talked to the horse she was brushing.

"Why did they take my memory from me. I wish I understood."

Then a hand was place on each of her shoulders. Angel went right into their arms.

"This has been hard for the two of you. Raymond brought us here because of his wife. She misses her mother and father. Her father can't get away until Christmas. These two families will have Christmas together. Right now, no magic can block your heart. Your heart will tell you if this is right. Today your part of my family. We are your grandparents if you like. I hear that the two of you can dance. Maybe you and Mic could dance for us. You can dance also for Christmas. Will that be all right with you?"

"Yes! That will be wonderful." Mic and Angel put on a grate show for the two families.

The school year went by fast. The two schools brought home many trophies. At Christmas the two families came together. Before school brake Mic and Angel put a show on with a few of their best dancers. This was Angel's first Christmas without her family. Her mine told her that the two families weren't hers. Angel still felt joy. Her heart was telling her that this was right. This was all she needed.

With magic! Bill and Raymond were able to let the family watch Mic and Angel dance at school. Christmas was wonderful. It was as if she was back home. James and Joseph with their wife's where in the Highlands. This was the first time both families were in the Highlands together.

It was Mic second year of school. He will be fifteen in January. When Mic and Angel wasn't around the family talked.

Bill had brought up about Mic's age. *"Mic will be seventeen when he gets out of school. He must be older to work on the ship."*

"Thank you, Bill, for pointing that out. If we add two more years Mic will be nineteen. He could go for his master's in engineering. Angel will have one year left. She will be eighteen when Mic leave school. Then two years with his grandparents to help with the horses and roses."

"That will be the best for the two of them. Bill have you talk to them about this?"

"Yes Joseph, I have. Angel thought she would like to take a course in first aid. She could also be working on her programming. It would be good two extra years. Then she like to stay with her grandparents for two more years. Angel was talking about working in a hospital. She would like to work on the children's floor. Angel will also have her art and photos besides a book she wrote. She like to try to get it publish and sell her art and photos. I believe she is going to beery herself in work. When she gets out of school. She didn't know how long it will be when she can find Mic. The two of them is doing well in school. Their getting stronger every day.

This summer. Angelica and I like to take them camping. Will take the horses with us. We have a lot to teach them. I think we could do some diving in May. Their doing quite well in there diving classes."

"I've noticed the two of them is getting closer."

"Bill do you think they're getting closer sexual?"

"Yes and No. They know it's not their time yet. I believe that they know of each other."

"Has the two of them taking care of the roses?"

"Yes. Mic hasn't said anything about a rose dropping in his hand."

Angelica said. "No Angel hasn't said anything yet. Wouldn't they be still too young?"

James said. "Remember in their dreams they came here for the rose. She has the power of the rose with her right now."

The two families watch them from the window. They saw Mic kiss Angel.

"Mic the grownups are watching us."

"I know. It's all right Angel. You're my girlfriend. Are you not?"

'Yes. I do love to be kiss by you. To feel you touching me. Can we walk a bit?'

'What do you have in mine Angel? You do know how I feel about you. My love for you is getting stronger.'

'I know Mic. My body wants to be touch by you.'

'That's a great idea. Let's go to the castle. There is a place that no one can see us. I know where the key is.'

It was Mic's last year in school. When school was out for the summer. Bill and Angelica made plans to take them camping all summer. This will be the last time the four of them will be together.

They will take the horses with them like all ways. There was a place to swim and do some diving. It will be Angel's birthday. She was going to be eighteen. Mic and Angel ask to talk to Bill and Angelica. It was Mic who did the talking.

"Bill what I'm about to ask you. You two will think it's crazy. Angel and I like to get married before I leave. I haven't gone to the roses yet. The two families told the story of the roses. They told me. If I ask the roses if Angel is my mate. A rose will drop in my hand. If it does. I like to marry Angel before I leave the Highlands. Will you two stand up for us?"

"What did you say Mic? I don't think I heard right."

"Angel and I like to get married."

"That's what I thought you said."

Bill held a hand up for them to wait. Then Bill took Angelica hand and they stepped away from them.

"Angelica what do you think?"

"Bill, in my heart I feel this is right. I haven't seen two people in love like those two. I believe if the rose drops in his hand. Mic and Angel will run away to get married."

"That is just what I was thinking. Who can we take them two?"

"At the campground there is someone that could marry them."

"Angelica we can ask Angel to take a picture. That's if the rose drops into Mic's hand."

"Bill we will hide and watch them. This way we will know what happens to them."

"All right. I'm still having to tell Raymond. He will have to take that memory away. It will be hell to be away from each other."

"Bill, I know why they like to marry. To be able to make love to each other."

"Will have to get something so he won't get her pregnant. Will make the summer their honeymoon"

"Bill are we going to do it?"

"Yes. Now what name should he give her."

"I think the two of them will know what to do."

Bill and Angelica went back to them. "We will do this for you two. Go to the roses this weekend."

There was only four weeks left for school.

"I need to talk with you. Could you get me a doctor's appointment?"
"Is this for birth control?"
"Yes. I want to mate with Mic on my wedding night."
"Angel I can't do that for you. I believe Emily can. She may do it for you. I know when Raymond fine's out that you got married. He'll be upset with all of us."
"I understand. I hope you understand this. I will marry Mic one way or another."

Everything was being wrapped up at school. This week Bill was training his replacement for the one class he taught. Next week he had to get the class their finals. Angelica was going to take over the two-diving classes. Only until they can find someone else for the boys. Mic and Angel was helping with the senior ball.

"Mic this is going to be my senior ball also. I don't think I will go to mine. I'm not going to dance with anyone next year. I will still teach when they need help. Like you I have been training a few of them who I think could teach. If I had my way this would be my last year here."

"Angel we better make this one the best one. If I could come back here, I would take you to your senior ball."

"Mic I don't want to be here without you. I like to take a nursing class. Then work in a hospital on the children's floor."

"Angel no. You got to stay here. It's only one year."

"Then I like to teach the ballet. I could work with the two teachers for the competition. Maybe work at the hospital on the children's floor near Raymond's home."

The word went out. Angel's not going to dance in the *competition*. This will also be her senior ball. A few of the group came to Bill and Angelica. They were having trouble with the lights. They like to make it special for Mic and Angel. One of the girls heard Angel say she's not going to her senior ball.

"Thank you for telling me. Now show me how it would look in a drawing?"

They didn't have enough lights to pull it off.

"I'll get some more lights for you guys."

Late that night Bill went to see the set-up of lights. With the lights off, he waved his hand. When he turned the lights on. It looked just like the drawing.

They were going shopping for a dress for Angel and Angelica. Angelica and Bill had to chaperone at the ball. It was a girl's night out. They made it a day. Emily daughter Tammy found Angel's dress. It was a long pearl white dress. It fitted Angel in all the right places. In Angel's mine she would ask Raymond to make the dress a golden yellow. She would ask Bill to put it back to a pearl white and shorten it after the ball.

It was getting harder for Mic to keep his hands-off Angel. They had tried every way to make love. This was the week Mic took her to the roses. Today he was going to see if it worked. Angel was with him. She loved the castle. She wanted to paint this place. One of her dreams she remembers seeing Mic near the castle on a horse. He was looking at the mountains. She started to take the picture she needed. She was taken pictures all-around.

Bill knew what was going to happen. He places a safe zone around Mic. Know evil could see him. Angel had turned to take pictures of the roses. She was able to catch the rose dropping into Mic's hand. The next shot. He was breathing in the scent of the rose. The last shot was of him falling to the ground. It had scared Angel. Bill and Angelica watch them. He knew what was to happen next. He took Angelica's hand.

"They're going to be fine. We have to let this go to the end."

"Bill, she looks to be really scared."

"Just watch."

By the time Angel was able to get to Mic. He was already on his feet. Mic was a MacGregor. He had drawn that woman. It was Angel. Only much older. The story she told me was of Eleanor and Thomas. She is my grate-grandmother. Mic knew Raymond will have to take their memories away from them.

"Mic are you, all right?"
"Come here I have something to give you."
Angel stepped into Mic's arms. He drew her close to him.
"Angel you have been my mate from the day you were born. I hunger to mate with you. I love you so much. Take this rose for it is a part of me."

"Angel…you are my beautiful Angel.
My heart is heavy knowing our time is drawing near.
I was lost, and you found me. You had touched my very soul.
Each time we dance, we flew to the heavens.
I will always be with you, my sweet Angel.
For now, you have my heart.
Call me in your mind. For I will be there in your dreams.
Keep this rose close to your heart. Our love will not know time.
The power of this rose is within you. Without you I will be lost forever.
I will not say good-by. For one day we will find each other.
I love you my sweet Angel.
You will always be my beautiful Angel."
03/31/2009 By A.E. Fortin

Tears filled Angel's eyes. How could she go on without Mic in her life? She knew she shouldn't cry.
"Mic I love you so much."
"Angel take this rose. This rose is a part of me. Make it a part of you."
She knew that she had to do what Mic had done. She lifted the rose to her nose. When Angel breathed in the scent. In Mic's arms she went limp. He picked Angel up and carried her to the bench. Here in his arms was his mate. Mic took a pedal from the rose. He placed it in the locket. This locket came from the magic rose back home. When she woke up, he kissed her. With cloudy eyes Mic told Angel how he felt.
"Angel I know you're scared. I need you to believe that the magic this rose holds will lead us to each other. We must believe in this magic no

matter what. I love you, Angel. Never forget that. We will find each other again. We must believe that. If we fail, we will be lost forever. Right now, I can remember the first time our eyes met. You were a baby. A newborn. When you looked into my eyes you took my breath away. The day you dance for me. I knew then you captured my heart.

"Angel… You are my beautiful Angel. I love to feel my fingers run through your long silky hair. For it's the color of honey. Your golden-brown hair shines like sunlight. What I will miss mostly is to be able to touch those sweet lips. Your kisses are of the taste of honey. Your lips are the color of this red rose. Each time we kiss I hunger for more. I will remember this time we had together. This is until we meet again."

"Bill, they need our help. Mic and Angel are going up against evil. Until they get their powers, we must keep them safe. When they are together, they can keep each other safe. You and I were a part of all this. Are four family's go's way back in history. It was my father who's keeping them a part. He has all of us intertwine. Marcos blood is in part of these families. I believe Mic and Angel is changing things. It was Marcos who wanted Angel's virginity. If Mic marries Angel, he will take her virginity."

"Angelica you may be right. Mic knows who he is. I think I know who told him. His grate grandmother. I was checking on Mic. His drawing paper was out. He had drawn and older woman. I believe she was in her eighties. She looked like Angel. Only older then Angel. Mic had said there was an older woman at the castle. It was on the day he cleaned the roses. He said she told him a different story about these roses. She must want Mic to know who he is. She must know what is going to happen. Come on we have to get back at the ranch before they do."

"Bill do you think that bubble will keep them safe. Evil ears must not hear."

"Yes! At least until they get to the ranch."

Back at Raymond's home. Angel was outside. She was looking at the stars. She held her locket in her hand.

"I wish when Mic and I marry. On that night. I would like to feel him come inside me. Why can't I have his seed that night? Grandfather you have the power to stop me from getting pregnant. I would like to make love to Mic as often as we like. Yes, I can have him in are dreams. Let me have him this summer."

'Hello Angel.'

"Hello, do I know you?"

'Yes. Just look at me.'

In the background was Mic. 'Angel how did you get Eleanor here?'

'I asked my grandfather a question. He sent your grandmother to me.'

"You're the lady that told Mic about the rose? I saw the drawing Mic did."

'Yes, my child. Do you know who I am?'

"You are Eleanor. Mic's great grandmother. I look like you."

Emily was at the door. She saw Eleanor and wonder why she was here.

'Angel you cannot ask a man something like that. Your grandfather told me to tell you to ask Alicia.'

Emily open the door and stepped out.

"Angel what do you need?"

"I want to marry Mic. I want to be able to mate with him that night. Right up to the time he leaves Scotland. Isn't there something to stop me from getting pregnant?"

"Yes, there is. It's called a birth control pill."

"Eleanor what is going on here."

Then Raymond came outside.

"Hello Eleanor."

'Hello Raymond. It's good to see you again.'

"Angel what is happening? How did you get Eleanor here?"

'STOP... Raymond before it's too late.'

Eleanor saw that Mic was ready to go after Raymond. She shook her head no. Right then Raymond paused Angel. Now she couldn't hear them talking. He waved his hand and sent Angel into her room.

"Grand come in please."

Then Raymond wave his hand again. Bill and Angelica were in the room. Another wave of his hand. The house had a bubble around it. No evil ears or eyes could hear or see what was happening.

Bill was surprised to see Eleanor. "Raymond is there something wrong? Eleanor why are you here?"

"That is what I want to know also."

Eleanor put up her hand. 'Mic and Angel would like to get married. Their feelings for each other is stronger. My husband and I didn't have these feelings at their age now. I still thought of Thomas as a brother. Angel thinks of Mic as her mate.'

"Eleanor why is everything changing?"

'Because you will have to take these memories from them. They won't remember each other. She will believe she is a virgin. This will draw Marcos out. The day Mic fines Angel. Something is going to happen inside the house in Vermont. Mic will believe that the house has a spell place on the ranch. He will be told by a psychic. There will be a young woman. He knows her by Angel. This young woman must stay a virgin. She is the only way to get back inside the house. This is Mic's land I'm talking about. Raymond, they have their powers. Mic will marry her on her birthday.

When Angel goes back home. There will be a lot of trouble happening. They will need this time with each other. We can't see what will happen. However, we can give them what they need. Mic knows that I'm here. You have the power to keep Angel safe. Give her the pills she needs. For Mic knows how to get married. He will merry Angel. With or without your help.'

Mic went back to the ranch. He went to his room. In his mine he called to Angel. Now they were at the waterfall.

'Angel tonight we are going to get married.'

'How can we do that?'

'In the spirit world we have are powers. We will make our family believe that you are twenty-one. I have the marriage license.'

'Mic how did you fine this out.'

'Bill had said I can get to you through the spirit world. Like the way we did for are fathers. This is going to work.'

The minister outside the school was at the castle. Angelica and Emily had gotten the birth control pills for Angel. Her father and mother were there. The castle was all done up. Mic watched Angel and her father walk down the aisle. It was really happening. Bill was next to Mic. He saw his father and mother. Both families were there. Mic gave Angel his name Tom MacGregor. Angel use Ellen Angel Heart on the license.

That night Mic made love to his wife. He took off Angel's dress slowly. The only thing she had on was the ring Mic made with his magic. In the morning. Mic made love to Angel before the sun came up. Her arms were around Mic. Then she felt him climax inside of her. When she got up. Angel went to the bathroom. She saw her pills. She had been taking them for a while. It wasn't a dream. Angel was now Mic's wife.

"You are my wife and I need to take care of you. This warm water will help."

Mic filled the tub. He took Angel's hand and guide her into the tub. She laid her head on his stomach. There were bubbles covering their bodies.

"This feels like a dream. If it is, I don't want to wake up from it."

"I know what you mean. When Eleanor was talking to Raymond. Your grate grandfather was talking to me. He told me how we could get married. That's why our family will think it's a dream. Only Bill, Angelica along with Raymond and Emily will know were married. We have two nights together before we go back to school. You see the powers we have we can use them in the spirit world. When people look at us were older. Raymond wasn't surprised. He said when we leave you and I won't remember this. It will be taken from are mines. The six of us will not have any memory of this. The weekends we can take the horses in the woods. I'll make love to you as often as you let me. I'm having a hard time keeping my hands off you. I love you so much. Just remember to take those pills. This way I'm able to come inside you."

Bill had bus duty. He had to take the boys to pick up their dates at the girl's dorm. At the gate Angelica waited with her girls. One by one the boys took their dates hand and help them onto the bus.

All the teachers were at the ball. Angelica and Angel went to the lady's room. One of the girl's ripped her dress and it needed fixing.

In the girl's bathroom. Angelica had fixed the girl's dress. She started to ask Angel if Bill had talked to Mic.

"Angelica about what?"

"About Bill and me. We been together for a while. Bill talks about getting married. He never says when. I just thought he would marry me before he leaves with Mic."

"Bill will ask you. Angelica I'm going to fix my make up."

Looking in the mirror she called to Mic.

'Mic, Angelica asked me if Bill had talk to you.'

'About what?'

'About getting married to her. She wanted to be married to Bill before he leaves. When will he ask her?'

'I don't know, he hasn't talk to me yet.'

'Mic if he does. Tell him do it to night. That's if he has the ring.'

Standing near the door the two of them were waiting for the girls to get back. Then Mic turn to Bill.

"Bill when are you going to ask Angelica to marry you?"

"I don't know where to do it."

"You could do it here. That's if you have the ring."

"Oh, I have the ring with me. Why here?"

"Beautiful lights to stand under. Maybe to let some of the men here know she is yours."

"Where are you getting your information from? Don't tell me Angel and you are talking to each other right now?"

"Angel had told me what Angelica said. She was hoping you were going to ask her tonight. She had asked Angel to be her maid of honor. At least the four of us will be in the same boat. The other day. One of the teachers asked me if you too are seeing each other."

When Angelica and Angel had left the room. Bill remember that he couldn't take his eyes off Angelica. He had been thinking he would like to ask her to marry him. The two of them had been together every night while at the ranch. The more he thought about it. Tonight, would be a good night for asking her.

"Bill, I wish the time here didn't go by so fast. I enjoyed the classes and teaching with Angel. How am I going to be strong enough to leave her?"

Mic had saw Angelica walk into the room.

"Bill when are you going to ask her to marry you? Bill did you hear what I said?"

"Yes, I heard you. How am I going to be able to leave Angelica? Mic the magic rose gave you the ability to go to Angel. You always know when she needs help. She has Raymond and Angelica. She also knows how to fight back. I know you wish you knew why this was being done to you two. Forgive me there is a beautiful woman I like to dance with."

Bill lowered his voice. "I think you better go get your wife. Before one of the guys gets the first dance. By the way would you stand up for us. I'm going to ask Angelica to marry me tonight."

※※※

Mic thought. 'Mrs. MacGregor. You are so beautiful tonight. I'm a lucky man too have a beautiful wife like you. I love you so much.'

When the lights hit her dress. The yellow made her dress glow. She was his angel. Mic walked over to her. How can he leave her?

'No! I will always be with Angel. Bill's right.'

Mic couldn't take his eyes from Angel. If they were alone. He would take her to the floor.

'Mic I know were married. I wish you could make love to me. If we can't make love to each other. Can we at least dance my love?'

'Angel, when we fine each other again. We will have a big wedding.'

'Mic we don't have to have a big wedding. I just want to be with you.'

The two of them dance. Then it was the time to crown the King and Queen. For the King they picked Mic. For his Queen. Everyone picked Angel.

"I give you Mic and Angel are new King and Queen."

"Angel don't cry. This is our time to enjoy ourselves."

"Then you better kiss me. I believe our subjects would like to see us kiss."

Mic took Angel into his arms. The King and Queen gave their subjects what they wanted. After the King and Queen dance. Everyone joined in. Bill worked his way to the center of the room. He held Angelica in his arms. Then he took out the ring he made. Getting down on one knee Bill open the box and said.

"Angelica would you become my wife?"

"Yes. I thought you never ask me."

Bill took the ring out of the box and place it on Angelica's finger. He had also got their license to marry. After the dance Bill took them to the little church. The church was down the road from the two schools. With the license the minister married them.

Then the day came when Mic graduated. Both schools were there. All the parents would be there later. This was for the two schools to say good bye to their classmates. Awards were given out. Mic and Angel was called up. This was the highest award that was given for teaching, teamwork, in dancing and competitions. Mic had high honors. He got awards for his paintings. There was one painting that he could give to anyone in the two schools. Mic gave it to Angel. Without anyone knowing. Mic had used his magic in the spirit world. He left a note inside the painting. It was time for graduation. Angel couldn't go to this one. But Bill made it, so she could be with Mic.

'Mic I'm here with you. Bill made me into a fly. Please don't try to kill me.'

'Where are you?'

'I'm in your hair. Near the top of your cap.'

'Don't move around too much. I don't want to forget you're the fly.'

'All right. I'm so proud of you my love.'

'Thank you. I couldn't do it without you.'

Then his name was called. Mic still couldn't have his name called out. It was Mic T.M.

'Will here we go Angel.'

Angel saw Mic's father and mother. He wore a gold ban. Mic was one of them who gave a speech to the class. Angel knew what he was going to say. On stage is where he sat. At the end of his speech.

"Good luck everyone in what every you do."

The Fairy Rose in America

The hold class through there hat into the air. Angel took a ride into the air. That's when Bill send her to her room. At the end of summer Mic and Bill will be on their way to America.

※※※

Now that school was out. The four of them got ready to leave for the campgrounds. For graduation. Brandon given Mic a motorcycle. This motorcycle the three of them had rebuilt it together. There was a horse that Mic and Angel was getting ready. It was for Mic's grandfather. Bill had told Mic and Angel to make them self-look older. They were going to have a week together. Raymond had given Mic and Bill money for their honeymoon.

Bill and Angelica had set up the camp. They had the horses bedded down and watched for them. The four of them enjoyed their honeymoon for that week. Soon the four of them won't remember that they had gotten married. They had an RV to camp in. Inside was set up with two bedrooms. Bill made shore that he couldn't hear Mic and Mic couldn't hear Bill.

Time went by too fast. Mic and Angel painted a mural on the motorcycle gas tank. The girls enjoyed laying in the sun. While the guys played football. The best time was seeing different places and going shopping in town. They did some diving and went over their training. Triger was doing well. The training with Angel paid off. Just being with each other. It was wonderful having so much fun. With just two days left. It was time to head home. The four of them knew Raymond had to take some of their memories away. What they didn't know. New memories were going to be put in place.

Back at the ranch. There wasn't anyone home. Mic and Angel took care of the horses. They rubbed them down and fed them. Bill and Angelica took care of all their things. Angel was having a bad feeling about not seeing the family. Outside they watched the sun starting to set.

"Mic, there is something coming. It's scaring me."
"Angel what kind of trouble?"
"I don't know Mic. Please hold onto me."

Then they saw it. It looked to be just a black cloud. Slowly it changed. Now it was a twister coming over the mountains. It was heading right for them.

"Angel we got to get somewhere safe."

Try as they may the two of them couldn't move.

"Mic I can't move."

"Do you feel if it's evil? I can't feel anything can you."

"No! The sound is getting louder. Mic this is magic. Hold on to me."

Mic wrapped his arms around Angel. Now he could feel the power coming at them. The magic they had. Couldn't get them out of this one.

"Angel whatever happens. Remember I love you so much. Honey this magic is from your father and brother."

"I know. I can hear Raymond."

In the air she heard. 'Sorry sis. Dad and I we have are orders.'

"Please don't take are dream world."

'Never daughter. This is all you will have. Kiss your man and hold on.'

"I love you Mic. I will find you somehow."

Chapter Thirteen: The Tornado Change Everything

THEY DROVE FOR QUITE A WHILE. Angel had fallen asleep in the van. There was a sign that read: Welcome to Rose Hill. There are over 150 acres to see.

Miss LeClair said, *"Angel the castle is coming into view. It will be on your left if you'd like to take some pictures."*

Angel could see that the children were outside playing football. She was pleased to see the teacher being involved with their students. As they got closer. Why didn't the teacher look like a teacher? What caught Angel's eyes was the Dale Earhart jacket and hat. She saw one of the boys throw the ball to the teacher. With her camera-ready. She caught the shot when he leapt into the air. There was so much power in that jump. Only someone who took ballet could have leapt that high. Angel's mind raced. He had a tan hat with the number three on it. Mic has a tan hat with the number three. She couldn't see his face with those sunglasses. It cannot be Mic. They wouldn't let the two of us be together at the same place. When Angel looked up. She had seen Miss. LeClair looking at her through her mirror. She didn't dare to look back to see if he was following them. Angel knew Mic would run all the way to get to her. They drove over a mile and a half down the road. She saw the mountains that was from her dreams. Along the road was a large fence. In the field were many horses. At the end of the fenced in area. A beautiful ranch houses. The van pulled into the driveway. What a beautiful photograph it made. She could see the mountains still in the background. Angel thought how wonderful it would be to stay here. To wake up to that view of the mountains every morning.

Miss LeClair drove up next to the barn. There in a smaller fenced in area was a beautiful jet-black horse. What was happening? Everything that was in her dream was here. What does it mean? She felt strong emotions. It felt like it was far away. However, it was coming closer quite fast.

'No! Mic can't be here.'

Angel knew in her heart it was Mic. She stared out the window. Miss LeClair had stepped out to speak to the MacGregors. They had to sign some papers. Now she was back. She had put her arms around Angel.

"It's time to meet the MacGregors."

The day was hot. In the van it got hotter without the air conditioner on. Her emotion was tying her stomach into knots. She felt nauseated. Outside the air felt good. As Angel got closer to Mr. MacGregor. He looked like the man who came to their home. She was a little girl back then. This man doesn't have a tattoo on his arm. The same tattoo as her daddy's. The man had black hair not light brown. Now Miss LeClair was introducing her to the MacGregors. Angel gave them a big smile. She was having troubles with her emotions. Every part of her body knew it was Mic.

"Hello Angel. I'm so happy that you chose Rose Hill. Please call us Aunt and Uncle. This will make it easier for our granddaughter. I've been told that you have a way with horses. There is this horse of ours that needs help. We were told that you could help us with him."

'No, it can't be the place that Mic stays at.' Angel told herself to stop it. Fine out if it is Mic first.

"Hello Mr. Mrs. MacGregor. Thank you for having me. May I ask you who told you about my skills?"

From the corner of her eye. Angel could see Miss LeClair shaking her head no.

"Angel I'm not the kind of man that lies to people I just meet. The person is living with us. He told us about you saving Nightmare from

being killed. The same young woman was asking to come to Rose Hill. I said yes."

'Why Mic? How am I going to say good-bye this time?'

"Angel is there something wrong?"

Angel looked at her and mouth I'm sorry. Then turn to Miss LeClair. She tried to keep her voice under control. She spoke in a soft voice.

"You knew he was here. This is where Mic stays. You were one of them that saw me brake down."

Miss LeClair could see the pain in Angel's eyes. Mic knew she was going to do this. She felt like crying herself.

"What can I say. Yes! Mic is here. Yes! He was the one at the school playing football. We got out later then we should of. Mic thought you found out that he was here."

When Angel drop to her knees and cry out. "No!!! I can't do this again. It tore my heart in two the first time. To see Mic trying to get to me. All the teachers holding him back. Why are you doing this to me? You should have told me. You knew how I felt about Mic."

Miss LeClair felt if she knew Mic's hold name. She would have told Angel.

Now Angel was screaming every word out *she said.* "Why are you doing this to me? Do you like to see me fall apart…please answer me?"

Angel's answer didn't come from Miss LeClair. It had come from Mic. Quickly she turned. Angel could hear Mic calling to her.

'Angel please it's not Miss LeClair's fault. I told them not to tell you.'

She turned back. Angel had bent her head in defeat. Then she looked up at Miss LeClair.

"I'm so sorry. I should have known. Mic knew I wouldn't have come. He told you not to tell me. What am I going to do? I can't say good-bye to him. If I do. I feel we may never find each other. You may think were just children. You think we can bounce back with no trouble. If this is so. Please tell me how to handle these feelings. I could stand being apart from him for a little while. If we could write each other. I know we can't. Please tell me how to deal with losing him. I can't do this it hurts too much."

Angel's eyes were pleading for help. Miss LeClair came over and pull her to her feet and into her arms.

"Angel could you tell me what just happen? How did you know it was Mic? He told us not to tell you?"

"Miss LeClair I can't tell you. Please don't ask me anymore about this. Please."

"All right Angel. The day we had to talk with Mic. We had given him your sketchbook. The moment he took it. He closed his eyes and told us it was yours. We asked him how he knew without looking inside. He said it's energy. That's all he could tell us."

"Miss LeClair please take me back to school. Mic is almost here. I can't face him. I saw the pain in his eyes. To say good-by to him. I can't do it. My heart believes those words mean forever."

In the background. The McGregor's were listening to what the two of them were saying. They knew and couldn't say what was happening to Mic and Angel.

"I'm so sorry that the two schools failed, to stop this. We knew there was something very special about the two of you. We try to keep the underclassmen away from the upperclassmen. To prevent this from happening. This time it couldn't be helped. The schools shouldn't have let the two of you work so closely together. We were enjoying taking first place every year. Our schools closed their eyes to what was happening. The more you work together the closer you got. As a couple. You two knew what the other needed. Your timing was so much in harmony with each other. Their schools will not change their policies. Until your parents who work in high office change their minds. These parents have a need to protect their children. You must understand. There will always be people that use children. To force parents to reveal secrets."

"Angel it's been hard on Mic. He couldn't get you out of his mind. Not working with you or helping others with homework. It's up to you if you stay or go."

Angel could hear Mic calling to her. He was pleading for her to stay with him for this week. She knew time was running out. Five miles was nothing to Mic. To run full out in this heat. With a hat and coat like he had on. It would feel like he ran ten miles. Angel knew he wouldn't care if he dropped.

"Please! What should I do? I'm scared to face Mic."

Miss LeClair spoke. "Angel, you told me that you dreamt about this place. You believed that you had to get here soon. It had something to do with your future. If you dreamt this. Then stay to find out why it was so important. Who knows it may help you to find Mic in the future?"

Off in the distance they could hear someone hollering her name. In Angel's mind. She tried to tell Mic to slow down. It was too hot to run this way. Now she could hear coughing behind her. She pictured him bent over. His hands on his knees gasping for air. Tears ran down her cheeks. All she could do was listen to his coughing. Mic tried to say something. As he gasped for air.

"Angel I'm …sorry. I didn't want… to leave you this way. It's… been eating me up inside. I can't …eat or sleep at night. I was going to ask your …school if I …could talk to you. That's when they told me … you were the …winner of the …art show. You asked to …come to Rose Hill."

Mic had a moment of coughing. "I'm sorry …Miss LeClair …I thought that …Angel found out. I was going …to be at the ranch when she came. I knew if …she found out. She would decide …not to come."

"Mic stop talking and rest. Your gasping for breath. We had troubles that delayed us. You had told me that Angel would lash out. She does this when she scared. It's okay Mic. Catch your breath.

"Angel it's hard growing up. There is so many changes that you will be experiencing. Life is not always fair. It's very hard to say goodbye to someone you love. Right now, you have a second chance. All I can tell you. Take hold of the moment and run with it. The way you said good bye the last time. You had said. It was hell on earth. The path you're on you can stay on and run away. With this second chance. You can make it right and find out why you dreamt of Rose Hill. Angel there are other words you can use. So, it won't sound not so final. Who knows? The two of you may find each other down the road. I don't know of any crystal ball that could tell your future. Think about it before you act. Let me know what you decide. Now! Go over to Mic and take care of that young Man. He ran a long-ways in this heat just for you."

Miss LeClair gave Angel a hug. She turned to Mr. & Mrs. MacGregor.

"Would it be all right if I could use your phone? I must let the school know I'm running really late."

"Yes! It's this way. I must check on my granddaughter. She went back to sleep after her daddy brought her over. May I offer you a cup of coffee?"

"Thank you, Mrs. MacGregor. I would love a cup."

"Call me Kimberley."

"Then you can call me Eva. Thank you for asking me to stay for coffee. This way I can give them some time."

The two women were looking at Kimberley's husband.

"Brandon, would you like a cup of coffee too?"

At first her husband didn't hear her. She punched him in the arm to get his attention.

"Brandon would you like a cup of coffee too?"

"Yes dear! I would love a cup. I'll be right there."

All this time Brandon was watching his nephew. It was upsetting him that he couldn't help Mic.

"Angel it's always hard to say good-bye. We also will miss Mic. He's been a part of this family for six years. There is not much I can do. The school rules have tied my hands on this madder. What I can do. You and Mic can stay here for one week. This way you could spend some time together. Maybe next year you could come to the ranch for a visit. I could always use a horse whisperer. Angel I would love to have you stay for Mic and Trigger. Trigger needs someone to help him. The people that owned him before. They had done something to him. Trigger will become a gift to my father. I will be sending him to the States. First, I have to find someone to help him."

Brandon was watching the two of them. He could see Angel was having troubles to look at Mic. It was getting hard for Mic to stay standing. He was unsteady on his feet after that run.

"Mic sit down before you fall flat on your face. Right now, you're slowly heading to the ground."

"Yes sir. I do feel a little lightheaded.'

The moment Brandon said that. Angel's head turned quickly to look at Mic. She could see he was sliding down the van to the ground.

"Angel Mic had told us that you have been dreaming about this place. He said it's been two years you've been looking. If it was me. I would jump for a chance to get some answers. What I would do is kiss Mic and speak. I will be waiting until we meet again. Angel think about it. Your dreams brought you here. There are many people that thinks you should stay with Mic."

"*Thank you, Mr. MacGregor. I know everyone would like me to stay. Even my father thought it was a good idea. I promise to give it a lot of thought.*"

"*Angel that is all I can ask for. Remember it's "Uncle Brandon." Now go over and take care of Mic. He looks as miserable as you do.*"

When Brandon went inside the house. Angel went to the van without thinking. She grabbed all her things and brought them over to Mic. The first thing she did was give Mic a bottle of water. He took it quickly and drank more than half of it in three gulps. Angel pulled a towel from her bag. Mic's hair needed to be dried.

The next thing came out of her bag was a sweatshirt. Angel helped Mic take his coat and hat off.

When Mic got a look at the sweatshirt. He spoke "*Wait a minute. This is my sweatshirt. I thought that I lost it.*"

Angel looked at Mic and smiled. "*You did. You lost it to me. This sweatshirt was the only thing that helped me. I wore it to bed each night. It had your scent on it.*"

Angel gave his back a rub. "*There! That should replace your scent. I would like it back before I leave.*"

Angel could feel the tears rolling down her cheeks. Does this mean she was going to run again? She tried to give Mic a smile. When she picked up his hat and placed it on her head. With the towel she started to rub Mic's hair dry. Once dried Angel went back to her backpack. There she found what she was looking for.

"*I have another hat. You can wear it if you like.*"

Mic was drinking the last of his water. "*Wait a Minute. It's not one of those girlie hats? Is it?*"

"*Yes! It's all pink,*" and she gave a little giggle.

Angel turned to look at Mic. "*Did I ever tell you that I'm also a fan of Dale Earhart?*"

She smiled when she saw the surprised look on his face.

"*No! You never said anything about that. Angel there so much I could learn before we part. I was going to kiss you, but you left. If we were alone, I would kiss you now.*"

"*Mic, please stop. All I've been doing is crying. Is this your plan to try to keep me off balance? To make me stay?*"

"*Yes! If it would help to get you to stay with me.*"

With the knowledge of him kissing her. Angel closed her eyes. She needed to take a deep breath before talking.

"This hat came from Loudon. I went to a race there with my grandfather and brother. That's when I bought this hat. I was looking for a white or tan hat. The only hat they had was this black one. If you like it, I'll take the tan hat. You can have this black hat with Dale Earhart on it."

Mic could feel his eyes trying to water up. He took the hat from her.

"The hat smells like you. Yes, I'll take it. This hat goes better with the coat. My grandparents bought me this on my birthday. Angel I will always wear this hat with the coat. I will think of you and my grandparents. I love the three of you so much."

It was too much to take. She sat back on her heels. Angel placed her hands over her face and bowed her head.

"Mic I'm sorry I shouldn't have run from you that night. When it came time to say good bye. I got scared. It felt as if someone was pushing a knife into my heart.

She picked her head up and looked at Mic. *"I'm sorry Mic that I took the coward's way out."*

Mic took hold of her hands. They were facing each other. He saw a tear rolling down her cheek.

"Angel you're no coward."

With his lips. He took the tear drop from her cheek. She through her arms around his neck.

"Mic I'm so scared to lose you."

He pulled her into him. *"I know that feeling. I had it when I was reading your note. Only then I realize this was it. Know more dancing with you. I couldn't hold you close to me. I can't go for a run on horseback with you. It was over, and I couldn't turn back the clock. All you did was end it the best way you could.'* Mic was rubbing her back. Then he pulled her away.

"You got to stay with me this week. I have my license to ride that motorcycle over there. It's all plan out. I was going to take you on a picnic today. Please we can't end this. Not yet! Your dream must play out first."

Before Angel could answer him. They heard the screen door open. Then they heard Mrs. MacGregor call out. *"Mic, Lilly's on her way to see you. Could you take care of her."*

Angel was watching Lilly run to them. Her little legs were going as fast as they could.

"Angel do you remember I told you about Lilly. I watched her for Uncle Brandon at times? She so funny. You see she can't say Uncle. It comes out as Gunkel. Angel I'll be right back."

Mic had got up. She brushed the tears away and grabbed for her camera. She was taking some pictures of Mic and Lilly. Now she was looking for a closeup of the two of them. When she zoomed in on Lilly's little face. She could see Lilly was a beautiful child. With her long blonde hair and blue eyes. Angel could see Mic loved being Lilly's uncle. She heard the squealed of delight. When he ran toward her and scooped her up into his arms. Lilly threw her little arms around his neck and cried out.

"I love you Gunkel."

She had given him a kiss on the cheek. Mic had put Lilly on his shoulders. The two of them headed toward Angel. As she put her camera down. Something was happening. Lilly was changing before her very eyes. There was a different little girl on Mic's shoulders. This sweet little girl had long black hair like Mic's. She looked like her niece Katie. As they got closer. She could see her eyes were the color of Mic's eyes. What was happening? Could this be what she needed to know? This was a vision of her and Mic's child. When Mic sat down. He could see that Angel was staring at Lilly. It was as if she was somewhere else. There were tears running down her cheeks. When he took her hand, he felt Angel jump. Could she have been day dreaming?

"Angel are you okay? You looked as if you saw something."

Quickly she wiped the tears away. When she looked back at Lilly. The other little girl was gone.

"I'm fine Mic."

Then she turned her attention to Lilly. *"Hello Lilly. It's nice to meet you. Your uncle told me all about you."*

All this time Lilly sat close to Mic. She just stared at Angel. She was holding tightly to Mic's hand. She didn't move or say a word.

"*Lilly tell Angel to stay with us. Help me to convince Angel to stay. Please Lilly help me.*"

Angel wondered why it was so hard to decide. Then Angel jumped when she heard the door slam.

Time was up. She saw that the three adults were heading toward the horses. Mic took Angel's hand.

"*Angel please stay with me. We can do so much together. There is one place I would like to show you. Besides you can help Uncle Brandon with Trigger.*"

What was Angel waiting for? Tell Mic you'll stay. Say those words. I will stay. Angel couldn't answer him. Why can I say those words? All she could do was just stare at Lilly. Mic bent his head. He had made the decision for her.

"*All right Angel. It's okay. I'll have Uncle Brandon take me back to school. I really need you to stay and help him with Trigger.*"

Before Angel could say anything. Lilly reached out her arms to Angel. Her little fingers moved for Angel to take her. In that moment. The other little girl was back. Now she was holding hers and Mic's little girl. How wonderful it felt to think this was their child. Could Lilly see what she had seen in her. Never underestimate a two-year-old. All Lilly knew Gunkel and Angel was sad. Lilly new just what to do. Her way to fix things was with a hug. Then everything would be all better. Now Lilly stood between Angel legs. One hand was holding Angel's neck. Her other arm was stretched out toward Mic. Her little fingers were wiggling for Mic to come closer to them.

"What sweetie?"

"Gunkel," she cried.

Mic moved closer to them. Lilly grab him around the neck. She started to pull him closer to Angel. For a two-year-old Lilly was one smart cookie. She knew how to fix this between Mic and Angel. Somehow, she knew Gunkel would leave. If Angel didn't stay. Lilly knew pulling them closer together. Angel never took her eyes off Mic. The two of them was surveying each other's face and lips. With one more tug of Lilly's arms. Angel felt Mic's lips touching hers. The moment her lips parted. Mic deepened the kiss.

Lilly must have thought that was enough. For the next moment. Her little hands were pushing them apart. Angel never felt like this before. Her whole body seemed to cry out for more of Mic's touch. Everyone was telling her to stay. It took a two-year-old to open her eyes.

"All right Mic I'll stay."

"Thank you, Angel, for doing this for me. I know Uncle Brandon could use your help with Trigger. I'll go and get my things and have him take me ..."

Before Mic could say anything else. Angel placed a finger over Mic's lips. As she watched her finger trace his lips. Slowly... her eyes met his.

"You don't understand. I didn't say you have to go. I mean. I would stay only if you stay with me."

"Angel do you mean it?"

"Yes Mic, I mean it."

Mic was so happy. His hand went behind Angel's neck. There he pulled her and Lilly into him. This time the kiss was quickly given for Lilly pushed Angel and Mic apart.

"Gunkel you're squishing me."

The two of them laughed. Mic kissed Lilly on the cheek. As he got to his feet. He lifted Lilly and tossed her into the air. Each time Mic caught her she giggled with delight. Angel caught an action picture of Mic tossing Lilly into the air. The three adults knew that Angel was staying.

Mic cried out. *"Angel is going to stay. Lilly got her to stay with us. This is the best gift Lilly and Angel could give me."*

She knew now why this happen. There is hope of finding Mic again. When Miss LeClair walked over to Angel and gave her a hug.

She smiled, *"I'm happy for you and Mic. I believe in my heart the two of you will find each other."*

From the corner of her eye. Angel could see Uncle Brandon talking to Mic.

"Angel the two schools and your parents. They are going out on a limb for you two. Listen very carefully. I must make this part very clear to you. Angel many girls think if she gets pregnant. The school will have

to tell her the name of the father. Others get pregnant in the heat of the moment. None of this will give you his Identity. Your child… If you get pregnant. Will grow up without his father. It may take time for you to find Mic. I'm speaking to you confidentially. I will deny I ever told you such a thing. You two may know of each other. You should not know him completely. You will not get pregnant if he touches you there with his hand or finger. Here are some papers that the school drew up. In these papers you must give your word. If you don't. You will come back to school as a virgin. If you don't sign. This trip will be all for nothing. I will have to bring you or Mic back to the school. Yes, it is unfair to do this to the two of you. Are two schools have no choice. Read the papers and sign them."

Angel remembered wishing she didn't have to give her word. She bent her head and sign the papers. When she looked over her shoulder. She saw Mic signing the papers also. After the last paper was sign. Something was going to happen. The adults disappeared.

"Mic what is happening?"

"Angel it's all right. Our time is all most up. Did you find what you were looking for?"

"I think so. Mic I'm scared."

"It's going to be all right Angel. Remember what we done together. I will always be with you, my sweet Angel. For now, you have my heart. Call me in your mind. For I will be there in your dreams. Keep this rose close to your heart. Our love will not know time. The power of this rose is within you. Without you I will be lost forever. I will not say good-by. One day we will find each other again. I love you my sweet Angel. You will always be my beautiful Angel."

"Mic the black cloud is back. It's changing. The twister it's back. Hold on to me."

Mic wrapped his arms around Angel. Now he could feel the power coming at them. Their magic they had in the dream world can't change what is going to happen.

"I love you Angel. I will find you before your twenty-one. Stay safe for me."

"I love you Mic. See you on my twenty-first birthday. Until then my love."

The End

Dictionary: Scottish words and English words

I thought it be better put in a sentence.
Aye: Yes, I will go with you. *Aye, I will go with you.*
Ye: I love You. I love Ye.

Characters in the Story

Meghalaya: The storyteller. She told Thomas about the Magic Fairy Rose. It started a quest for the MacGregor family. Who will bring the roses to America?

Father Sinclair: He placed the cross and rose on Garret chest in 1700. The family wears the birth mark. So, they know when demons are near. Garret gave his powers to the Magic Fairy Rose. This way they kept their magic through the roses on their chest. If a member uses the cross on someone to keep demons away. They will not have any powers.

Marcos: Is a demon. He's been trying to kill all the MacGregors. Now they call him Marcuse. Joseph and James with their team of Navy Seal. Is going after Marcuse. Because he is trying to bring down America.

Thomas MacGregor: He's a ghost now. He spoke to Neil about his parents. Also, about protecting Alexander to take the roses to America. Eleanor MacGregor: She's a ghost. She is also Thomas wife. She spoke to Alexander her grate-grate grandson. He called her Granny.

Garret Heart: Gave his magic to the roses. He gave the mark of the cross and rose to all his Children. Leslie: Is the sister to Garret. She and her brother wrote the Leslie letter with magic. The letter told Alexander to go to Dorset Vermont. There is land to bye.

Alexander MacGregor: His older brother will stay in Scotland. He will take care of the first magic roses. Thomas MacGregor found the magic roses. Alexander will be taking the next magic roses to America. He married Ginger MacKay. John and Sue her father and mother. Ben is her brother. When they got off the ship, in New York. They bought horses. They headed to Vermont. The town of Pittsford to find Ginger Mackay for Alexander. He is also Tom great great-grandfather.

Neil Heart: When the ship land in New York. He change his name to Angel Heart. They called him the demon hunter. He has magic through his birth mark. Through the cross and rose. He protects Alexander from demons in America. Neil Angel Heart: Is the great grandfather to Ellen Angel Heart.

Joseph Angel-Heart: 1950 the year he was born. Became a Navy Seal. His sister is Desiree. She was adopted as a baby. Her mother was distant cousin of Eleanor's Heart. She ran a way to America. Because she has Marcos blood. Joseph has magic through his birth mark. Only the one born with the mark. May give the mark to his mate. He married Malaya. Their children are Raymond and Ellen the two of them have magic. Ellen will be twenty-one when she has her powers. In the dream world she has her magic.

James MacGregor: 1950 the year he was born. Became a Navy Seal. His sister is Malaya. James married Desiree Angel Heart. She was adopted as a baby. Desiree mother was Albert Huascaran grate granddaughter. Desiree mother she got pregnant by someone who had magic. Their son is Tom in school his name is Mic Colman. When Tom is twenty-one, he will have his magic.

Tom MacGregor: His sister is Alicia. He married Ellen Angel Heart in Scotland. He was nineteen and just out of school. Ellen was eighteen and still in school. Her school name is Angel. After getting married. The time they had together. Before Mic had to leave Scotland was just the summer. Tom still had to use the name

Mic Colman. Bill Colman has magic he is a cousin to Ellen. Bill watches over Mic and keep him safe from demons.

Ellen Angel Heart: Is name in school is Angel. Her brother is Raymond Angel Heart. Angelica McKinnon watches over Angel to keep her safe from demons. Angelica has magic through the cross and rose. It was given to her by Bill Colman her husband.

Uncle Emile: Is a cousin to Joseph. He told James and Joseph about the Navy Seal. He lives in Dorset Vermont. On the MacGregor's ranch. Emile looks after James father and mother.

Arthur Stanley: Took care of Ellen and Tom in school. He knows there really names. He will bring them to the ship.

Murdock McKinnon: The officer that in charge of Arthur, James, Joseph, Bill, Mike Corban, Angelica. They are part of the Navy Seals. Angelica McKinnon: Is also his daughter. She married Bill Colman.

Raymond Angel Heart: Wife is Alicia. Their daughter name is Emily. His sister is Ellen. Her school name is Angel. Raymond has power like father Joseph and his grate grandfather Garret. His sister will have her magic when she is twenty-one.

About the Author

A.E. Fortin: Born in Sanford Maine. Right out of bootcamp she married her high school sweetheart. For twenty years he served. We had three beautiful children. Two boys and one girl. His last duty station was NAS Oceana in Virginia. As a family. We got involved in car shows on the weekends. When her daughter went to school. She went to work for the Hilton. After a few years there. The manager liked the way she clean the rooms at checkout. Without her knowing they time her. Checkouts was always the same time. They ask her if she was timing herself. She told them no. This is how she got a taste of writing her first manuscript. On the right way to cleaning a room at checkout. At the end of her husband career. They had to come back to Maine to help his parents. This is where are children found their mates. They gave us seven grandchildren. Six girls and one boy.

Her last job was machine operator at Parker. In 2010 she had a motorcycle accident. She all most had to have an operation on her back. She missed that bullet. However, the next bullet she didn't miss. She had a concussion with brane damage. At the time she was learning how to write stories. My first book she wrote need to be made into three books. This is what she is doing now. The concussion did its work. She started to forget how to read a blueprint. After her accident she got to work one more year before she lost her job. She had to prove to herself. She could do anything she put her mind too. This would be her legacy to her children and grandchildren. With her concussion and her handicap with reading and writing. She thought what better way to learn by writing a book. The world of computers. Opened a new world for her. Now we have things that read what a person writes. There is one lesson she leaves her children and grandchildren and anyone like herself. If there is a will… there is a way… to do anything you put your mind too. Never give up. No matter how long it takes. To the love of my life. My husband of fourth-seven years of marriage. Thank you Honey.

www.ingramcontent.com/pod-product-compliance
Lightning Source LLC
LaVergne TN
LVHW021047100526
838202LV00079B/4665